SCARS FORGET Us

A SMALL-TOWN WESTERN REDEMPTION ROMANCE

Greta Rose West

COPYRIGHT

Scars Forget Us: A Small-Town Western Redemption Romance

Cover by Sarah Kil of Sarah Kil Creative Studio
Edited by Peter Senftleben at PESeditorial
Cover model photography by Eric McKinney / 6:12 Photography
Cover Model Christian G.
Release date: June 4th, 2026

Ebook ISBN 978-1-955633-29-1
Print ISBN 978-1-955633-31-4

PUNK
ROSE
PRESS

DEAR READER

The hero in this book is an amalgamation of many people I've known and still know who have struggled with substance abuse, alcoholism, and the disease it causes within families. I think Dixon has been hiding in a deep cave in my mind for a long time. When I first wrote his name, back in *Light Betrays Us,* that's all he was—just a name. But then I wrote *Roads* and *Forever*, Dixon's brothers' stories, and he became real to me. His heart broke mine, so I had to write this book. I hope you enjoy it.

Avery Jane was a character I first dreamed up back when I wrote my very first book, *Burned.* I won't give away direct spoilers in case you haven't read it yet, but there are some bonus scenes on my website, and in one of them, the characters from *Burned* needed a florist. AVery Pretty Petal was born. She was mentioned briefly in *Rivers Between Us* when she gives little Gracie Morris a book one day on Main Street.

The characters from Cade Ranch and Wisper, Wyoming have been filling my head and my heart for almost seven years now. I knew it would be coming time to say goodbye to them, and it terrified me. They've become friends, and I realized, a security blanket. So this (**I think**) is the last book in the Wisper Dreams series. There are still so many characters in town who could inspire a love story. Never say never, but for now, I think we'll let them rest and grow, and we'll head to a new place, with new families, a new town, and a whole lotta cowboys! If you read *Roads Behind Us*, Bea mentions the town in her first chapter.

I've already started writing the next series, and I'm already deeply in love. The landscape is different. The view changes and the characters will be new, but they will capture your heart and wrap it up in the pastel skies and dusty earth of the eastern Wyoming grasslands.

Oh, and also, I'm told by a very trusted source that I'm about to offend British people the world over because the characters in this book heat water for tea in the microwave. I'm sorry! Please forgive the faux pas, but that's how I was raised. We zapped everything in the microwave. I'm a child of the 70s and 80s, what can I say? But I do make up for it, because Avery Jane has a pink tea kettle. ;)

TRIGGER WARNING

In this book, you'll find talk of past illicit drug use and alcoholism. The main character, Dixon, is a recovering addict. There's also talk of child abandonment, abuse from Dixon's childhood, neglect, and co-dependency. Additionally, Dixon's mother recalls a past abusive marriage and cheating. None of it happens on the page but is discussed between characters and in inner thoughts. There is stalking and mild violence.

But as with any of my books, love wins in the end, family comes together, and the good guys live happily ever after. Thank you for reading!

Narcotics Anonymous https://na.org/
Alcoholics Anonymous https://www.aa.org/

ALSO BY GRETA ROSE WEST

Wild Heart: Welcome to Wisper

Subscribe to the newsletter for this short introduction into the Cade Ranch world and for extra goodies and scenes. Sign up at gretarosewest.com.

THE CADE RANCH SERIES IN ORDER

BURNED

BROKEN

BUSTED

BRAVED

BLINDED

THE WISPER DREAMS SERIES IN ORDER

RIVERS BETWEEN US

STORMS INSIDE US

MOUNTAINS DIVIDE US

LIGHT BETRAYS US

MIDNIGHT SURROUNDS US

ROADS BEHIND US

FOREVER FINDS US

SCARS FORGET US

WYOMING LOVE EBOOK BOXSETS

LOVE AT CADE RANCH (Cade Ranch Books 1 - 3)

CADE RANCH IN LOVE (Cade Ranch Books 4 & 5)

LOVE IN WISPER, WYOMING (Wisper Dreams Books 1 - 3)

ACKNOWLEDGMENTS

I can't believe I'm at the end of another series. I would never had made it through these last thirteen books without Peter Senftleben, my editor: Thank you!!! It fills me with pride every time I send you a MS and you send back shorter and shorter edit letters. But don't you go thinkin' there will come a time I don't need you. Publishing a book without your input would feel like streaking naked through Walmart. I'm just not gonna do it. ;)

To the kids and my little Westie: the adventure you have us on is wild. Thanks for letting us be a part of his daily life. It means everything to Papa and me. Hearing, "That's a red Mack truck, Grammy?" and "Life is a Highway" will never get old. Love you.

Stephie, love you. I'm glad we get to sisser again and find new coffee shops. I may miss my mountains, but I love you and Westie more. ♥

Beta readers, Barb, Geri, and MJ. Thanks again. I think you all know how invaluable your feedback is, but I hope you know I mean it when I say that these books are better because you read them. I have to send an extra shoutout to MJ cuz I keep throwing books at you left and right. You are the busiest mama bear, but you never tell me no. Love you. Thank you.

To my ARC team: YOU ARE THE BEST. Thank you so much for always showing up for my latest book, even though I suck at social media and you haven't seen much of me online for a hot minute. Thank you for the email check-ins and all the reels and memes in DMs. I love every single one.

Sarah, thank you for a beautiful cover once again!

Tradition now dictates that I thank the musicians who made the music on my Scars playlist, the artists who inspire me every damn day. And I'm nothing if not a sucker for tradition. To the Cowboy Junkies, Twenty One Pilots, Madonna, Sam Barber, GAI, Zach Bryan, Jonah Kagen, The Castellows, P!nk, Eminem, Lord Huron, Shania Twain, Jaymes Young, TOOL, and Anna Graves to name a few: Thank you. And Hozier, on the off .000001 % chance that you will ever read this, I want you to know that I cannot count how many times I sing-screamed the lyrics to "Abstract (Psychopomp)" in my car. Thanks for that.

For Terre.
Love & Light.
Miss you.

“Do not kill him even now. For he has not hurt me. And in any case I do not wish him to be slain in this evil mood. He was great once, of a noble kind that we should not dare to raise our hands against. He is fallen, and his cure is beyond us; but I would still spare him, in the hope that he may find it.”

–J.R.R. Tolkien, *The Lord of the Rings: The Return of the King*

PROLOGUE

DIXON

"D, why don't you start us off today?" Mo said.

It looked like he'd showered and combed his hair, brushed his teeth, but he was probably three cups of coffee deep this morning, so there was a discolored tinge to them. Drugs and drinking hadn't left them pearly white anyway. His button down was rumpled, as usual, and his khakis weren't the wrinkle-free kind by any stretch of the imagination.

I asked, "We're tellin' memories? Good or bad?"

"What comes to mind?"

But Mo was a good guy. Maybe the nicest person I'd met since I got sober. He always had a kind word, even if his day had gone to shit. He had real, true belief in his fellow man, and if you needed it, he'd give you the shirt off his back even though he didn't have a pot to piss in.

A memory? I had to think about it. I had lots of those. The therapist told me to let the bad ones come, that I couldn't avoid them forever if I wanted to stay clean, but today had been a good one up till now, as far as memories went, and I didn't want the bad ones to sour my stomach quite yet. I'd just eaten shitty diner bacon and eggs, and if I let the bad memories flow, I'd chuck.

If I thought about Candy and my brother's baby, what I'd done to them, what I didn't do…

No, today, I wanted to think about something good. Something sweet.

Memories of my brothers and sister from when we were kids hit me like a bullet train. My oldest brother, Bax, was off limits, though, because he was attached to the memories of Candy and their baby. He wasn't safe. My other brother, Brand, was a good man. Maybe a little self-centered, but I loved him. I always had. And I wouldn't be clean if he hadn't flown down from Wyoming to California and paid up front for rehab.

I loved all my siblings, and maybe Brand had his own demons to wrangle and that was why he'd always been a little standoffish and stiff.

My sister, the youngest in our family, Abey… What a beautiful soul.

I ached for her. She'd gotten the worst of our dad. He'd made her feel like she didn't even deserve to live—

No. My brothers and sister were out of bounds this morning if I wanted to keep my day on track, and I sure as shit wasn't going to give myself permission to remember Kel, the dead mother of my kid.

Stay positive.

"There was a girl."

The tired, beat-down group of men around me mumbled their agreement. Didn't it always start with a girl?

"Yeah," I said, "but this girl was a kid. I was a kid. She didn't have anything to do with why things got dark for me. She was a light. Her grandparents lived near our family farm, and she used to stay out at their place during the summers.

"Her hair was the color of cornsilk. The sun made it that way. And she had this tinkling laugh. Her name was... I don't remember. It won't come to me. There's too much bad and hurt between now and then." The hurt made the good memories blurry and out of reach. "But I remember that laugh.

"She loved flowers, was always picking the wild ones, even picked 'em from her grandma's prized garden, and she'd make these bouquets for the squirrels and birds, deer and elk. Now, I knew they didn't give a shit about flowers, but she insisted on leavin' 'em for the animals. She made beds of flowers and strung the stems together to make strands we'd hang from tree limbs. She said when the wind blew through the trees, she thought her flowers made the animals happy."

Next to me, Nesty chuckled. He thought shortening his real name, Ernesto, to Nesty sounded like Posty. He was always doing that, comparing himself to celebrities, even though he was the scrawniest, least-famous dude I'd ever met. He was strong though; he punched me once when we were high after I called him Ernie. Most guys didn't, but I hoped if he stayed clean this time, he'd rethink the nickname.

"Don't think I've ever seen you smile like that," he said.

I elbowed him. "Shut up. Mo said good or bad memories. This is my good one.

"Anyway, I think about that girl when I can't sleep. I always told her she should take over her grandma's flower shop. I wonder if she did. I wonder if she's happy. If she still laughs like that, like a wind chime."

Or was she like me, broken and sorry and scarred?

I prayed like crazy I'd stay clean, like it wasn't up to me.

But it was. And this time, I had the best reason to beat my demon into submission.

A son.

A beautiful, soft, perfect baby boy.

He had a family, people better than me to look up to. My brother and his girls were raising my Stuey. He had love around him. Before my car died, I'd driven up to check on him, to make sure my family had come through for me this time.

They had. Stuart was happy and healthy. He was up on my family's land right this very minute, and when he grew big enough, he'd run free like I had when I was his age, laughing and learning, maybe picking flowers with his own memory girl.

But he needed his dad in his life. Even if my brother would always be Stuey's *daddy*, his father figure, and I could only be his friend, if it was all I could give my son, I would.

I'd be his best friend if that was what was healthiest for him.

I loved him enough to do that for him, no matter that just thinking about him never knowing the real me made me ache like I'd never ached before.

And I'd known plenty of fucking ache in my life.

But my baby boy didn't need to know anything about that.

He needed smiles and tinkling laughs, mountain air, dirt to dig in, grass to roll in. He needed birds singing to him from the trees and evenings spent around a happy dinner table. Nights filled with stories from books with silly cartoons on the front and bubble baths.

My son deserved good dreams and good memories, and I intended someday to give those to him.

But I still had to make it through these first thirty days. And after that?

Well, I wasn't sure. I didn't have a pot to piss in either, or any kind of direction about the path my sober life would take.

But I was goddamned determined to figure it out.

CHAPTER ONE

DIXON

Four and a Half Years Later

HOPPING down from the seat I'd ridden bitch in for the last five hundred miles, I planted my boots on the pavement and breathed deeply, steadying myself with my hand on the mud-covered fuel tank.

Home was a place I'd avoided for too long—Wisper, Wyoming, a little-known corner of the Jackson Hole Valley. Up here in the mountains, the air was thin, but the weight of it felt thick and heavy in my lungs.

"Don't forget your pack," Ken said.

He'd been hauling lumber, and before we delivered his last load yesterday, he agreed to drop me off on his way back to Rock Springs. Wisper was a little out of his way, but he said he didn't mind seeing the Tetons before he headed home to his wife.

How he'd known I was in recovery was a mystery to me. I hadn't said anything to him when he picked me up at a truck stop outside Winnemucca, Nevada, but he said I just had that look. The ex-junkie look, but it never failed—fucked-up had a tendency to find fucked-up.

Like me, Ken was a recovering alcoholic, but the difference was that he quit before his love of alcohol escalated to other shit. He'd been sober twenty years, but he admitted he still thought about the burn from a shot sliding down his throat.

I'd been sober more than four years, and I still thought about the rush of dope in my veins. More than that, though, I craved the numbness it provided, the ability to let demons and fathers and disappointments fade away. Most of all now, I wished it could wash away my family's shame.

But if I let the chemical bliss take over, I couldn't remember my son. And fuck if I was letting Stuart get any further away from me.

Ken dropped me off a mile from the south side of town, like I asked him to. I needed the last stretch of road to prepare myself for my impending, unknown future.

It had come time to face my mother. My brothers and sister. It had come time to face all of them and to apologize for lying and stealing and abandoning them.

It was time to face Stuart.

Five years old now, Stu had probably already started school. He probably had friends and dreams and wishes. He wouldn't understand addiction. He couldn't understand the part I'd played in his mother's death, even though I wasn't the one who'd injected the heroin into her vein.

Some days, the jealousy I felt toward my oldest brother and his wife could swallow me whole. Yeah, I was the one who gave up my kid. I handed him over to Bax when I knew I couldn't take care of a baby, but that fact didn't make my absence in my son's life hurt any less. All the things I'd missed gutted me on a daily basis: birthdays,

Christmases, bad dreams, maybe his first lost tooth. His first laugh.

I'd missed it all, and there was no going back. That was the hardest pill to swallow, and God knew I was damn good at swallowing pills. This one, though, it just wouldn't go down.

Walking along Highway 20 with the morning sun beating down on my face, all those precious, missed memories ran through my head, and I tried to picture Stu's face when he saw Santa for the first time. Did he smile? Was he excited or scared shitless? I had a vague memory from my own childhood of seeing jolly old St. Nick and then running in the opposite direction, screaming. He was just so big and tall, and my mama had told me so many times that if I was bad, Santa would know, and he'd be pissed.

All my life, it seemed everything I'd done was bad. At least that was how my "father" had seen it. It didn't seem to matter to my subconscious that he was dead. His disproval had followed me everywhere I went.

Learning to live without his voice in the back of my mind, berating me and telling me all the ways I'd let my family down, had proven to be easier than I thought it would have, but that was only because *my* voice had replaced his, and now it was me who berated myself—for leaving my kid, for failing his mama, for failing my family, for being a fuck up.

For falling in love with my brother's wife and then bailing when she died in my arms.

Candy had loved me, too, but not in the same way. It had taken me a long time to realize that I'd loved her because she was the only good relationship in my life. Eight years had passed since she died of an aneurysm on the side of the fucking road in the middle of downtown Wisper. Eight years since I broke her ribs trying to give her CPR and bring her back to life. Eight years since my brother asked me to tell him what happened, but instead I drowned myself in cheap liquor, then pills, and things only got worse after that.

"Fuck," I breathed, wiping sweat from the side of my face with my hand.

I don't know if I can do this.

Pulling out the tiny, folded scrap of Stu's baby blanket I'd been carrying in my pocket for over four years, I squeezed it in my fist. It had worn thin between my fingers over time, but the red cartoon tractors and the frayed edges of the fabric soothed my fears and anxieties. The only picture I had of Stu had been rubbed clean of its ink long ago. Now, the only image I had of him was the one fixed in my mind, the one I'd stolen when I creeped on my family's land, trying to catch a glimpse of his smile as my brother hoisted him over his shoulders, and Stu sat up there, thunking Bax on the head with his little fists.

If I could just get through the rough part with Bax and his new wife, and with my mama and Abey and Brand, maybe I could be a part of my kid's world. Maybe they'd let me see him sometimes. Maybe then I'd know what his laugh sounded like.

When I made it into the center part of town and spotted the sheriff's station, where I knew my sister would likely be, my heart began to pound. My mouth went dry, and as I leaned against the wall of the building across Main Street from the station, I realized I'd finished off the last of my water.

But it wasn't a wall behind me; it was a door with a loose latch, and I stumbled through it.

"Can I help you?" asked a quiet voice behind me as I tried to stop my backward momentum and not fall on my ass.

I spun around and looked right into the eyes of my memory girl, and then her name hit me like a ton of bricks:

Avery Jane Harlowe.

AJ. My flower girl.

When she was little, she hated her first name, so she'd introduced herself to me as AJ, and it stuck. I used to weave wildflowers together and drape my homemade garland around her neck. She wasn't a girl anymore though. She'd grown into a stunning woman, with hips made for a man's hands.

"Hello-o-o?" She lifted her hand and waved it in front of my face. "Oh, I'm sorry. Maybe you don't speak English. Um, hablas inglés?"

"Yeah," I grunted. "I speak English."

"Oh. I'm sorry. It's just, you weren't sayin' anything, so I thought— Never mind. How can I help you?"

She hadn't recognized me. I wasn't surprised about that. It had been a long lifetime since we'd last seen each other. She had no way of knowing the bright sound of her laughter was the last thing I thought about every night before I fell asleep. After a long day in the woods, that light, glittering sound had been a balm to my soul and my aching back.

I couldn't exactly tell her I'd stumbled into her store because I was trying to avoid facing my family a few minutes longer.

Instead, I looked around.

"So is this your store, or…?"

Her store. She'd gone and done it, just like we'd talked about when we were little kids.

I felt like I'd fallen into an enchanted faerie land. The light seemed filtered somehow, dusky and peaceful. A quiet, lilting song played from a speaker somewhere, but it was so low that I imagined if I listened hard enough, I'd hear crickets chirping and birds singing.

Just like we'd made decades ago, strands of flowers lined

one whole wall. They had to be fake flowers; there was no way she'd have the time to string that many flowers every day, but they looked so real.

Bouquets topped mismatched tables and pot stands everywhere. Live greenery seemed to be growing right out of the wood, and buckets of fresh stems lined the wall near the door to the back storeroom, filled with multi-colored roses and lilies, dahlias and daisies, and so much baby's breath.

When we were young, we used to have the run of downtown, and we'd be out there for hours in the summers, exploring and adventuring, and we'd stop at the store every now and again to check in with AJ's gran. She'd give us water and always had a healthy snack or PB&Js waiting.

AJ stared at me now, really looking at the man looming in front of her, sweating and flustered. She was probably worried I'd come to rob her.

"Yes, it's my store," she said carefully.

"Nice place."

"Thank you. You still haven't said what you need."

Wiping the sweat off my brow with the back of my hand again, I mumbled, "Oh, uh, right. A bouquet."

When I didn't say anything more, her eyebrows furrowed over the prettiest hazel eyes I'd ever seen. Flashes of those eyes sparked in my head, and I realized I hadn't only been dreaming about the sound of her voice; I'd been dreaming about AJ's eyes too.

"A bouquet for my mama," I said so she wouldn't think I'd lost my mind. "I haven't seen her in a while. Figured I'd better bring her some flowers. Somethin' small." Small enough to be cheap. I'd been saving the money I'd earned working a farm over near Medford, Oregon, and after that as a timber faller, but I needed all my resources so I could buy a used car and rent a room. I wouldn't ask to stay on my family's land. They probably wouldn't want me anywhere near there, and I couldn't blame them for that.

Reaching around Avery's waist, I grabbed a premade bouquet of bright orange daisies off the display table behind her. She'd tied them together with a baby-blue ribbon. "How 'bout these? How much?"

She scrunched her nose, and the freckles smattered over the bridge twinkled like stars in an evening sky. "You love your mama, don't you?"

"Yeah. 'Course I do."

"Then you can't give her those. They're cheap and boring. Your mama likes pastel colors anyway."

"Yeah, but how much are those gonna cost— Wait. You know my mama? You know who I am?"

"Yes, Dixon. You were my best friend in grade school. It took me a minute, but did you think I'd forgotten?"

"I-I… Well, yeah. It's been a long time, and I'm not— I don't look the same. I'm not the same person I used to be."

Her eyes slid down my chest but quickly lifted back up to mine.

"I'm not the same either, but I could never forget those blue eyes." She reached up tentatively and touched the tip of her finger to an overgrown lock of my hair that had fallen over my shoulder. "You should get your hair cut before you see your mama."

Looking down at her finger still playing with my hair, I felt my cheeks heating with embarrassment. Another flash of heat ran through my body, much lower, but I shut that shit down as quick as I could and took a step backward.

She might have known me all those years ago, but she didn't know me now. I wasn't someone a beautiful, successful woman like her should want to know.

"The orange ones will be fine," I said, and I pulled a

sweaty and crumpled wad of cash from my front pocket, embarrassing me even more than I already was.

If AJ knew who I was, then she'd likely heard the gossip around town about me; there was no way Wisper hadn't talked when I brought Stu to stay with Bax. And I was sure no one had forgotten my teenage years and my twenties. None of that would've been good.

"Suit yourself," she said, seemingly disappointed at my mundane choice of flowers, and she grabbed the bouquet from my hand and whipped around to wrap them in tissue paper and ring me up at the cash register.

Her barely waving, blond hair fluttered out behind her, and the ends licked my forearm. The movement pushed a rush of air in my direction, and when her sweet, floral scent hit my nose, I groaned. She still smelled the same, like wildflowers and fresh air, and the memories of the two of us exploring the woods as kids sucked the breath right out of my chest.

God, how I wished I could go back to that time, when I was nothing more than an innocent boy.

Suddenly, I wanted to hear AJ's laugh. I wanted the happy, tinkling sound to wrap me up and carry me the rest of the way home. Maybe it could wash away the evidence of my sins, like God himself had kept a tally score, every wrongdoing marked in cuts and fading needle marks on my skin.

Maybe then the fear would go away.

Maybe then I could face my son and my family with more confidence than I currently possessed… and a straight back.

CHAPTER TWO

AVERY JANE

"WHO WAS THAT?" Mama asked when she and Gran walked into AVery Pretty Petal after their run to José's Diner for a late breakfast.

Dixon held the door for them, and Gran craned her neck so far up and over her shoulder to get a good look at him that I thought I should warn her not to get a crick. As soon as the jingle bells announced the door had closed, my mama asked the question, and Gran's head whipped right back around. Her curious eyes landed on mine.

It wasn't lying if I didn't answer verbally, right?

I shrugged.

"He looks familiar," Mama said. "Who was it?"

"A guy."

"What guy?" Gran asked, her eyes narrowing.

"Just a guy. He said he was buyin' flowers for his mom. Isn't that nice?"

"Who's his mother?" my own nosy mama asked.

"Oh my gosh, you guys. I was tryin' not to lie to you. And I'm not answerin'. You two are the biggest gossips this side of the Continental Divide, and some things don't need to be announced over a bullhorn through town."

Gran gave up trying to coerce information out of me, but only because she knew I'd tell her later. She had more patience than a saint. She walked into the back room and picked up her knitting project, then relaxed into her rocking chair and her hands became a blur of loops and pulls.

Mama, on the other hand, pressed her nose to the front window. "That man's walkin' into the sheriff's station. Maybe he's a criminal. I wouldn't be surprised. All those tattoos, and did you see his hair? Ain't no men around here wear their hair like that."

"Oh my God, Mama," I said, rolling my eyes. "Just 'cause someone has tattoos and long hair doesn't mean they're bad. It just means they have tattoos and long hair."

"Yeah, but then what's he doin' at the station?"

"Maybe he's reportin' a crime someone else committed." I laughed. "Maybe he's there to report that *you're* stalkin' him."

"Avery Jane Harlowe! I am not."

"Looks like you are."

She turned away from the window and crossed her arms over her chest. "Well, I'm not."

"Okay, good," I said, waving my hand toward six buckets of flowers on the floor, "then you can help me get these lilies into the fridge in the back before their edges start to curl."

My childhood best friend had probably gone into the sheriff's station to see his sister, Deputy Sheriff Abey Lee. If he'd just arrived in town, it seemed like a good place to start. I hadn't seen or thought about him in a long time. Years. Not consciously anyway, but he'd always starred in my dreams.

The last anyone knew, he had brought his son to town for his brother to raise, and then he ran again.

Dixon and I hadn't been friends in a long time. We'd grown up and grown apart, as kids do, but then I watched all through middle and high school as he became someone entirely different than the sweet little boy I'd spent my summers with. He became distant and angry, and he did every single thing the adults in his life told him not to.

He'd gotten into more fights than I could count, and he'd been on track to waste his life. And I'd heard that was exactly what he'd been doing since he graduated high school by the skin of his teeth. He'd become an addict. He'd run away.

But now he was back? And he looked… healthy. He looked strong, which was the complete opposite of how he'd looked the last time I'd seen him, two days after I graduated a year after him. I had been preparing to start business classes at the community college in Jackson. I hadn't even waited until the fall semester; my first college course began two weeks after high school ended.

But Dixon had been drunk that night at the local diner, causing a ruckus with his friends. They actually managed to break José's front window when they chucked a chair at it. Dixon was lucky no one had been hurt, but he and his stupid friends had spent the night in jail anyway.

That misguided, angry guy felt miles away. Now, Dixon seemed the opposite, quiet and stoic, mindful and… sad.

If I was honest, the tattoos were kind of hot. One had been visible peeking out of his T-shirt on the side of his neck, and it looked like he had a dragon on his left forearm, but I imagined he had a lot more under his clothes. A mountain rose up the sides of his wrist and peaked at the center point of his right forearm, and he had numbers or markings on his fingers that made me curious. I kind of liked his long hair. His older brothers were pretty clean cut. They were both good men who treated their wives well and bought flowers for them regularly, like partners should.

Dixon was different. He always had been.

And that had never been more apparent than it was today.

CHAPTER THREE

DIXON

THE HEAVY SHERIFF'S station door slammed shut behind me from the momentum of its own weight when I entered, and the only person in the room looked up from a mass of papers on her desk.

She was my brother's girl, the one he'd brought with him when he came out to California four years ago to try to talk me into coming home. I hadn't been ready then, though, and Brand showing up had made that pretty clear to me. He'd wanted me to face my past, but when they'd left and I spent the next week wide-eyed and jonesing at three in the morning, I knew for sure I wasn't ready. Not even close.

That was when I really went off the grid—Idaho, Alaska, and then I ended up in the PNW, acting like a fucking lumberjack in the Cascades, chopping down trees for a guy who gave me a cabin to live in and an honest wage.

It was there I finally came to terms with myself in the dead of winter, when I couldn't get down the mountain for food or water, nursing an empty stomach and frostbit fingers. That was when I finally knew I needed my family again and that I was ready to face them… and ready for them to need me.

My brother's girl—*shit, what's her name?* For the life of me, I couldn't remember. She didn't say anything, but she looked up at me, and I watched as realization dawned in her eyes. She lifted the phone on her desk so slowly, it looked like she was moving in slow motion, and she pressed it to her ear, hit a button with a long finger, then spoke quietly, "Get out here *right now*."

She hung up the phone and stood, smoothing wrinkles out of her uniform pants with flat hands. "Dixon."

"Hello. I'm sorry, I don't remember your name." Looking at the nametag over the pocket of her stiff brown shirt, it read R. Fitts-Lee, and then I remembered. "Wait. Roxanne? You were my brother's girl."

"Roxi." She nodded. "And now I'm his wife."

A door slammed somewhere in the back hallway. I still remembered what that long, daunting corridor looked like from my teens and all the times I'd been dragged back to the sheriff's office.

I wasn't in trouble now, but my tongue felt thick and my heart started racing again. "Y'all got married?" I said to Roxi, but my eyes didn't stray from the hallway. "I'm sorry I missed it. That's great. Congrat—"

But my best wishes stuck in my throat when my baby sister appeared at the end of the hallway.

Tears filled Abey's eyes, and she rushed toward me and threw her arms around my neck, reaching up on the tips of her work boots to hug me.

I had been right to find her first. My sister was the embodiment of light and love, and her acceptance of me bolstered me and infused me with the confidence I needed to face the rest of our family.

She held on tight, and tentatively, I hugged back, letting feathery wisps of her hair that had frizzed out of its bun tickle my cheek while I remembered the last time she'd tried to hug me, when I broke my arm because I had been too drunk to stand upright on my own.

But I'd pushed her away then, and that broken arm was the reason I'd been in the passenger seat of my sister-in-law's truck the day she died. And it was maybe the reason the CPR I'd administered hadn't worked.

The pain pills the hospital had given me for the break had been the reason I'd discovered heroin. And for a long time, I blamed those doctors for my dependence, but the truth was that my addiction was my own damn fault. I knew the first time I took one that those pills would lead me to Hell if I kept taking them. I remembered the moment I held the pill bottle over my toilet, but I didn't dump them. I pocketed them and shoved two in my mouth.

It was the last decision I remembered making before Hell really had rained its fire over my life. And it was the decision I regretted more than any other because it led to the most dire mistakes I'd ever made.

Abey let go and began patting me all over, like she was trying to make sure I was real and at the same time check me for weapons or drugs. She pulled back and looked in my eyes. "Are you okay? When did you get here? Have you been home yet?"

"Yes, I'm okay. I just got here, and no, I haven't been home yet."

"Shit," she said. "Mama's gonna lose her mind."

"How is Merv? How's her health?" I asked, using the nickname we'd given her years ago. She wasn't "Mama" in my head anymore. Good manners would make me call her "Mama" to her face, but inside, the name was too vulnerable, too painful, because mamas were supposed to protect and defend. Mervella Lee hadn't so much, and part of the reason I'd come home hinged on being able to flip some darkness from my past into the light of day. Merv would be pretty integral to that objective.

But she wasn't the main reason I'd come home. That honor went to Stu.

And to me.

"She's good. Older than you'll remember, but she's healthy. Um, okay, can you wait for me? The mayor's sittin' in my office right now and we're on a video call with the governor. Or Roxi could drive you to the ranch."

Abey looked at her deputy, and Roxi nodded agreement, but I didn't want to inconvenience her.

"Thanks, but I need to stop in at the community center next door. I checked online, and they have AA and NA meetings there. I wanna get the schedule. I'll wait for you, if that's alright? I might grab somethin' from the coffee shop."

"Yeah," my sister said, wiping an escaped tear from under her eye with her index finger, "that's fine. I'll be a half hour probably." She grabbed hold of my hand, squeezed, and smiled so widely that my heart ached. "Just… don't leave, okay?"

Shaking my head, I promised, "I won't."

No, I wouldn't be doing that. No more running. I'd come home to stay. It was fixing to be painful and uncomfortable, but my son was a bright and shining tether to my hometown, and there was no goddamn way I'd risk losing my grip on it again.

WHEN I LEFT the station and headed across the alleyway to Ace's House, Wisper's community center, the midday sun blinded me. I'd left my sunglasses in a roadside john somewhere in northern Nevada and hadn't bothered to replace them, but now I wished I had.

There used to be a sundry shop down Main Street. Henly was the owner's name, and if he was still running it, I was betting they'd have some cheap shades. If I had time after talking to the community center people, I'd head that way and see what I could find.

When I was a kid, the building I had just entered housed the local newspaper's offices. Merv could probably tell me when that had gone out of business and been bought by whoever turned it into a community center, but somehow, it still smelled the same, like musty, yellowed paper and wet ink.

As my feet crossed the threshold, a memory bubbled up from the depths of my subconscious of my dad dragging me along to place an ad in the paper for summer help on our sheep farm. My brothers and I helped after school, but we had been young and Noah Lee needed grown men with muscles and lambing experience.

Usually, I worked hard not to let memories of him enter my active thoughts, not unless my ass was glued to the seat of a chair in a therapist's office, but this memory seemed innocent enough. There were no fists shaping the memory or words of degradation, just a little boy following the man he looked up to more than anyone into an old brick building, hoping that after, his dad might take him for an ice cream cone or a milkshake.

The memory was too fuzzy for me to see through it, so I couldn't remember if the day had ended with a dairy overdose. It was doubtful, though, since the man had never deigned to acknowledge me unless he was cussing me, but it felt fitting to me that as I came to inquire about NA meetings at the community center, a memory of Noah Lee would creep up.

His love—or more precisely, the lack of it—was the catalyst to my addiction, and the original reason I needed meetings in the first place.

"How can I help you?" a man asked, and I shook the memory away as I focused on his face. He wasn't familiar.

"Yeah." I cleared my throat. "I heard y'all hold meetings here?"

"We do," he said. "What kind of meetings are you looking for? We have all kinds of meetings here."

The knowing look in the man's shrewd eyes told me he'd taken one look at me and knew exactly what I was asking, but he wasn't about to let me off the hook.

"NA or AA."

He nodded. "Come with me," he said, and he turned and didn't wait for me to follow him to an office.

I shut the door quietly behind me when I entered, and he sat behind a big mahogany desk. He pulled open a drawer and took out a piece of paper.

"The meeting times are listed here. They don't change often, but if there's ever a scheduling issue or we have bad weather, you can find updates on our website. The address is there." He set the paper on the desk, pushed it in my direction, and pointed to a blur of print at the bottom.

"Thanks," I said, grabbing the paper. I folded it and shoved it in my back pocket.

"Right now, we only offer AA meetings. We had a guy who ran the NA meetings, but he and his wife recently moved, so until we find someone else, you're welcome at

AA. The meetings aren't formal, and there's usually cross-over anyway."

"It's cool," I said. "An addict's an addict, and I'm no stranger to alcohol."

"Me either," he said. "I'm Theo by the way. Are you new in town?"

Reaching across the desk, I shook his hand. "Dixon. Technically, yeah, I guess I am. I grew up here, but I've been away a long time."

"Welcome home, Dixon."

"Thanks."

"There's a meeting tomorrow morning if you're interested."

"I'll be here," I said, thinking that, after facing the rest of my family, a meeting would be more than necessary.

CHAPTER FOUR

AVERY JANE

"WAS THAT *HIM* AGAIN?" Gran asked after I hit Deny Call on my phone and tucked it back beneath the counter.

Shrugging but not looking at her, I said, "Don't know. I've blocked him, but he gets a new number and then it just shows up on my screen like any other local number."

"You haven't talked to him though? Lately, I mean."

"No, Gran. I haven't spoken to Cody in weeks, thankfully, and I don't plan to, but I can't help it if he finds ways to get through."

The truth made my heart drop into the empty pit of my stomach and my knees weak with unease.

Cody Mahone had found countless ways to contact me even though I'd asked and screamed and then demanded that he stop. He worked on the ranch his family owned east of Jackson, so he was always too close for my comfort, and that fact was never far from my mind.

A month ago, when he showed up at my little cottage behind Gran's house with my least favorite food, escargot, if you could even call it "food," from a French bistro in Jackson and a bottle of expensive merlot, I called the Sheriff. She'd come out quickly, but Cody dropped the food and wine and ran when I yelled through my locked and deadbolted door that she was on her way. The purple stain left on my porch was a daily reminder to keep my eyes open for the asshole.

I'd given two years of my life to that man, but when I told him I was leaving him because he couldn't bother to engage in our relationship, *then* he decided to be obsessed with me?

What even was that?

Maybe it was the thrill of the chase. Maybe it was that I'd injured his pride when I left him and he was embarrassed, and that made him act a fool. I had no idea. I didn't care to know, but what I did know was that there was a determination in his eyes now I'd never seen in him before.

For whatever reason, Cody wanted me back, and it seemed clearer and clearer to me that he wouldn't stop until I gave in. Which would be never. I liked my life better without him in it, without his constant need to control everything I said or did. Both Gran and Mama couldn't stand him, probably because, since the first date, they had been able to see through his charms and how bad he was for me, and my relationships with them began to break down until I dumped his ass.

When we were dating, it never would've occurred to me he could be violent or inappropriate, but like the clearing of debris after a fire, I knew it was true. He'd never hit me or hurt me in that way. But I knew it was inside him now, especially because he was used to getting what he wanted, and I found myself looking over my shoulder for him at every turn.

That night, the sheriff had given me her cell number and her deputy's and told me, if I ever needed to, I could call and they'd come. Even if I wasn't sure Cody was lurking nearby, "Call or text," she'd said, "day or night."

This morning, when I'd seen her brother for the first time

in almost twenty years, I had to stop myself from imagining Dixon coming to my rescue.

It was difficult; he was all brawny muscles and tall steadfastness, but I knew that was just his outward appearance. Inside, I had a feeling Dixon was still the little boy I remembered from childhood, the little boy who never wanted to go home and who would sneak out of his house at night and sleep in between the bales of hay my grandpa kept for his horses.

"Are you okay, Avery Jane?" Gran asked. "I know this whole Cody thing weighs heavy on you."

"I'm okay, Gran. I'm sorry I snapped at you. It's just that I don't know what else to do."

She hummed behind me. "Sheriff Lee told you to file a restraining order. You should do that."

I scoffed. "A piece of paper? That's the weapon you think I should use against my creepy ex-boyfriend? What good will that do?"

"I said nothin' about weapons, but that piece of paper is a shield. You need to have that in place for when he crosses the line. And when he does and he violates the order, then the sheriff can lock him up. Right now, all you've got is your word against his. His family has money. You know this. They've got clout around here. A restraining order won't hurt him physically, but it would give clear boundaries to all those dicks."

Spinning, I tried not to let surprise show on my face, but Gran never cussed.

"What," she drawled. "you think I can't come up with some swear words of my own for that foul man and his foul family? *Please*."

"Okay, Gran. I'll do it. I'll file a restraining order, *if* he shows his face again. You have to have just cause and proof that someone has been doin' bad things. You can't just slap anyone with a restraining order 'cause you feel like it."

"Next time might be too late, Avery Jane."

I ignored that warning. "In the meantime, I'll do somethin' else to protect myself. At the last Small Business Association meeting, Manny Perez told me he'd teach me some self-defense. That's a good thing to know, right?"

Gran nodded and looked back down at her knitting project. I had more knitted gloves and beanies than I cared to admit, but I would never refuse something Gran made for me because everything she created was made with love.

"Don't tell Mama Cody called again, okay?" I said as I turned around when the bell on the front door jingled, indicating a customer. The squeaking of Gran's chair rocking on the floor stopped. "She'll just get up in arms, and it's not good for her stress level."

Gran mumbled something under her breath as I greeted my customer. I knew she hated keeping things from her daughter, but she'd keep this to herself because she knew I was right.

"Everlea, hi. Long time no see," I said to the woman who walked into the store with a little boy following and her daughter perched on her hip. We'd become friends six years ago when she asked me to help her with her wedding at Cade Ranch. Somehow, I managed to procure thirty tall, skinny potted pine trees and a boatload of peonies in the dead of winter.

Gran mumbled her usual "H'lo" behind me.

I handed little Mirabelle a loose daisy from the bunch I'd been using to make a bouquet a local cowboy had ordered for his wife, and Mira immediately stuffed it in her mouth. Jack Jr. went directly to the display of cacti and succulents I kept in the window for maximum sun exposure and began pressing his finger against the spines.

"Ow!"

Everlea sighed and tried to dig the daisy petals out of Mira's mouth with her finger. "Jack, c'mon. Do you have to touch *everything*?"

Jack shrugged, touched the cactus again, then pulled his finger away and stuck it in his mouth to suck away the sting.

"Sorry," I said. "I didn't think she'd eat it."

"Hi." Everlea took a deep, stress-releasing breath and laughed. "Two months ago, I was worried she'd starve because we couldn't get her to even eat candy. She's at the end of her terrible twos, and I just know they're gonna follow her to her threes. She's more stubborn than her dad, but now she eats literally everything."

Mira smirked all too knowingly.

"Well, what can I do for you? Need somethin' to brighten your day?"

Everlea smiled. "Yeah, actually. That'd be nice, but what I really need is a centerpiece. We have some new people starting the veteran program at the ranch next week and a new employee, and I thought it might be nice to add some color and cheer to the bunkhouse."

"That's a great idea. Do you have any flower preferences?"

"No, please just do your thing. I know whatever you make will be beautiful."

"Thank you. Size?"

"Whatever you think. It's going on a long, beat-up dining table that seats twelve. Nothing too over the top, I guess, but I trust your judgement."

"Great. I've got some ideas already."

She shifted her daughter on her hip, pulled a credit card

from her pocket, and handed it to me as she spun to see what had just fallen and shattered on the floor. "And ring up that cactus and the clay pot my son just dumped on your floor. I'm so sorry." She turned back toward me, wincing. "I'd offer to clean it up, but if I put Mira down the mess will only get bigger."

"No worries. I haven't sold a cactus in ages. It's on the house."

Everlea and the kids left, and after I cleaned and swept up the mess, I grabbed my wallet from my purse under the counter.

"Watch the store for a few minutes for me, Gran? I'm gonna run down the street and grab a snack."

"Those sugary candies are gonna ruin your teeth," Gran said like I was Mira's age as I ducked out the front door and headed up Main Street.

The August sun was hot on my face, but a cool breeze whispered down from the Tetons and soothed the heat. Walking beneath Your Local Bookie's awning, I waved through the window at my fellow small-business owner, Aubrey, and let the cool shade rush around me for a second.

It seemed funny because it hadn't occurred to me until he arrived back in town, but ties to Dixon were everywhere. Aubrey married Rye Graves, who was co-owner of Spitfire Ranch with Dixon's brothers, Bax and Brand. The sheriff was his little sister, and Deputy Roxi was Dixon's sister-in-law. It felt like I couldn't throw a rock in Wisper without hitting someone related to Dixon somehow.

And when I made my way up to Henly's and pulled open the door to get my candy fix, the man himself stood there, blocking the entrance, his body like a big boulder in my way, emanating heat that canceled out the gust of frigid, conditioned air rushing out of the store.

An intensity pulsed around Dixon, and it made me press the tips of my toes to the sidewalk beneath my feet, like somehow it grounded me and made me less likely to fall for him. He wore a pair of Ray-Ban knockoffs so I couldn't see his piercing blue eyes, but my memory of them had always been clear in my mind.

"Hi again," I said.

He nodded and stepped back to hold the door open for me, and I passed by him, trying not to feel the heat from his body on my bare arm and thinking I should've worn a long-sleeved shirt instead of a tank top, but that was silly. In the middle of August?

Dixon still carried the bouquet he'd bought, and now I noticed the backpack slung over his shoulder. Was that the only possession he'd brought with him when he rolled back into town? But he had to have a truck or something somewhere with the rest of his stuff, right? Surely, one backpack wasn't big enough to carry everything he owned.

"Avery Jane," Mr. Henly greeted me from behind the counter, which still looked like we were living in 1987, with little cardboard boxes on top filled with Snickers and Milky Way bars. The only difference now was that they cost a dollar fifty instead of fifty cents. "I suspected I might be seein' you today. I've got your candies right here."

"Still like Smarties?" Dixon asked quietly, and the corner of his lips tipped up into a little half-smile.

That stopped me in my tracks. He remembered my favorite candy? And how dare he smile at me like that? Something about the curve of those lips made me lose all the grounding I'd just been doing, and I felt like I might fall over like a plank of wood.

"Sweet Tooth AJ strikes again," he said, and he walked out the door and disappeared down the street.

CHAPTER FIVE

DIXON

"NICE TRUCK," I said as my sister drove us toward the farm I'd grown up on.

Although, the fleece farm our old man had started before Bax was born had become nothing more than a memory. My brothers and their friend, Rye, had turned it into a cattle ranch, and my family ran a cabin rental business on the property now too.

"Comes with the job," Abey said as she pulled to the shoulder of Old Fish Creek Road and flicked on her hazards, though there wasn't a lot of traffic on these old ranch roads on a Tuesday in the middle of prime work hours, with the sun high in the sky. "Why are you here?" she asked, turning in her seat to face me.

Fair question.

"I wanna see him."

"Stuey?"

I nodded. Who else?

"Okay, I understand that, but Dixon, you left. Bax is Stu's dad now. I don't know how else to say this to you, but you can't just waltz back into town and expect to…"

"To what?"

"To be a dad."

"I know that. And I'm not here to interfere or to take Stu away from Bax, but I've spent a long time preparing for this, and I want to *know* my kid. Is that wrong?"

Abey shook her head. "It's not wrong. And please don't misunderstand. I'm glad you're home. You look good. You look… healthy."

"I'm sober. That's what you really wanna know, ain't it?"

"Yes. It is."

"I've been sober more than four years," I said.

Her jaw dropped. "*Four* years? So you've been sober since Brand found you in California? And you didn't come home till now? Why?"

"Just 'cause I wasn't high, it didn't mean I had my shit figured out. I had a lot of demons to come to terms with, and I wasn't about to dump that on my kid's front door."

"I wish you would've called us though. I've been so worried about you."

"I'm sorry, but that didn't feel safe for me. Y'know?"

"Okay, but I just wanna make sure you're prepared for what's about to happen. Merv is gonna lose her shit and cry, and you can't just walk into Bax's house and announce that you're Stuey's dad. He doesn't know you."

"I'm not stupid, Abey. I wouldn't do that. I-I… I just want to be part of his life. However I can. In whatever small way I'm allowed to be. That's all. Did they… H-have they adopted him? Legally?"

She shook her head. "No. They tried but it was denied. The judge wouldn't do anything without talkin' to you."

"Oh." I wasn't sure how I felt about that. Elated in one sense, but when I left Stu with Bax, I assumed if I ever saw them again, they'd be father and son. Officially. It was part of the reason I had to stay away. I didn't know if I could see that, see their bond with my own eyes, and not run to the first dealer I could find.

Touching the tips of her fingers to the back of my hand resting on my leg, Abey smiled. "Have I told you I missed you?"

"I missed you too, sis. Now, drive. Let's get this home-comin' over with."

BEFORE ABEY and I left the station, I saw Roxi on her cell phone, whispering to someone. I assumed it was her husband, and now, when we pulled up to my brother's house, listening to the slow pop and crackle of gravel beneath Abey's tires, I knew I'd been right.

Brand opened his front door and stepped onto the porch. He whistled loudly, and after a few seconds, bullets of white came running to me from the trees. It took me a beat to realize the fluffy, flying fur balls were Tilly and Zephyr, the two Pyrs I'd trained back in Mad River, California after I first got sober.

As I stepped out of the truck, they rushed me, jumped on their hind legs, and tried to hug me and lick me to death, which, considering they were full grown Great Pyrenees and one of the largest breeds of guardian dogs, was like two non-violent polar bears converging on me.

"Mangy mutts," I whispered, smiling, scratching behind their ears and pulling thistle out of their coats. These goof-balls had been friends to me when no one else in the world was.

Brand had built himself and Roxi a log A-frame, nestled at the tip of an outstretched finger of the forest, surrounded on three sides by deep green pines and firs. The wood almost looked red against its mountain backdrop.

He descended his porch stairs slowly, taking me in. I couldn't decipher the look on his face. He had to be angry with me. I'd promised him four years ago I'd come home, but all my promises back then had been hollow. Not that I made many. I didn't know my sober self well back then, but I knew enough not to trust anything I said.

Things were different now. I'd spent the last four years learning who I was, what I was capable of, and what I wasn't.

But if I made a promise now, I knew I could keep it.

I gave the command for the dogs to sit, and surprisingly, even after all the time that had passed, they did.

"Brand," I said, and my voice cracked as I addressed the brother who'd tried to help me when I barely had the strength to accept it. When death, degradation, and despair had weighed me down like someone had dragged me to the edge of the ocean, wrapped me up in wool, and tied a brick around my shroud.

"Dixon. I thought we'd never see you again."

Abey stepped from the truck and closed her door quietly, and the three of us stood there, just looking at each other silently.

Something clicked into place inside me. It was something I had dreamed of and imagined a million times but never dared hope.

I was home. The land had accepted me back. I felt it inside my bones, and a settling crept up on me slowly, like it was afraid to startle me for fear that I'd react.

I didn't. I just breathed and let it coat my soul.

"I'm sorry," I said to Brand and Abey both. "I'm sorry I promised things I didn't know how to give."

Brand came closer, looking in my eyes, trying to decide if

he could trust me. He probably thought he could trust me four years ago and look what that had gotten him.

"Before I see Merv and Stu, I wanna tell you both that I'm home. I'm not leavin', even if it's hard to stay. I'm not here to take Stu from Bax and his wife. I'm just here. I wanna know y'all again, this time sober, and I want to earn my place in the family again, if that's even possible."

Tilly whined at my feet, looking up at my brother like she was begging for me.

"Of course it's possible," Brand said. "We love you. We've missed you and worried about you. I'm glad you're here." He took the last few steps separating us and wrapped his arms around my back. I couldn't help my reaction; I clung to him. To his forgiveness and acceptance, and I clung to the hope that we could be brothers again. Quietly, he said, "Give Bax time. Give him space and go slow with Stu. He'll come around."

"I will."

Abey joined our hug from the outside, but I pulled her between us so we could squish her in the middle like we had when we were kids. She laughed and squirmed to get free, but that just made us hug harder, until she reached up on her toes, maneuvered her arms around my shoulders, and held on tight.

No matter the division in our family, the way our father held me separate from my brothers and sister, the way he spent his life dismissing me— With my siblings, I never felt different. When it was just us, Bax, Brand, Abey, and me, I had always felt accepted.

As Brand backed up to allow us the moment, Abey whispered in my ear, "I'm so happy you came home. It hasn't been right here without you."

And that was when my tears began to fall.

TILLY AND ZEPHYR chased Abey's truck as she drove Brand and me to Merv's house, and he explained that he'd driven back to California to adopt the dogs from the couple I'd worked for, the Coulters, after I disappeared and left them without a dog trainer. They'd given me a place to live and a job when no one else showed me kindness because I was a four-time rehab flunky and I'd been in jail. I'd known my brother had adopted the dogs. Brenda Coulter told me when I went to ask her forgiveness for bailing on her and her husband when they had been depending on me.

The Coulters offered their forgiveness, but I still had a lot of amends left to make to a lot of people.

Merv's house wasn't much more than a mile away from Brand's, and when we got there, the dogs flopped in the grass in front of the house next to a water bucket left there for them. Tilly inched toward it on all fours, slopped up half the volume, and then rested her big head on the rim in case she decided she wanted more. Another dog, a German Shepherd, came trotting from the opposite direction. He sniffed Zephyr and Tilly and then lay between them with his head on his paws, as if settling in for a long babysitting session.

The new house Brand had built for Merv was beautiful. Rich, deep blue and set against the stark mountain in the background, it was exactly the kind of place I'd always dreamed for my mother. She lived in a run-down trailer for years after our joke of a father died, and I hated that place. It looked on the outside like I had felt on the inside, busted up and pathetic, and I'd known Merv deserved better.

A better house and a better son.

For a long time, I was angry and bitter at Brand for being able to give our family what I knew I never could. Now, I knew that what he'd given them was a blessing. Just like whatever it was that I would give them. I'd never be rich; anything I had to offer couldn't compare monetarily, but that didn't mean my worth was less than my brother's.

It was just different. I was different, and I knew now that was okay.

Not that coming home again would be easy. I wasn't under any false impressions about that. I'd left messes in my wake since I was fifteen years old, and it would take more than a little—

"Son?" Merv appeared on her porch, and the screen door clacked closed behind her. Abey had been right; our mama was already crying, her eyes red and puffy. "Dixon? Is that you?"

"Yeah, Mama," I said as I got out of the truck, reaching back in to grab the flowers I'd brought for her from the dash, and I walked slowly toward my mother. God, how she'd aged. Her hair was all silver now, and I could see the years passed on her face like a road map to her heartaches and joys. "It's me."

She nodded. "You look different."

I climbed the stairs somberly, like a funeral procession to a grave, but I held the bouquet out toward her, even though I knew a handful of daisies couldn't fix what I'd broken, or what she had.

"So do you."

She patted her hair. "I'm old."

"You're beautiful, Mama. You always have been and you always will be. These are for you. They ain't much but—"

The flowers fell to the porch as Merv flung herself into my arms. I wrapped them around her shoulders and held her close while she cried.

Between sobs, she mumbled, "I'm sorry. I prayed for this

day, and I promised myself and God I wouldn't blubber, but I can't help it. I'm so thankful to have you home. You don't know what it's been like without you."

But I did know. I knew all too well what it felt like to be alone, without my family. Without love. Without hope.

That was the kicker; having hope again was a catch twenty-two. It could take me higher than any drug and drag me down lower than any rock bottom I'd ever faced. The hope that had embedded itself under my skin, the hope that my kid could ever love me, had the power to eviscerate me.

It was the scariest feeling I'd ever known. I hated it, but somehow I loved it, too, because if my son could learn to love me, I would be the richest man to ever walk the earth.

CHAPTER SIX

DIXON

ABEY AND BRAND sat on the Adirondack chairs on Merv's porch while she took me on a tour of the house. She'd lived in it for several years, but it was new to me.

It felt weird to be in a home with her again, one I'd never seen the inside of, and memories of my childhood in the farmhouse Bax and my son now lived in flooded my mind.

For so long, I believed I deserved every bad thing in life, and if enough bad things weren't happening to me, then I went out looking for more.

So many arguments and punishments flashed through my head, dinners I'd been denied because my father hated me and deemed everything I did to be wrong. I had no clue how many nights I'd gone to bed hungry, but however many, it was wrong and cruel, and it had taken me all my life to accept that those punishments came from a mean man with a mean heart and that I hadn't deserved them.

AJ starred in those memories too. I wondered if she had any idea how much comfort she'd given me back then, when I was a little boy lost, when she brought me a blanket and a pillow in her granddaddy's barn and slices of bread and butter and cookies because I'd been so hungry, I cried. And she'd wake me up before dawn so I could climb the gutter next to my bedroom window and sneak back into my own bed.

As I followed behind my mama, listening to her chatter about window coverings and nice furniture Brand had bought her, I wanted to know why she'd never stopped the abuse. I had a pretty good guess, but something inside me needed to hear her say it out loud.

She guided me to sit at her dinner table and sat next to me, but then she jumped back up.

"Coffee," she said awkwardly. "I'll make us some coffee. You still drink it?"

"No, ma'am."

"Oh. Well, I'll make some anyway. I still drink it, but decaf since my heart attack—" She stopped and looked at me. "Did your brother or sister tell you I had a heart attack? It's been almost four years."

"Yeah, Brand told me. Are you okay? How do you feel now?"

"Oh fine," she said as she turned again and headed for her coffee maker. "I'm healthier now than I've probably ever been, but when it first happened, I had to make a lot of changes. I'd already quit smokin', so caffeine was the next to go."

"Good for you, Mama. I'm proud of you."

As she waited for the coffee to start, she turned and leaned against her counter. "I'm proud of you too. A-are you… Do you plan to stay?"

"Yes, ma'am. I'm home for good, and I'm healthier than I've ever been too. That's why no caffeine for me either."

"I can see that. You're like a different man."

"No, same man, but now I know how to look after myself and make healthier choices."

Jesus, could this conversation get any more uncomfortable? But an argument on the front porch interrupted us, and then I heard Brand raising his voice and telling Bax to wait.

He didn't. Merv's front door banged open, and then my oldest brother was there, standing right in front of me with dirty hands on his hips. He must've come from working the ranch.

After too many years between us, all he said was, "You're here."

"Yes," I said, but I kept my ass in the chair because the anger and confusion pulsing out of him like a beacon needed space. I didn't want to appear confrontational in any way. Not with Bax.

"Why? What do you want? You can't have Stu."

"Bax," Abey and Brand pleaded quietly in unison behind our brother.

He shook his head. "No. It needs to be said. He left his kid on my goddamn doorstep. He can't just breeze back into town and expect us to—"

"Bax, *stop*," Merv begged.

Bax threw her a scowl. "Why are y'all actin' like I'm the bad guy here?" Pointing at me, he barked, "He abandoned his son!"

"I did." Finally, I stood, but slowly and I held my hands in front of my body. "But I'm not here to take him away from you."

"Good 'cause you can't. You signed your parental rights over to me. He's not yours anymore."

It was true. I knew it, but the words stabbed me in the heart all the same.

Resisting the urge to clutch my chest and fight against the pain, I let it run through me. I would have to get used to hearing the truth.

"I'm home, Bax. For good, but I don't wanna do anything to hurt Stu. Please believe me."

He laughed humorlessly. "I'd love to, little brother. I'd love to stand here and shoot the shit and trust everything that comes out of your mouth, but I don't. I don't know if I ever will. You've lied, you've cheated, stolen, and you ran away. You can pull that shit on me every goddamn day of the week, but I will not let you do it to my son. You hear me?"

But before I could answer, Merv's screen door squeaked open again, and then a little brown-haired head peeked around Abey's hip.

"Why's my daddy mad?" the little boy asked, and I froze.

My little boy. I *made* him. I knew him in my soul, knew the sound of his voice and the warmth of his skin. I knew his happiness as if it were my own. I still remembered his tiny bean toes and the way his eyes, still untrained and free from images that could hurt him, searched my face. There hadn't been anything good for him to find, and that was just one more reason I had known I needed to give him up.

Stuey stared up at his aunt but pointed at me. "Who's that guy?"

Abey looked at me and then Bax. "Um…"

Bax's wife rushed in behind Stu, and when she saw me, she stopped dead in her tracks. We'd met once before, but I'd looked a lot different then, and I'd barely spoken to her. But Stu was my spitting image. His hair was the same wavy brown, his eyes the same shape and shade of blue. Somehow, I thought I saw the same curiosity in them I'd had as a boy, so Bax's wife had to know who I was.

Bax groaned. "Dammit, Bea. Didn't you get my text? I told you to take Stu straight home."

I knew I liked her the minute she spoke.

"Put a lid on it, husband. We got a flat tire on the way

home. You try changin' a tire with that one"—she pointed at Stu—"jumpin' around and tryin' to dart out into traffic. I didn't have a chance to check my texts."

Bax's hands dropped from his hips, and he hung his head. Bea walked beside him, and he turned and leaned down to kiss her cheek. "I'm sorry. Please, would you just take Stu home?"

"Mama, who is that guy?" Stu said again, and regret coursed through me. Bea *was* Stu's mama, the only woman lucky enough to raise him, but he used to have another mama, and it struck me for the millionth time that he would never know her.

"Um, that's your uncle, Dixon. He's your daddy's brother."

His uncle. It seemed the easiest explanation, but it stung.

"I have another uncle? Cool! You wanna go fishin' with me?" Stu asked me, and I almost fell right off my feet.

I pictured it: my son and me sitting at the end of a dock or in a canoe, fishing poles dangling over a lake, eating sandwiches and talking about our day.

"No," Bax said. "Maybe another time. You have homework."

"Dad," Stu groaned. "I'm in kindergarten, and school just started. All I gotta do is color a picture and call it a day."

I snorted. I couldn't stop it because my kid was funny! I hadn't expected that.

"Right," Bax said. "So then I'm gonna go with the classic 'Because I said so' excuse."

Stu rolled his eyes but then looked at me and shrugged. "Maybe next time."

"Maybe," I agreed. "And maybe your dad can come with us?"

Bax glanced at me, trying to gauge if I really wanted him

to come. I did. I meant what I said. I wasn't here to take over. And I wouldn't do a goddamn thing if it would hurt my kid. Bax needed to know that.

I wasn't the man who'd raised us. I wasn't cruel, and I loved my big brother more than I could ever tell him for a lot of reasons, but most of all for raising my child when his mama and I couldn't, for loving Stu and providing him with the care and comfort I'd had no clue how to give.

Bax didn't respond. He turned and nodded out the door to his wife. She flashed me a sympathetic smile. Maybe she believed what I'd said was true, but she hadn't grown up with me. She hadn't been a witness to my descent into addiction. I'd never lied to her or stolen from her. I'd never let her down.

"We'll discuss it later," Bax said like the steadfast father he was, and he walked out the door, following Bea and Stu without a look back in my direction.

When they were gone and the happy sound of Stu's questioning chatter faded away, we heard Bax's truck grinding gravel behind Bea's. Merv sat at the table, and I fell into my chair. I was surprised I hadn't fallen straight down to the floor on my ass.

My kid!

God, he was beautiful, and his squeaky voice and wit filled me with so much unearned pride that I felt like I could burst into a million happy pieces. I saw his mama in him too. He had Kel's nose and a little bit of her stubbornness and sass that I remembered from when we'd first met, but all of that had disappeared by the time she died. Addiction had stolen all her good parts, but now I felt them again with every sound and every move Stu made.

"Are you okay?" Merv asked as Abey and Brand took seats at the table with us.

I couldn't speak, so I nodded.

"He'll calm down," Brand tried to assure me.

"It's okay if he doesn't," I said quietly. "I'm pretty pissed at the same guy Bax is for the exact same reason."

"Dixon," Abey said, grabbing my hand and squeezing. "Maybe it would be good for you to *show* Bax that you're different. What are your plans for work and housing? We have an inn on the property now. You could stay there or in one of the cabins."

"He'll stay here with me," Merv said. "His room has been waitin' for him since the day I moved in."

"No," I said. "Thank you, Mama. I appreciate the offer, but I need space. And I won't stay on the farm. It's too close to Bax and Stu. I don't wanna push Bax. For now, I planned to rent a room in town."

"A room?"

"Yeah. Didn't there used to be a boarding house close to downtown? Is it still there?"

Abey nodded. "Mrs. Ellison's place."

"What about money?" Brand asked. "A weekly rental won't be cheap."

"I've got it covered," I assured him before he offered to pay. He'd spent enough of his hard-earned money on me.

Merv frowned and shook her head. "Don't you want to be here with me? Won't you be lonely?"

"I've been alone for a long time, Mama. I like the silence, and Abey's right. I need to prove to Bax and Stu both that I have no plans to mooch off anybody or invade their lives uninvited. I meant what I told Bax. I'm here to stay, but I don't wanna disrupt Stu's world or cause trouble. I just want to earn the right to be in his life in some small way." I turned to Abey. "Can you give me a lift to the rental place?"

"Right now?"

"Yeah."

Abey's eyes darted to Merv. I knew my mama would be disappointed. She'd always fussed over me, even more than my brothers and sister, and it felt like she wanted to now, but I'd just seen my son for the first time in more than four years, and I needed to process the clusterfuck of feelings bubbling up inside me.

If Merv crowded me and smothered me the way she used to, I'd be right back where I was before the drugs. Until she and I could talk and hash out our past, I needed to maintain a careful distance. It was the only thing keeping me sane.

The last two hours had been filled with more emotion than I'd let myself feel in a very long time, and it was starting to be too much.

"But you just got here," Merv said, the wounded sound of her voice making my decision to get some space even more right.

I stood and promised, "I'll be back, but I need to find a place to stay and a car. Tomorrow, I need to start lookin' for a job. Once I do all that, I'll come back to tell you about it. There's a lot you and I need to talk about."

Merv's eyes lowered for a few seconds, but then they lifted back up to mine. She took a deep breath. "Yes, there is."

CHAPTER SEVEN

AVERY JANE

THE FIFTH CALL in two days from the same unknown number told me exactly who had been calling.

It was risky since a lot of my customers contacted me on my cell, but I had a feeling I knew who it was, so I didn't answer, and the caller never left a voicemail. A customer would have, or they'd text when I didn't answer. It wasn't Cody's style to leave a message. Whatever he wanted to say to me, he would say it to my face, whether I wanted him to or not.

It was exhausting trying to predict when that might be, so instead of waiting around for the unpleasant inevitable, I called Manny Perez to talk to him about starting my self-defense lessons. He only lived three blocks away, and he said, "No time like the present," so I walked to his house after work with a bouquet I whipped together from garden clippings for his wife, Yolanda.

Wisper in late summer was a slow, quiet, all-American haven. Birds twittered and chirped beneath a clear blue sky, swooping in and out of cottonwoods. Kids raced by me on their bikes as I walked, and every few houses, neighbors were out tending their lawns. Mrs. Darby and her husband Bo planted a garden every spring that could win contests. A fair few of the arrangements I'd made over the years had been inspired by the whimsical, English-cottage vibes of the Darbys' garden.

I waved to them sipping iced tea on their front porch, and they waved back a hello.

"Your lavender and lilies look amazing this year, Mrs. Darby."

"Thank you, dear!"

"Welcome," I called back as I turned the corner and started counting the familiar sidewalk cracks I'd been keeping track of since I was eight. I ran my hand along the Darbys' freshly painted fence, but before I made it all the way to the end—one hundred and fourteen wooden slats and thirty-seven cracks later—two large, worn cowboy boots appeared in my view, straddling the thirty-eighth crack and blocking my path.

"You'd think the county would've repoured these sidewalks by now," Dixon said as I looked up and into his sunglasses, trying to see the depths of the blue behind them. He removed the glasses and let them dangle from his fingers next to his thigh, and somehow, seeing the lifetime in those eyes felt like home, even though now they showed years of a hard life, told in lines and creases of his skin. "How many cracks now?"

"Dixon, I know you know this because you're older than me, but I'm almost thirty-five years old. I don't count cracks in the sidewalk anymore. I haven't since we were kids."

He cocked an eyebrow. "How many?"

I rolled my eyes and conceded. "You're standin' on number thirty-eight." Looking around the large bulge of his bicep, I noticed the sheriff on her phone by her truck parked next to the curb, and then I looked at the boarding house behind the Darbys'. "Are you stayin' here?"

"Yeah. Just checked in. You still live at home?"

"No. Well, yes, technically on the same property, but I stay out back in the guest house. Gran let me renovate it. It's small, but it's all mine. I even have a cat, Fancy."

Swinging his arm toward the bouquet I'd made, he said, "That's pretty. You make it?"

"Yeah."

He smiled, and I tried not to gasp out loud. The way his eyes lit up and the curve of his mouth reminded me how much I used to love him. By the time he turned fifteen, Dixon had already been headed down a much darker path than me, but it hadn't stopped me from admiring him from afar and wishing we could be close like when we were little.

He'd always possessed the talent to make whatever he did seem effortless, but I had known the truth—that the hurt and the fear raging inside him made everything harder. Honestly, I'd never really been surprised he'd turned to drugs. Dixon was an empath. He always had been. He felt every single emotion so deeply, and he took on the emotions of the people around him, whether he wanted to or not.

It had to be a lot to shoulder. And on top of all that, his dad had been awful to Dixon his entire life. I never understood why. Dixon tried everything in his power to make his dad happy when we were kids, but it was never enough.

There was a story Dixon used to tell. He told it to his brothers and sister, to anyone who'd listen, about a magic man who had come to the Lee farm to find his faerie princess. Everyone scoffed and laughed at Dixon. Magic didn't exist. Not for the people of Wisper, Wyoming, not back then. They worked crap jobs, drove crap cars and trucks. Farms and ranches failed all the time, and half the stores on Main Street had been vacant. If you needed something, you drove to Jackson. So, if magic existed, why wouldn't it fix all those horrible things?

But Dixon said all his naysayers were wrong. The magic man *did* find his princess—Dixon's mama, Mervella Lee.

When she was young, she had flowing hair of gold and eyes the color of the blue Wyoming sky. All the men in town lusted after her, desperate just to hear a kind hello from her lips, but her husband was possessive and mean, and she didn't dare speak to any of those men.

But the magic man believed in fate, and he fell in love with Dixon's mama. She fell in love with him, too, because he made her laugh and forget about all the things that made her sad.

And then they made a baby.

When the faerie princess's husband found out, his anger grew so big that the whole town of Wisper felt it. The ogre's anger grew and grew until it was the size of an evil, fire-breathing dragon, a dragon with one mission: to find the magic man and vanquish him from the earth.

And that was what the dragon did, or so Dixon used to say, because the magic man was never heard from again.

"And your mama and Gran," Dixon asked, yanking me right out of my memories, "how are they? I was kinda flustered this mornin'. I didn't say hello to 'em."

"They're good. They were really curious about you. They didn't recognize you."

"Tell 'em I'm a travelin' acrobat, and I've come to swing from mountaintop to mountaintop until there ain't no more mountains to conquer."

Laughing, I said, "I see you're still makin' up stories. You probably got a ton by now. You should write a book."

"I could tell a story about a guy who writes a book, but

actually writin' one? Naw. I wouldn't have the first clue about that." He kicked at the crack in the sidewalk between us with the tip of his boot. "So, where you headed this fine afternoon?"

"I'm takin' a self-defense class. Well, it's not really a class. Do you remember Manny Perez?"

"Uh, yeah. You mean the guy who dragged me by my hair to the sheriff's station when I snuck into his bar and he caught me stealin' from the cash register?"

"Yep. That's the guy," I said, regretting that I'd reminded Dixon of something he probably wanted to forget.

But he laughed. "Yeah, I remember Manny."

"He's gonna teach me how to protect myself."

Dixon's stance changed. He stood straighter, and I watched as his muscles bunched and tightened beneath his threadbare T-shirt. "Why do you need to protect yourself?"

But I wasn't about to dump my problems on him. He had enough of his own to contend with.

I waved away his concern, flapping my hand in the air between us. "Oh, no reason. It's just somethin' I've always thought about learnin'. You know, just in case."

He relaxed, his fists loosening the grip on the imaginary balls they'd just been squeezing, and out of the corner of my eye, I noticed his sunglasses, now in pieces.

The daydream I'd had earlier floated to the surface of my thoughts, the one in which Dixon became my rescuer like I was a fair maiden held captive in a baroque tower. I shook my head, trying to wipe the daydream away.

To Dixon, I probably represented safety and good memories because I'd taken care of him when we were young, but he'd never felt the same way I'd felt about him. He'd never lain in bed at night, picturing our imaginary love story. He'd never looked at my body and thought that if he touched me once, he might combust and become a wild inferno of desire.

And God as my witness, that was ten times worse now. Just looking at him made my heart quicken, and my tongue peeked out between my lips to lick them like Fancy with a bowl of tuna in her sights.

The little boy I used to know was still in there somewhere. And the young man who didn't know who he was, where he belonged, he lived inside Dixon too, but now, a grown-ass man stood in front of me. It was clear *he* was the one leading the horse, and he was *fine*. His old, used-up clothes didn't bother me, nor did his unkempt hair, the scuffs on his boots, or the wear showing on his face.

What I saw when I looked at him now was the strength he'd fought tooth and nail for and a knowing ease, because maybe he finally did know where he wanted to belong, but there was no pretension because he still didn't think he deserved to belong anywhere.

He was an island, and I was an idiot for thinking so, but in my view, his island was a sexy, humid hideaway in the tropics, with aqua waters and the greens of the leaves in the trees so bright and vibrant, they left me blinded and breathless. Rare flowers bloomed in deep, rogue reds and punchy purples. The air sweltered, the sun baked, and *everything* was hot.

But there was no way in hell I was going to clue him into the fact that I'd spent the entirety of our teenage years and most of my adult ones imagining him in my bed.

"Well anyway," I said awkwardly, "I better get goin'. Manny's expectin' me. See you around?"

"I expect you will," he replied, and he smiled. He lifted the sunglasses to pop them on again, but he noticed that he'd broken off the arm, so he shoved them in his pocket instead. "See you later, AJ."

I waved as I walked away, and when I passed his sister still talking on her phone, she nodded at me and covered the speaker with her hand. "Still have me on speed dial?" she asked.

Looking over my shoulder, I wanted to make sure Dixon was too far away to hear us. He was, but I nodded silently anyway.

"Good," she whispered, but she looked the picture of the town protector, especially with her gun holstered to her thigh, when she said, "Call any time."

I thought about Dixon and his sister the rest of the way to Manny's. I wondered if Abey had gone into law enforcement because of Dixon. I wondered if she had known how sad her brother had been when we were kids, so sad that he had to make up stories about himself to get through each day because reality was so horrible for him that lies were the only way he could cope.

CHAPTER EIGHT

DIXON

"YOU SHOULD WRITE A BOOK."

How absurd was that?

Me, a fucked-up, recovering heroin, alcohol, and pain pill addict. An asshole who'd abandoned his son and his family. Who'd lied and stolen and cheated. Who had spent more nights locked in a jail cell than he wanted to admit.

Write a book?

I was no writer. I was a misfit, a ne'er do well, like my old man used to say.

I'd watched people die. I'd caused three people's deaths. Four if you counted that son of a bitch, Noah Lee, who I hoped died as a direct result of the anguish he felt about how he'd treated me. I wasn't sure if it had any effect on the prick 'cause I was high as a kite outside his hospital room when he took his last breath. I couldn't have told you my name that day for all the shit coursing through my veins.

Only blood flowed through them now as I pulled the hardback chair to my room's window. I sat and tried to get comfortable, watching and waiting.

Three nights I'd sat at this window. The first time it was

because I didn't know what else to do with myself. The room I'd rented was so goddamn small, it felt like I was locked up again. I needed air and space, but I'd already walked miles around Wisper. I had nowhere else to go, so I opened the window and let the hot, claggy, evening shadows rush in and surround me.

Listening to the utter silence of Wisper at midnight, it reminded me of my cabin in the Cascades. That place had been so silent and dark there at night that if my power went out, which it often did, I couldn't tell if my eyes were open or closed.

I had just decided to shut the window and sweat myself to sleep in bed, when *she* walked by.

AJ.

Assuming she must've been having an uncommon bout of insomnia, I didn't expect to see her again the second night, but I did, and I watched as she patrolled the street, counting her cracks again and touching every plant and flower she passed on her way.

Tonight, I'd come prepared with a cup of steaming chamomile tea Mrs. Ellison had fixed for me before she'd gone to bed that was lukewarm now but would hopefully still be effective. Her only other tenant had checked out and left town, a birdwatching guy from over somewhere in Idaho, so there wasn't even the sound of the videos he played on his phone to distract me from my thoughts. Mrs. Ellison watched *Jimmy Kimmel Live!* before bed every night, but the TV was in her room and not available to me. She told me I could get my own if I wanted to, the noise wouldn't bother her, but I'd never been much for TV.

I liked the stories in my head better.

I hadn't been back out to the ranch yet. I spent the last three days pounding the pavement, looking for a job, and I walked out to Mickey Finkle's used car lot. He sold me an old, like *really* old, El Camino. But it wasn't like I planned on back roading anytime soon, so the beater would do for now to get me around town. It needed a new exhaust, and the upholstery had been ripped to shit, but I'd always been good at fixing stuff like that, and it would give me something to do on days I wasn't working.

Mrs. Ellison said she'd knock some money off my rent if I fixed the shower in the upstairs bathroom, which didn't so much spray water as it did leak it, so that was first on my to-do list.

When I showed up for my first AA meeting in Wisper, I also inquired at the community center about available work, and Theo said I was in luck because his handyman had just quit and opened his own Mr. Fix-It business. The handyman position paid well, and Theo even offered health insurance.

While I was there, I took advantage of the center's clothing donation room, found me a few new shirts and two pairs of jeans that looked worn, but not so bad that anyone might notice or scoff. I still had a hard time spending money on new things. I'd tried to convince myself it was because I was trying to give back to the earth, recycle, protest grotesque capitalism and all that bullshit, but that was a thin lie. I still didn't think I deserved new things. Boxers and socks, though, those were my big splurge. Found a pack of each over at Henly's my first day back.

Before I left Ace's House, Theo also offered me the NA meeting leader position he still needed to fill. Of course, that job was a volunteer thing and didn't pay bupkis, but I turned him down because I had no clue how to be a leader. He said I should think about it and decide once I'd gotten settled, but it wasn't for me.

I was glad for sobriety and grateful for AA and NA.

Those meetings and all the addicts attending them day after day in every city in America had been my saving grace more times than I could count. Knowing millions of people were out there fighting the same fight as me made me feel a little bit less alone, but it was better for me to distance myself from people's pain. If I got too close, I took on their worries and sorrows like they were my own, but I had enough of my own burdens. The weight of everybody else's was too heavy to bear anymore.

Instead, I took a second, part-time position at the animal clinic on the weekends, tending the animals boarded there or recovering from treatment. Now that was a job I knew I'd be good at, especially if I got to be around dogs. I'd always had an inexplicable connection to them. They understood me, and I understood them.

All that work would keep idle away. I'd found the busier I was, the less I allowed myself to wallow. Like now, as I waited for AJ to walk past my window again, my thoughts kept straying to Stuart. I wanted to know what he looked like when he dreamed. I wanted to know what his nightly rituals were. Dinner, maybe a TV show before his bath, a book, and then bed? Did Bea tuck him in or did Bax? Or did they both? Did Bea sing to him like Kel had the few weeks she managed to stay sober after she gave birth to Stu?

What was the song she sang…

"Hush, Little Baby."

Humming the melody, I made up a story for Stu in my head about a little boy who had so many people who loved him, and all that love made him grow bigger and stronger until he was so big he became the king of the land. The love rained out of him and down to all the people in town, but the rain was so beautiful and warm, so they tucked away their umbrellas, smiling and laughing, and loved him right back so that his love never ran out.

I didn't see AJ at first, but I heard her as she rounded the corner, cussing up a storm to the night. When she appeared at the end of the Darbys' fence, she stomped on the cracks in the sidewalk instead of stepping over them.

Something's wrong.

Grabbing a T-shirt out of my backpack, I pulled it on as I ran down the stairs, hoping I hadn't woken Mrs. Ellison. When I got out to the porch, the squeaking screen door scared AJ. As I made a mental note to WD-40 the shit out of it, she stopped and whipped her head around to find me.

She squinted, trying to see me under the dark eave. "Dixon? Is that you?"

"Yeah," I said quietly, moving into the light from a nearby streetlamp. "Just me."

"What're you doin'?" she asked nervously. "It's midnight."

Laughing, I said, "I could ask you the same thing. This is the third night in a row you've gone for a stroll by yourself in the dark."

She seemed taken aback that I'd noticed.

"I can't sleep either," I explained.

"Oh." She relaxed, her stance loosening a little in relief that I wasn't some creepy stalker, tracking her every step. "Why not?"

I shrugged. "Dunno. Sleep's never come easy for me, I guess. Too much goin' on in my head."

"Well I love sleep. If I could sleep twenty hours a day, I would."

"So then, why the midnight walkabouts?"

She sighed, and her shoulders dropped what seemed like twelve inches.

"What's wrong?" I asked as I stepped off the porch and joined her on the sidewalk. "Somethin' to do with the flower shop?"

"No. It's not that. It's a… a guy."

"Oh." I hadn't expected that answer. I didn't *like* that answer.

"It's not a big deal. He's just a little persistent, and I'm kinda fed up."

It had been a million years, but the old urges I'd had when I'd seen her at school or around town when we were teenagers came back. We didn't speak more than a word or two in passing back then; our happy childhood had faded with the years. My anger at my family, my mother, the world, had washed them away, but I still noticed AJ. She grew taller, curvier, and she'd always been so smart.

Maybe I was creepy because I couldn't stop noticing now how her hips swelled and dipped in around her waist. Her thick hair fell behind her slim shoulders. It dusted her shoulder blades and shone under the moon. And her lips? Full, pink, and perfect. And God, those freckles on her nose — I wanted to kiss each one. She wasn't much taller than five-five, and if I held her, she would've fit in my embrace like she was made to.

Holding her hand like I had when we were kids, the touch of her skin on mine felt magnetic. I wrapped my fingers around hers, took a tentative step down the sidewalk, and she followed. We walked together slowly, and it felt so much like old times and peaceful, it almost scared me.

"He live around here?" I asked, thinking if he did, I'd be glad to go this jackoff's house and have a *conversation*.

"No. He lives east of Jackson, but he keeps callin' me."

"Can't you block his number?"

"I have many times."

Stopping and turning toward her, I asked, "Don't you only have to do that once? I admit, I'm no cell phone expert. I don't own one, but I thought that was a one-and-done kinda thing."

"You don't have a phone?"

"Not anymore."

"How do you talk to your son?"

"I… I don't."

CHAPTER NINE

AVERY JANE

JESUS, *Avery Jane! How many times are you gonna remind this man of all the wrong he's done? Pretty sure he's quite aware.*

"Sorry," I said, pulling on his hand and dragging him with me as I continued walking.

"You know about Stu?" he asked.

"'Course I do. I've met him a few times."

Dixon pulled my hand this time and turned me. There was so much hope in his eyes. "You have? What's he like?"

"He's… delightful. Funny and caring. He and his mom came into the shop once when I was teeterin' on a ladder and hangin' up my strands of flowers on the back wall. I dropped my hammer and a box of nails, and Stu crouched down and picked up every last one.

"Sometimes I see them all walkin' downtown, and he always waves to me and smiles."

The matching smile dawning on Dixon's face was so beautiful that I wanted to reach up and touch my fingers to his lips so I could feel his happiness.

Looking up at him, I said, "He's a storyteller, like you."

Staring into my soul, Dixon whispered, "He is?"

"Yeah."

"What kinds of stories?"

"Well, he's only personally told me one about the fish in the lake by his house and all the silly stuff they get up to, but my friend Everlea has a son, and sometimes the boys play together at the park. Her son's a few years older than Stu, I think, but Everlea says Stu can jibber jabber with the best of them. She says he's a hoot."

"God. I've missed so much. What else?"

"I'm sorry," I said, "but that's all I've got. He comes into the store with his da—I mean your brother every now and again, and he always gives me a hug."

"It's okay," Dixon said. "Bax *is* Stu's dad. All I am is his DNA donor. I didn't raise my kid. I didn't hold him when he was scared or couldn't sleep. He thinks I'm his uncle."

"But you're back now. You'll make it right, won't you?"

As a rush of warm, slow wind caressed us, he shrugged. "I want to, but I'm not sure I know how. I can't take Stu away from Bax. I won't do anything to hurt my son, but then how can I be a dad to him? He can't have two dads."

"Why not? I think he'd be lucky to have two devoted dads who love him like crazy. I wished my whole life for a dad, but two? That'd be like winnin' the lottery. There's gotta be a way for all of you to coexist and love Stu together."

"Maybe," Dixon mumbled in a gruff voice that told me he wasn't so sure he believed me, but then he tilted his head, and the look on his face turned wistful. "You're still a ball of light to my dark, you know that?"

"I am?" I asked as I watched him lick his lips.

"Yeah, and I wanna kiss you right now."

That admission had my eyes rising to meet his gaze. He

leaned down and tucked my hair behind my ear, letting his other hand cup my jaw.

"That okay?"

I couldn't speak, so I nodded slowly, thinking for years I'd imagined what his lips would feel like on mine, and now I would know. Those years between us didn't matter. The bruises on his soul, and on mine, didn't matter.

I needed him to kiss me like I'd never needed anything in my life.

"Please," I breathed, and his hair brushed over his shoulders and tickled my chin as he pulled me closer. I closed my eyes and pressed up on my toes until I felt his soft, wet skin on mine, and when my knees went weak, he wrapped his arms around my back and held me up.

Expecting simple lip-on-lip action, I was utterly surprised when his tongue swept into my mouth. He tilted his head and *really* kissed me, and butterflies began to flutter deep inside.

Suddenly, I was fifteen again, and he was my ex-best friend, the one I watched every day at lunch with his friends, talking about rodeos and hunting. But he was also the same guy I'd noticed sneaking off to hide in the back of the gym when he was having a bad day, the one I'd wanted to comfort but didn't know how.

"AJ," he groaned, bringing me back to the present, "you taste like heaven."

A moan was my only response as he kissed me harder, pulling my body against his. His hands snaked through my hair, his fingers molding to the shape of me, and he held me there, trapped in his embrace with no escape.

But the last thing I wanted was to get away from him. I felt his erection under his jeans, pressing against my belly, and tried to pull him closer, too, with my hands on his arms so I could better feel the desire he felt for me.

Kissing him and wanting him felt a little dangerous. I knew he'd lived a harder life than me, had been in jail, and was an addict. But I also knew his soul. He and I had been connected since childhood, so I didn't need him to tell me he was sober. I knew it in my heart, and I knew he was fighting like hell to be a good man.

"Stop," he whispered. "You have to stop this. I don't think I can." His mouth moved to my neck, and he licked and groaned and tucked his nose in my hair while his hands moved lower down my back.

"I don't wanna stop."

"We have to," he murmured, rubbing himself against me now, not trying at all to hide his desire.

Sex had been seriously lacking in my life. I hadn't been with a man since Cody, which meant I hadn't been properly screwed in way too long, maybe ever, and now that the image of Dixon and me tangled up under my bed sheets had worked its way beneath my skin, I wanted to be properly fucked. Damn if I couldn't imagine the kind of hard, angsty fucking Dixon would give me.

"Come home with me," I breathed against his lips, feeling their wet warmth and trying not to rut myself against him. "We can help each other sleep."

"No."

Taking two steps back, he disentangled our bodies, and a grave look grew in his eyes. "You don't want me, AJ. I'm no good for you."

"Wait. What? You just kissed me."

"I'm sorry," he said. "That was a mistake."

A mistake?

A surge of anger and a whole boatload of humiliation had me stumbling backward, and I caught my heel on the edge of the sidewalk. Dixon reached out for me, but I pushed his hands away and regained my balance on my own.

"How dare you say that to me, Dixon Lee?"

"Wait, AJ, I didn't mean—"

"No," I said, turning to storm away. "I don't care what you meant. That hurt. I've spent way too long hurtin' over you. I'm not doin' it anymore."

"AJ, please wait. Don't go. Let me explain."

"No. Screw you, Dixon. I've waited my whole life to experience a kiss like that with you. You don't get to offer that to me and then rip it away."

"Your whole life?" he said to my back, but I was halfway to the Darbys' already.

Waving my hand in the air, I called back, "Don't come to my shop for shitty bouquets anymore. Get them at the Food Mart like every other stupid man from now on."

"AJ. Wait!"

When lights began to flicker on in houses along the street, I picked up my pace. If Mama and Gran learned that I was the cause of the late-night commotion, I'd never hear the end of it.

And besides, when I turned the corner and peeked back at where Dixon had just been standing, he was gone.

CHAPTER TEN

DIXON

SHIT.

"Shit. Shit. Shit."

Walking in the opposite direction, I was lost. Something about AJ was my compass. Hurting her, owing her amends was unacceptable. For her and for me. She had no idea how much she'd shaped my recovery. And now, here she was, all perfect and pristine, a petite wonder.

She didn't deserve the confusion I'd just caused her.

"Shit."

I rounded the end of the block and headed back the way I'd just come, and when I got to the Darbys' fence, I walked faster, trying to avoid the sleepy, prying eyes of neighbors.

I still remembered where AJ's Gran had lived when we were in middle school, after AJ's granddad died and they sold their farm. AJ and her mom had moved in with Gran in her downtown bi-level soon after that, and it had put an end to my nightly wandering, when I'd curl up in her grandpa's barn and wait for her to find me.

Three generations of Harlowe women in one square block? The world better look out 'cause that was enough power to fuel a rocket. I wasn't at all surprised that AJ had taken over the flower shop, and I wasn't surprised that it was successful and thriving.

Standing outside her Gran's gate, I used a breathing technique to slow my heart.

AJ said she lived out back in the guest house, but I felt like a prowler walking back there uninvited. Her family probably wouldn't recognize me in the dark if they woke up and spotted my ass in their yard.

But this was too important, so I opened the gate, walked quietly to the path that led to the backyard, and followed the worn stones. An orange and white cat peeked its head out of some kind of low bramble bush, and as I walked, she followed carefully, but every time I turned to get a look at her, she darted back into the leaves.

Quietly, I asked, "Is this your mama's house?"

She peeked out again and then emerged, but she kept a careful distance and stayed low to the ground, ready to run if she needed to.

"C'mon then. Follow me home, kitty kitty. That bush can't be comfortable. Look at all its spikes."

The garden alongside AJ's cottage was a thing of whimsical dreams, especially in the dark and bathed in moonlight. I had no idea the names of the flowers blooming there, but they were delicate and beautiful, and Kitty rubbed against them as she followed me down the path. The greenery looked lush and healthy, and a flashback of AJ and me in this yard when we were ten or eleven came at me so fast, it left me flat-out gasping:

"Do you know my dad?" AJ had asked me.

I shook my head as I crouched by the fir tree behind her gran's house and fiddled with my shoelace, which had come undone again. No matter how many times I tied the dang thing, it always unraveled. Mama would be mad if I was late when she came to pick me up at the library, and if I had to stop twenty times to tie my shoes, I'd be late for sure.

"He's gone," AJ said, "but I thought you might've met him before he left."

"I don't think so."

She shrugged, and tendrils of her golden hair bounced on her shoulders.

Centering myself in front of her door, the memory dissipated, Kitty rubbed against my boot, and I knocked softly. When AJ opened it slowly, looking like a spooked lamb, Kitty slipped inside and disappeared.

"Please forgive me," I said, but my eyes were already scanning the inside of her cottage behind her, and the scared look on her face told me something more was wrong than it had been earlier. Very wrong. "What happened here?"

Glancing over her shoulder, she shrugged just like that day all those years ago.

"Has someone been in here?" I asked.

"I'm not sure. It could've been the wind."

"Did you leave your windows open?" I asked as I stepped forward over the threshold, and AJ stepped back to allow me in.

"No. The air's on."

"So then how did that vase end up on your floor?" I said, pointing at a crystal vase that had fallen off AJ's hall table and splintered into chunks that now lay in a pool of water on the hardwood. The bushy, yellow flowers that had sat in the vase looked like they'd been ripped apart and strewn all over the place, which led my eyes to a four-seater dining table that had been upended. "And why is your dinner table layin' on its side?"

She chewed the inside of her lip and focused on the door behind me.

"AJ?"

Sighing, she turned to walk into her living room, and I followed and watched her kick off her shoes, plop onto her couch, and tuck her feet beneath her. "I think it's that guy I told you about. Cody."

"You think he broke in?"

She shrugged again.

"AJ, say somethin'. Stop shruggin'. It tells me nothin'."

"Yes, I think he might've been in here. He's mad that I broke things off with him. Well, not mad exactly, more like unhinged."

"What does that mean?"

She shook her head and pointed to the opposite end of the couch.

"Hold on," I said. "Have you checked the rest of your house?"

"Of course I did. There's no one else here but you and me."

"Okay, good."

Awareness of how much I didn't fit into her beautiful home itched under my skin as I sat. Except for the vase and upended table, her place was clean and organized. The six-year-old AJ I remembered had left her mark all around me in sweet colors and light wood tones, framed photos of wildflowers on her walls, and accents of plush, soft pillows and fabrics. It didn't feel expensive exactly, more like homey and girly. I sat, but I couldn't relax. By just sitting on her overstuffed, light-colored couch, it felt like I was painting her world with my dark influence.

"We dated for a couple years," she said, "but I broke it off because things were goin' nowhere between us. He wasn't invested in our relationship. He acted like I was just a fill-in girlfriend until the woman he *really* wanted to marry came along. His parents are rich, and he told me once that they expect him to marry a rich woman. I don't know. It all seemed so stupid to me. You love who you love. Who cares if they're rich or poor?

"Anyway, after a while, it seemed like maybe he'd bought into all that stupidity. He was always lookin' at other women. He even flirted with them when we went out. Like, right in front of me. So finally, I broke up with him."

Hearing her talk about this douchebag pissed me off, but I was still confused. "So then why would you think he was here?"

"I told you I blocked his number, but every time I do, he gets a new number, and then the calls start up again. Gran and your sister think I should get a restraining order against him."

"Wait. Abey knows about this guy?"

"Yeah. I called her the last time things escalated with Cody. He showed up here and wouldn't leave, so I locked the door and called the station, and your sister and Deputy Roxi came out. He was gone by the time they got here, and until tonight, I didn't think he'd been around. But now I'm not so sure."

"You have your phone on you now?" I asked.

"Yeah, of course."

"Call my sister right now."

"It's so late, Dixon. I don't wanna bother her, and Cody's not here now. What's the point?"

"AJ, the point is that someone else needs to know he was here. All this stuff adds up. The calls, the mess," I said, swinging my arm out in the direction of the broken vase. "Abey will want to know he was here. And if she can prove it was him somehow, then you can get that restraining order easy. Call her, please."

I'd been holding out on getting my own damn phone, but now I knew I needed one. If I'd had one tonight, I would've already called Abey.

"Fine." AJ sighed again heavily, then lifted up on her knees to reach her cell phone in her back pocket. She tapped it a few times as she settled on the couch again, moving inches closer to me. I scooted over, too, until we were shoulder to shoulder as she waited for Abey to answer her phone.

Abey must've been dead asleep because she didn't answer, so AJ left a message. "Hi, Sheriff. Um, it's Avery Jane… from the flower shop? Anyway, your brother's at my house and he said I should call you. That guy, you remember from last time, Cody Mahone? I think he's been in my house. I'm totally fine. There's just a broken vase, but Dixon said you should know so… now you do. Thanks. Okay, bye."

"It's not just a vase, AJ," I said when she hung up and set her phone on the coffee table in front of us. "We should check the rest of your house."

"Why? I think he broke in and figured out I wasn't home and then he left."

"Yeah," I said, a little overly dramatic, but she didn't seem to be getting the severity of the situation, "but he might've stolen somethin', and if he didn't, then what the hell were his intentions for breakin' in? Have you thought about *that*?" But then something occurred to me. "You were angry earlier outside Mrs. Ellison's. Why?"

She waved her hand in front of her chest, like she could wave this jerk out of her life. "Oh, he called. I didn't answer 'cause I figured it was him, but he kept callin'. I blocked that number, but then immediately, my phone rang again, and it was a different number. It could be totally random."

"Look at me."

She did. Her wary but beautiful hazel eyes focused on mine as she leaned her head on the back of the couch and looked up at me. She must've recognized the seriousness on my face because she whispered, "I know, Dixon. It was him. You're right. It's just that I don't know what to do about it. I just want him to go away."

That can be arranged.

AJ's phone rang, and we both jumped. "Sheriff Lee" flashed on the lit screen, and for a split second, I thought my sister had heard my silent vow to kill a man I'd never even met. Okay, maybe *kill* was a little dramatic, but I was ready to fuck the guy up if he came back. Probably not my best idea, considering my history, but this was AJ. She was innocent. She didn't deserve this bullshit.

She answered the phone, and I stood and looked around, hoping she didn't notice my nosiness as the overprotectiveness that it was. Quietly, I checked inside closets. I poked my head in her kitchen, then her bedroom and the bathroom across the hall, looking for anything out of place. Her sheets were messed up, and her happy wildflower scent was palpable in her bedroom. I wanted to go in there and coat myself in it so I could carry it with me when I went back to my empty, bleak room at the boarding house.

"No, I didn't see him," she said to Abey, and she listened as my sister asked questions. I couldn't hear what she was asking AJ, but I thought I could read the tone of Abey's voice, and it was very sheriff-y and all business. "Oh, um, I went for a walk," AJ said, "'cause my phone kept ringin'. The same number's been callin', three days in a row now. I couldn't go back to sleep tonight, so I went for a walk and ran into Dixon by Mrs. Ellison's house. We, eh, talked for a few minutes, and then I came home. But Dixon forgot to tell me somethin' so he followed me home, and that was when he saw the mess on the floor. Whoever was here knocked my dinner table on its side."

Abey talked for a minute, and then AJ sounded anxious when she said, "That's really not necessary. I'm fine."

Flipping on her bathroom light, I checked in there, looked behind the dark-green shower curtain with white daisies all over it and opened the lighted medicine cabinet over the sink. Everything looked normal, or at least what I imagined was normal for AJ.

As I closed the cabinet, it occurred to me that there were two orange bottles of medication in there, but I hadn't read the labels. In my old life, that was the first thing I would've done, and if the medications were for pain or anxiety, no matter what they were or why they had been prescribed, I would've pocketed them.

When I walked back to the couch, AJ looked uneasy. "Your sister's on her way. I told her she didn't need to come, but she insisted."

"Good. Everything else looks okay," I said, "but you should check, too, in case I missed somethin'. And you should ask your mama and gran if they saw anything."

AJ stood. "No. I'm not wakin' them up. I'll ask in the mornin'."

"Too late for that," a female voice said from the doorway. AJ's gran smiled at me, and she and AJ's mama walked into the house, their heads swiveling back and forth as they took in the mess.

AJ's mama, Miss Belinda, rushed past me and hugged AJ close. "Are you okay, Avery Jane? Why on earth did you take off your shoes? There's glass everywhere."

When Belinda said it, I felt like an idiot because I hadn't thought of it first. What kind of dad could I ever be if I couldn't even warn a grown woman to keep her shoes on so she didn't cut her feet?

"Oh." AJ glanced at her feet, but then she looked up so she could try to pacify her family. "I'm fine, Mama. I promise. I'm sorry I woke you."

"You didn't wake us. Gran and I were already up because we heard a car peel out in front of the house about twenty minutes ago. I wanted to call the sheriff, but Gran said we didn't really have anything to report except some noise."

Gran Harlowe sighed in the doorway. She'd aged, but she was still beautiful to me. The sound of her voice held kindness like it always had. "Obviously I was wrong about that," she said. "Dixon, it's nice to see you again. I thought that was you the other mornin', but you're all grown up now."

"Yes, ma'am. Nice to see you too."

"Well, I'm glad you're here. I feel better knowin' Avery Jane has a friend around in case that asshole comes back."

Miss Belinda scoffed at the curse, which was true to my memory of her. She'd always been harder to win over. Trust didn't come as easy to her as it had to AJ's gran. But I was in complete agreement. Just as it crossed my mind that I wasn't AJ's protector, that I couldn't be, her mama looked back at me, and in her eyes, I saw doubt. She didn't think I was AJ's best choice for a protector either.

"I'll wait on the porch for the sheriff," I said. "'Scuse me."

CHAPTER ELEVEN

AVERY JANE

DIXON SLEPT on my porch in my wicker rocking chair, with no blanket or pillow, his arms and legs kinked up and hanging over the sides like a bunch of melted puzzle pieces that didn't fit together anymore.

After she'd fingerprinted my door and the vase and table, I'd heard Abey talking to Dixon on the porch, but Mama and Gran stayed and insisted on helping me clean up, and by the time they left, Dixon was snoring.

When I woke up this morning on the couch, he had already gone.

But I didn't have to wait long to see him again, because five minutes after I opened the flower shop, he walked in quietly, carrying an old, silver metal toolbox.

All he said was, "This door needs tendin'. I nearly fell through it the other day because the latch doesn't engage properly, and all it took was one look to see the hinges are nearly rusted through. If you don't mind, I'll replace the hardware," and without another word, he removed the front door from its hinges and began to work on removing the hinges themselves.

He was kind and helpful to customers when they came in, but he stayed silent most of the time. Gran and Mama were in and out, checking on me all morning, too, so I suspected Dixon wanted to talk but wouldn't in front of them.

He worked effortlessly, like he hung doors every day. Maybe he did. I had no idea what he'd been up to since he left Wisper or where he'd lived before he came home. Wherever he'd been, it was clear the work he'd been doing was physical.

Cheese and rice! The man was built. Not like, 'Oh yeah, he does cardio four times a week in a gym somewhere,' but like he worked with his hands for hours every day, gripping things or manhandling things. I had no idea, but his hands were strong and sure.

And sweet Jesus in Heaven! When he bent or crouched, I came close to passing out. His ass! That perfectly rounded, toned backside had seen its fair share of lunges and squats.

By lunchtime, I was fanning myself with a paper flyer from the bakery down the street, advertising a class on how to make apple turnovers from scratch. My door had been rehung, the hinges now shiny brass, the glass had been cleaned, and the locks had been replaced and upgraded.

"I'll do the back door tomorrow," Dixon said as he turned to face me.

I tried desperately to conceal a squeak when he lifted the hem of his T-shirt to wipe the sweat off his forehead, flashing me six perfectly formed abs and those tiny muscles on the sides of his ribcage—*labs? Lats?* Whatever they were, they rippled and popped as he lifted his arm, but then he dropped his shirt, bent, and grabbed his toolbox from the floor. He handed me my keyring, now jingling with new keys, nodded, and left, and I watched him walk across the street to Ace's

House, where he said he'd been hired as a handyman. And that was the last I saw of him until now.

He knocked on my door for the second time in twenty-four hours, and I rushed to answer it because when Dixon was around, I felt safer than I did without him. I knew it was him and not my creepy ex because I'd heard him pull up, and when I looked out my window, I saw him getting out of an old, black El Camino he'd parked behind my delivery van.

"Did you buy a car?"

"Yeah."

"Interestin' choice," I said, nodding over his shoulder and giggling.

"Don't you make fun of me, Avery Jane Harlowe, or I'll be forced to remind you that you used to make flower garlands for forest animals and draw hearts around all your boo-boos with a scented marker 'cause you thought the hearts would help you heal faster."

"That's fair. Come in," I offered, opening my door wide and stepping back as he entered. I closed the door behind him and locked it tight. "Would you like somethin' to drink? Coffee, tea?"

"What kinda tea you got?"

"Peppermint or Earl Gray."

"Peppermint, please," he said. "I don't take caffeine."

"Probably not a good idea this time of night anyway."

"Right. Sorry. I should've called. Is it too late?"

"How would you call? You don't have a phone."

"I do. Bought one today."

As he pulled a gray, older model phone from his pocket, I said, "It's not too late. I wasn't gonna fall asleep anyway. Too much on my mind."

"Same," he said. "Here. Put your number in." He handed

the phone to me and walked further into my house, checking the dining table for scuffs and making sure everything had been put back into place after last night.

I typed my contact info into a new entry in his phone and texted myself so I'd have his number too. I followed him into the kitchen and watched as he found the box of teabags and mugs in my open-faced cabinet and located my tea kettle already filled and heating up on the stove.

"You know you could just microwave the water," he said, looking over his shoulder as I sat at my little fold-out island next to the kitchen window and set our phones on top.

"Yes, but a pink kettle is more fun and it's more whimsical, and you know I'm all about the whimsy. Did you know that in the UK, if you heat your water in the microwave, they'll try you for war crimes?"

He chuckled silently, adjusted the heat a little higher, then faced me and leaned against the counter.

"Didn't know that."

"So, you haven't said. Why are you here?"

"Oh. Uh, yeah, well I wanted to give you my cell number, and I guess I thought we should talk about what happened last night."

"I'm not sure what else there is to say. Your sister was here. The whole town now knows I had a break-in, and she fingerprinted and took my statement. I told her I'd email her my cell phone logs from my provider so she can try to track the phone calls, but I doubt she'll be able to. Cody's probably using one of those pay-as-you-go phones. At this point, he's probably got a whole box full of them so he can grab a new one every time I block him."

I rolled my eyes, but when I focused on him again, Dixon was smiling.

"I wasn't talkin' about *that* part of last night. Did you

already forget I kissed you and then you stormed away and yelled at me?"

"No. I didn't forget. But you said it was a mistake, so I wasn't plannin' on bringin' it up."

"Well then, I'm bringin' it up. And when I said it was a mistake, I didn't mean it was a mistake for me to kiss you. I wanna kiss you again right now. I wanted to this mornin'. I want to kiss you every minute of my day. But what I meant was that *you* shouldn't want to kiss *me*. The mistake was mine, though, because I never should've put you in that position."

"You wanna kiss me again?"

"AJ, did you hear anything else I said?"

"Nope." I gulped, reaching for the necklace around my neck that Gran had given me last Christmas and spun the tiny, rose gold dandelion between my fingers. "All I heard was that you think about kissin' me all day long."

Dixon's strong hands gripped the edge of my Bess's Bargains granite countertop behind him. His fingers flexed around the polished edge, but then he let go and walked to the island across from me, pulled out the other chair, and sat.

"I do," he said quietly. "You've been on my mind all day. But AJ, I'm not the man for you. I'm an addict and I've been in jail more than once."

He waited for me to react to what he'd said, but I didn't. I already knew all that.

"I abandoned my own fuckin' kid."

I knew that, too, but I didn't really see it as Dixon abandoning Stu. I saw it as Dixon giving his son a fighting chance in this life. Would it have been better if Dixon raised Stu around drugs? My dad left when I was only two years old, but from what Gran and Mama had told me, I was better off. So, if a bad father leaving was a good thing, certainly a sick dad leaving to get better for his son could only be good too.

I didn't acknowledge Dixon, so he went on.

"You think you know who I am because we were friends as kids, but you don't know a goddamn thing about me now."

There he was, my best friend, the boy who'd told me his every fear and desire, and the man who had long been the focus of mine.

"So, tell me. Talk to me like you used to."

Placing his hands on the island in front of us, he shook his head. "My family, my life—I'm a fuckin' mess, AJ. You don't want me."

"I work with dirt and manure, Dixon. Messes don't scare me."

He tried to one-up himself. "I barely graduated high school. The only job I could find was as a janitor. I don't have money."

"True," I said, nodding, pretending I agreed with all the dumb excuses coming out of his mouth. "And you bought an El Camino. That's a red flag right there."

"C'mon now. Don't joke. I'm bein' serious. I'm no good for you. Look at this life you've made for yourself." He looked all around the kitchen but, inevitably, his blue eyes landed on mine again. "I don't belong in your world."

Reaching across the island, I clasped my hands around his. "Don't you think that's somethin' I should get to decide for myself?"

Wordlessly, he laid his head on top of our hands, and his long hair spilled over the butcher-block top. I pulled one hand free, then gently and so slowly drew my fingers through the deep-brown strands. I pressed my palm against his head, and he moaned quietly and pushed into my touch.

"Dixon—"

The teakettle's whistle pierced the night air, and it startled us both. Dixon sat up, and he pulled his hands away, then stood and went to the stove.

I followed and slipped my arms around his waist, pressing myself against his back while he lifted the kettle and set it on a back burner.

"AJ, I can't even tell you how good it feels for you to touch me and kiss me, but"—he turned and put two feet of space between us—"we don't know each other anymore, and besides, I'm in no place to be the man you need. And there's Stuart. I need to figure out how to be his dad. Or his friend. Or… somethin'."

"Oh." *Right. Stuart.* That sweet little boy was way more important than my libido. "You're right. I totally understand that. But just for the record, you don't need to figure out how to be a man for me. You already are. You proved it today when you fixed my door. Just the fact that you noticed it needed fixin' shows me who you are now.

"But I don't want to come between you and your son. That wouldn't be right."

"No," he said, reaching for me. He pulled me close again and leaned down. But he hesitated before he pressed his lips lightly to mine. "I didn't mean you'd come between us, just that I'm so confused about who I am to my own kid, and I don't think I'd be any use to you as a boyfriend or a… whatever. I've let so many people down, AJ. I don't wanna let you down too." He tucked me against his chest and hugged me. "But I'm all in to be your friend, if you'll have me. I wanna get to know you again. Would that be okay?"

His warm breath on my cheek made me shiver, but I knew he was right, and I was proud of him for knowing what he needed.

"Of course," I whispered, hugging him, too, my long-lost

best friend, because I realized it might be the last chance I had to be close to him.

Dixon was home, but he was broken and beaten down, and before he could be anything to me or anyone else, he needed to figure out who he was to his son.

And to himself.

CHAPTER TWELVE

DIXON

JUST TO DRIVE, just to be somewhere that wasn't my little ten-by-eleven room at Mrs. Ellison's, I headed out of town down Route 20, and as I passed the vet clinic where I would start work in a few days, I couldn't stop hearing AJ's words in my head:

Of course. Of course. Of course.

AJ agreed with me that Stu was more important than anything else, but I heard the disappointment in her voice, and I couldn't help thinking that I had just lost the only chance I might ever get with her.

A week ago, she was just my memory girl. It had never crossed my mind she might be real, that she might be someone I'd want.

Goddammit! I was so fucking sick and tired of feeling confused.

I needed a meeting, but there wasn't one within driving distance of Wisper this late in the evening. I didn't know him well yet, but I knew Theo lived above the community center, so maybe he'd be awake. He might know of a meeting close by.

I wanted to call Nesty. I wouldn't have survived my last stint in rehab if he hadn't been there with me. I'd heard he'd relapsed again and had gone back in, but I assumed by now he'd gotten out and I *hoped* stayed sober. I had his old number written on a slip of paper tucked in my wallet, but he didn't know I had a phone again, and I had no clue if he had one either. His number could have changed five times since the last time we'd talked. There were probably fifty messages on cheap phones that had been lost or traded or forgotten from here to LA. No one would ever hear them.

And besides that, Nesty might be high. My sobriety wasn't as fragile as it used to be. I wasn't scared that my best friend being high would make me want to get high. It might, but I had coping mechanisms now that I didn't have in the past.

But talking to someone who was three sheets was draining. Exhaustion weighed heavy on me just imagining how the conversation might go. And I knew I'd end the call feeling angry and frustrated and scared for my friend if he really had relapsed.

No. Tonight I needed to talk to someone who had already figured their shit out.

Pulling to the side of the road, I grabbed my phone from my center console and looked up the number for Ace's House. I saved the number, and then it rang three times when I dialed, but a cold, robotic voice told me the center's inbox was full. That was the problem with fucking cell phones. If you really needed to talk to someone, they wouldn't hear their phone if they turned it off or turned down the sound. And how come everybody's damn inbox was always full?

I hung up.

Shit.

But I had AJ's number. A friend would call in their time of need, right?

I hit the widget thingie for my contacts and searched the meager list of names. I didn't see AJ's, but the list was only about an inch tall, and at the bottom I saw an entry titled "Tweedledee."

Smiling like a fool, I hit the little round phone icon under the name and waited.

AJ picked up on the first ring. "Dixon? You okay?"

"May I please speak to Tweedledee? This is Tweedledum."

She giggled into the phone. "I thought that might make you smile. Remember your brothers used to call us Tweedledee and Tweedledum?"

"I remember. God, that was lifetimes ago. Sometimes I wish I could go back."

"Are you at Mrs. Ellison's?"

"No. I'm on Route 20 somewhere. I didn't want to go back there yet, but I didn't know where else to go, so I drove."

"You can come back here," she said. "I feel like I came on too strong earlier. I'm sorry about that, but when you kissed me, I just… Well, I felt somethin', but I understand where you're comin' from. If you want to come back, you don't have to worry about that. We're friends and only friends. I promise."

"I felt it too," I admitted. "Don't you get it? That's why I had to stop it. I had to stop the kiss because— Fuck, AJ. From the first moment I saw you, I wanted you. But I don't want just a kiss, and that's the problem. Anything more than that wouldn't be fair to you. I'll fuck it up. I'll hurt you."

"I don't think you will."

I'd never known a more glass-half-full kind of person! She needed a wake-up call.

"I killed the last woman I loved. Stu's mama. Her name was Kel."

I heard AJ breathing over the line as she tried to process what I'd just said. "You killed her? How did you do that? The Dixon I used to know wouldn't hurt a fly."

"That Dixon is long gone, AJ. That's what I've been tryin' to make you understand."

"So, tell me about her. Tell me what happened."

I didn't decide to do it, but as I spoke, I drove back toward AJ's little cottage. It took me a minute, and I had to pull over again, but I finally figured out how to put the call on speaker and then set my phone on the dash.

"Kel. She was… Her name was Kellie Gale. It fit her 'cause she was fearless, like a gale-force wind. We were both sober when we met. She'd only ever done a little coke and pot, but I had just gotten out of rehab for… heroin. Sorry, you probably don't want the details."

"It's okay," AJ said. "I do want to know. I can handle it."

"Well, we kept runnin' into each other. Yeah, we were both sober, but neither of us were bein' smart about it. We didn't change who we hung out with, y'know? Which is the first thing you do after rehab 'cause all your old friends are the people you used to get high with. Anyway, we didn't do that, and our friends were friends, so we kept bumpin' into each other.

"Finally, she asked me out, but the love story only lasted about two weeks. We bonded over our families hatin' us. And like addicts do, we became inseparable because we confirmed for each other all the lies we liked to tell ourselves so we could stay sick.

"The next time we were together, she said she'd always

wanted to try H. I was feelin' strong and protective—and stupid—so I tried to talk her out of it, but she'd already bought some and brought it with her. So, then my dumb ass says, 'If you're gonna do it, at least do it with me in case you OD or need help or whatever.'"

"Oh no," AJ whispered. "I think I know what happened next."

"Yeah," I said as I parked behind the AVery Pretty Petal delivery van outside her Gran's house. "And by the next day, we were both hooked and high as kites."

AJ must've heard me pull up because she opened her front door as I walked toward it, but I still had the phone to my ear, so I admitted something that had been eating at me for years because maybe it wouldn't be so hard to say out loud into a phone instead of straight to someone's face.

"It's my fault. It's all my fuckin' fault, AJ. I could've flushed that shit down the toilet. But I didn't."

AJ clicked off her phone and slipped it in her jeans pocket, and when I stepped onto her porch, she grabbed my hand and tugged me inside. We sat on opposite ends of the couch again, not saying a word and just looking at each other.

"It's not your fault, Dixon," she said softly. "Deep down, you know that, right? You didn't force her to do heroin."

"I didn't stop her."

"Would she have let you?"

Sighing and shaking my head, I said, "No. She'd already decided to do it, and when she made up her mind, nothin' stopped her. It's what drew me to her in the first place. She reminded me of my brother, Bax. He's always known what he wanted. I was the opposite, and I hated that about myself."

I thought for a few minutes about Kel and all the things she had been so stubborn about, like when we left California and hitchhiked out to Nebraska because she said she just knew she'd be happy there and we could get clean. And then in Omaha, she insisted she was sober enough to drive the car she said she bought but I found out later she'd stolen. I was too high to realize she didn't have money to buy a car, even a shitty, used one.

She hadn't been sober enough—I should've known that too—and she got picked up a block away from where we'd been staying in a run-down motel we'd paid for with the last of the inheritance she received when her dad died a few months before. She spent ten days in jail until I could come up with the money for her bail, and not one red cent of that cash had been procured by legal means.

Still to this day I couldn't remember how we made it back to California, but that was where I found myself when I woke up one morning with way too much clarity for my liking. It should've scared the shit out of me that I had no clue how I'd traveled across five states, but it didn't. Heroin was thorough like that; it let all your fears and anxieties seep into the ground beneath your ass and made wherever you landed comfy as fuck so you never wanted to move again. And once Kel and I were back in Redding, it was like we'd never left. We were as high as ever, she didn't go back to Nebraska for her court hearing, and she died later with probably several warrants out for her arrest.

"When we found out she was pregnant with Stu, she swore she could handle it. She promised to stay clean for him, and I believed her because *she* believed. But I also knew better.

"And Stu," I said, "as soon as I saw him, I knew I'd get clean. Kel felt the opposite. It was like she went into shock after he was born. She couldn't figure out how she deserved such perfection. She didn't think she could ever be worthy of him, so she made it true.

"Those first two weeks feel like a dream to me now. Sometimes I doubt they actually happened, that she was sober for two whole weeks of his life. But it didn't take long for her to find some dope, and it didn't take much for her to convince herself that Stu was better off without her. After that, she stayed as high as she could until I took Stu away from her.

"But she must've known deep down that she was wrong, like her mama-bear instincts had been activated. He'd get so hungry and cry so hard, she tried to physically fight me to get him out of my arms so she could breastfeed him, but she had so much bullshit runnin' through her veins. I couldn't let her feed him that. His little body had already gone through too much, detoxing after he was born."

God, just remembering was making me edgy. Here I was, home and hoping for forgiveness, but I still hadn't forgiven myself, and I wasn't sure if I ever could. I shifted on the couch, trying to find a comfortable position, but there was none.

"The shit I put that kid through. I'll never forgive myself, AJ. I swear I won't.

"But that was when I started to believe in myself, because I knew what was right. Kel couldn't see it, but I knew how bad things were, and that's when all those lies I'd been tellin' myself began to crack and fall away.

"Stu and I lived in an abandoned barn on the edge of someone's property for a week so I could keep him away from her. The old man who owned the place found us out there, and he gave me food and water. He let us stay in his air-conditioned garage, and his wife bought formula for Stu. They offered to drive me up here when I told them I had family who would take Stu, but I needed to do it myself.

"By the time I got back to California after I left Stu with Bax, Kel was at the end. I tried, AJ. I tried so fuckin' hard to get her to go to the hospital. She wouldn't, and she died right in front of me.

"But it's not her I see when I get the urge to use again." I shook my head, letting the pain split me in two all over again. "It's Bax, holdin' my kid and the jealousy that caused inside me, because no matter how blissed out drugs can make me feel, seein' Stu for the first time was better, holdin' him in my arms, feelin' his weight. I've never loved anyone the way I love him. It's still crazy to me how fast I fell in love with him. It was faster than instantaneous, and now that I'm here, the hope I feel about getting to know him and be around him feels the same. I want that. I need him in my life more than any high."

AJ wiped away a tear that had fallen from the corner of her eye.

"Don't cry. Please don't cry for me. I don't deserve your tears."

"Yes, you do," she said. "You forget, I knew you before you told yourself all those lies. I knew you before your daddy damaged the sweet little boy you used to be."

"He was never my dad, AJ. He was just the sorry son of a bitch who owned the house I grew up in."

"What does that mean?"

But I didn't have it in me to explain all my conspiracy theories tonight.

Instead, I asked, "What about you? What have you been up to all these years?"

CHAPTER THIRTEEN

AVERY JANE

CLEARLY, Dixon was trying to redirect the conversation, and that was his prerogative.

If he wanted to talk about his dad and his childhood, I'd listen. Some of it was my childhood, too, but if he wasn't ready, I'd just show him that I would be there for him when he was.

I stood and stretched. He'd talked about Stu's mom for a while, but I noticed he never said he'd been in love with her. Which was kind of sad, and it made me wonder.

"Still want that tea?" I asked.

"Sure."

He followed me into the kitchen and sat at the island again as I poured filtered water into our mugs, but this time I zapped it in the microwave.

Handing him his peppermint tea, my fingers brushed over his, and Dixon looked up at me.

"Sugar?" I asked.

He shook his head and sipped the plain, weak tea, but I added a spoonful to mine and stirred.

"What do you wanna know?" I asked as I sat across from him. "There's not much to tell, really."

"Not much to tell? You're kiddin', right? It's been, what, almost twenty years since we've seen each other? Maybe less, but I wasn't exactly present the last few years I lived here." Swiping the hair up off his neck, he pulled it back into a loose ponytail, let it drop, and then reached for my wrist. He tugged the elastic band I wore there for the same reason and slipped it over my hand, then used it to tie his hair back.

"Well, I went to school locally to get my business degree. Gran wanted to retire and I always knew I would take over the flower shop, so when I felt confident enough, I did. It was kind of cool. I was in my last year of classes, and my professors and the other students were invested in helping me figure things out, so I got a lot of guidance.

"I graduated, then Gran retired officially, and all of a sudden, I was a full-time small-business owner." I shrugged. "That's about it."

"What about friends? Men?"

Men. Right.

"Friends faded away as we got older. They moved away or got married and had families, and I didn't. But I made new friends in the local business community. They're better anyway. They don't come with ancient high-school drama."

"What about that girl you used to hang with? What was her name… Bindy? Bobby?"

"Brandy?

"Yeah," he said, "that's the one. She had a weird last name."

"Brandy Noon. Everybody called her Nooner. She's married now and her name is Brandy Sheets."

"A nooner in the sheets?" He laughed and took a sip of

his tea. "But you two were thick as thieves in high school. Best friends, right?"

"Friends, yeah. I don't know about best friends. She was pretty shallow back then, and our friendship revolved around what was goin' on with her."

"But I always saw you two together—"

"Because that's what I wanted you to see."

"What does that mean?"

"*You* were my best friend, Dixon." Embarrassed to admit it to him, I sipped my tea, too, and blew at the steam rising from my mug. "But you were on a different path. You had all those friends and y'all were the life of the party. I was just the quiet, mousy girl you used to know, so when you looked, I acted like I had life all figured out. But I was just as lost as you, and I still went to bed every night thinkin' about you."

His eyebrows rose higher the longer I talked. "You did?"

I nodded slowly, remembering all the nights I pined for him, for the friendship that had shaped my childhood and the hurt I felt when it ended. It wasn't Dixon's fault. He was living in hell, but I still missed him and cried for him when I was alone.

"Yeah. I missed you even though you were right here. But we grew up and then you left."

Reaching across the table for my hand this time, he held it within his grasp, his calloused skin roughing over mine. "I'm sorry."

"It wasn't your fault." I smiled at him, trying not to let tears fall. Tears for the loss of our closeness all those years ago. Tears for the abuse I knew he'd suffered, and tears for the loss of what could've been.

"I'm not so sure about that," he said. "I don't know if I should tell you this, but I was the opposite. I *saw* you. I saw you clear as day back then, but I wouldn't allow myself to think about you."

Sadness must've shown on my face, because he rushed to explain. "But not because I didn't wanna think about you. I pushed the thoughts away because I always remembered your smile and your goodness, and I knew I was lettin' you down. Every time I started a fight at school or got suspended, I looked around for you, because I knew the disappointment I'd see on your face. Part of me feared your judgment, and the other part of me wanted to see it. If I knew I'd let you down, that meant I was doin' a good job of fuckin' up my life. That was my goal for a long time. If my dad didn't love me, then clearly, no one else could."

"I'm so sorry you had to go through that."

He dismissed my concern, shifting in his seat, and he angled his body away from me slightly.

"I'm damn tired of talkin' about myself," he said. "So, what about men? You scoffed when I asked."

"Yeah, 'cause there's not much to tell. There have been a few guys over the years. There was one in college, but as soon as we graduated and he realized my little flower shop would never be his cash cow, he took off. I heard he married some trust-fund princess in Texas. And you already know about Cody. He's the most notable because he's a nuisance, but there were a couple others before him. No one to write home about though.

"No, I focused on the shop. It's what makes me happy. Who needs love anyway?"

Dixon set his mug on the table. "Everyone? Literally everyone needs love, AJ."

Shrugging, I said. "Well, maybe I don't."

We moved back into the living room and took our spots

on opposite ends of the couch, facing each other, but this time I stretched out my legs, and Dixon relaxed his around mine and pulled my feet into his lap.

"So, if you don't date and you hate everyone from high school, what do you do in your spare time?"

Kicking his thigh playfully, I said, "I don't *hate* anyone. We just grew apart. But if you must know, Gran's been tryin' to teach me to knit. Although I have to admit, it hasn't been goin' well, and also, I volunteer."

"You do?"

"Yep, at Mountain Home, you know? The local retirement community."

"It's still there? It used to be pretty run down."

"It's still there, but they received a few large donations over the years, and now it's not just for the elderly. They added a second wing, and they take in rehabilitation patients after injuries or difficult surgeries. They even offer scholarships to pay for care if someone can't afford it or their insurance won't cover it. A lot of times it's kids. So, one day a week, I go and spend time with the residents, play games with them or take them for walks or whatever.

"And once a week, I deliver fresh flowers for the common rooms there. Gran still helps me put the bouquets together for the nursing home, and she jokes that when she can't pee on her own anymore and we stick her in there, at least she knows she'll have pretty flowers to look at. And then I deliver the bouquets, and it is the best feeling in the world, seeing the patients' smiles when they smell the flowers, knowin' somethin' I did brightens their world for a moment."

The smile on Dixon's face grew, and his eyes glittered and lit up like the sun reflecting off a crystal alpine lake. "That's the coolest thing I've ever heard."

"What is?"

"You. You're still the coolest girl, and you might think you don't need love, but you got it inside you, and you give it away in spades."

CHAPTER FOURTEEN

DIXON

GOING HOME AGAIN, this time in my own car I'd bought with money I'd earned legally, was weird.

But as I turned off Old Fish Creek Road onto the lane that would lead me to Merv's place, I realized the fear I used to feel every time I stepped foot on my family's land was gone.

It used to take at least three hydrocodone and two Xanax to get me up this road.

Now, though, I was clearheaded and free from all that bullshit. Noah Lee was dead, so that helped, but it wasn't him on my mind anymore as gravel shifted and settled beneath my nearly bald tires.

The only person on my mind now was Stuart.

He was probably at school. *Wait, is kindergarten all day or do they still go half days?* It didn't matter, though, because before I could see Stu and try to… whatever it was I was trying to do, I'd promised Merv I'd come back and we'd talk.

So that was my plan, but when I pulled up in front of her house, it wasn't Merv I found. It was Bea. And she was alone.

"Hi," she said as I got out of the El Camino. "Nice car. You gonna fix it up?"

"Yeah, I might. Just to give my hands somethin' to do."

"Cool. God, I still can't get over how different you look. Big change from the last time we met."

"You mean when I abandoned my kid in your cabin?"

She smiled, but pity laced her tone. "Yeah."

"Well, I am different. I'm sober, four years now."

"Good," she said, nodding. "That's good. Um, are you here to see him? The school year just started, so he's still there."

"Stu? I'd love to see him, but I wouldn't do that without talkin' to you and Bax first. No, I promised Merv I'd come back and let her know where I'm stayin' and check in. You're welcome to join us."

Bea snorted. "You're on your own there, captain. That sea's a little too choppy for me. I have to get back to work anyway. We got some mail up at the house for your mama, so I dropped it off on my lunch break."

Man, I really liked her. And now I had a clue where Stu had learned how to be funny. Bax hadn't influenced that particular personality trait; my brother was about as funny as a paper plate.

"Thank you," I said.

"For?"

"For lovin' my kid. For teachin' him everything he knows. For bein' his mama."

"I didn't do it for you."

"I know you didn't, but I'm still grateful you did."

"You're welcome." She nodded over her shoulder toward where Merv had just opened her screen door and stood on her porch. "Good luck in there."

"Thanks."

"By the way," Bea said as she pulled open her truck door, "Stu taught me everything I know too. He and Bax and Athena gave me a family and made me a mom. So did you when you brought Stu here, so I'm a little bit grateful to you too."

Bea's unexpected grace filled me up in places I never knew were empty, and I let it lift me up and carry me toward a hard conversation. She waved out her window as she drove away, and I smiled. It didn't feel forced or fake. Bea was real. Her words were genuine, and I knew I could trust her.

"I've been waitin' for you to come back," Merv said when I turned and headed toward her.

"I said I would, but I s'pose you're not used to me doin' the things I promise."

She tsked her tongue and waved me inside, and I followed. She had always done that, spoke in hushes and gestures so that I was never sure what she really meant.

"Is that not true, Mama?"

She sat in a plush, sage-green recliner in front of her big-screen TV. "I reckon it is true."

"Then what was the noise you just made?"

"I just don't like hearin' you talk about yourself like that. You were a good boy."

Okay then, guess we're just gonna jump right in.

"When I was little, I was a good boy. When I was a teenager, I wasn't so good. And as an adult, I've let you down in many different ways. I'm not a boy now, and I don't want or need you to treat me like one."

Merv froze and stopped her chair from rocking. Her knees popped. The sound echoed around the quiet house, and it was then I noticed how mangled her arthritic hands had become.

"Listen, I'm not here to blame anybody for anything. I made my own poor choices in life. But I've had to learn how to hold myself accountable, and I'd like you to try to do the same. I want you to expect good things from me, not excuse the bad things I've done."

"That's fine, I guess."

"No, Merv. It's not *'fine.'* I'm tellin' you what I need. You can give me what I need, or you can decide not to, but you should know that sobriety is my priority. Stu is my priority. Our relationship"—I wagged my finger between the two of us, but the hurt look on her face told me she knew exactly what I meant—"and the dysfunction that came with it was so unhealthy. And the way I dealt with it, the way I manipulated you *and* the way you manipulated me, helped me stay sick, so if you can't get on board, then I'll have to distance myself."

"I understand," she said. "You know, you're not the only one who's been goin' to therapy."

"Abey mentioned that. I'm glad to hear it." I sat on the couch, but I couldn't relax. There was just too much bad blood, and it flowed between Merv and me now, like the churning sea Bea had alluded to. I didn't belong in my mother's house. Sometimes I wondered if I belonged anywhere.

There was so much more to say, but the timing didn't feel right. I'd barely been home a week, and I couldn't risk upsetting Merv yet, in case she interfered with Stu.

It seemed she wasn't up to the harder conversation either. "So, how's Mrs. Ellison's place?" she asked.

"It's fine. It's just a room, but that's all I need right now. But I got a job."

"I heard. Devo tells me they hired you up at the community center."

"Yeah. Abey said Devo works there, too, but I haven't met her yet. I also took a part-time gig at the vet clinic on the weekends, helpin' with the animals."

"That's nice. I'm happy for you. Why don't you come for

supper Sunday? Everybody will be up at the big house. Athena wants to see you, too, and you could see your son."

"I might," I said, "but I'd like to check in with Bax first. Make sure he's okay with it."

Merv grumbled something but then started pushing her feet on the floor and rocking her chair again.

"Mama, say what you mean, please. The passive-aggressive bullshit doesn't do either of us any good."

"Fine. You're right," she said curtly. "I said that Bax needs to get off his high horse, and I'm not ashamed I said it."

"Bax has every reason to be angry with me."

"He can be angry if he wants to," she said, "but I wish he'd try for all our sakes. Most importantly for Stuart's sake."

"He's protectin' Stu exactly like I asked him to."

She sighed. "When did you get so level-headed? It's kinda annoyin'."

Shrugging, I said, "I dunno about level-headed, but you're just not used to me sober."

"That's true." She stopped rocking again and leaned forward in her chair. "Dixon, I know I'm not the best at communicatin' how I feel, but I'm workin' on that, and I want you to know that I'm so happy you're home. I'm proud of you, and if havin' you in my life again means I have to change, I'll do it.

"For you, I'd do anything."

THE OLD PLACE had been repainted and Bax and Bea had added a new wraparound porch, but the house was still the same ugly sunshine-yellow color, like it had been when I was a kid.

I parked between Bax's blue Ford he'd had for probably ten years and a tricked-out, black RAM, and as my boot touched the dirt beneath my tires, yips and barks filled the air. I heard cows too and sheep. Like I could ever forget the bleating sounds of sheep.

As I walked toward the new barn, I remembered the first time I'd seen it, when it had been newly built, right before I dumped my kid. But I'd hung around before that, with Stu strapped to my chest in a bed sheet, trying to get up the courage to face my family. In the end, I couldn't do it. I knew how ashamed they were of me and of the mistakes I'd made, but I knew they would love Stu and give him all the things I couldn't, so instead of facing them, I made sure Stu found his way into trusted hands, and then I ran.

I was ready to face them now, so I hung the second pair of sunglasses I'd bought in the past week from the neck of my T-shirt. The sun had slipped behind heavy rain clouds that cast dark, moving shadows over the land, like silent trolls emerging from their Hell caves. Thunder rumbled far in the distance, and I pictured the ugly ogre that used to inhabit this farm and his big footsteps shaking the leaves off the trees.

But that was make-believe. There were no trolls, no ogre. He was dead, but it surprised me how many times I had to remind myself of that, and it surprised me how, now that I'd come home with a clear mind, stories filled my head again, characters and settings blooming to life easily.

Chuckling, I remembered Nesty laughing at my stories late one night in rehab while we ate hard candies in our bunks, making shit up and trying to do anything we could to distract ourselves from detox. I'd told tales that night of ogres and princesses, of mysterious circus ringmasters and a band of brothers who traveled the West, saving little kids from evil. Nesty ribbed me, told me I was nuts, but whenever he had a bad day or a hard therapy session, he'd beg me to tell my stories.

A fine line existed between make-believe and reality, and trying not to fall on my ass while I walked that line like a tightrope was hard as shit, but it was the thing I needed to master if I wanted to stay sober.

Zephyr and Tilly came bounding in my direction from the northwest field, and my brothers and another guy followed slowly on their horses. When they came closer, I realized the other guy was Rye Graves, Bax's best friend since they were ten years old.

He dismounted from his horse, tossed the reins over the animal's back, and then he bounded toward me, too, threw his arms around me, hugged me, and patted me not so gently on my back as Zephyr and Tilly ran circles around us. The German Shepherd sat a safe distance away, watching it all like a silent King's Guard at Buckingham Palace.

With my hand, I gave Zephyr and Tilly the command to sit and was shocked again when they obeyed.

"Heard you were home," Rye said. He released me and stepped back, taking in an eyeful. "It's good to see you. Damn, man. I don't remember you bein' this big. Whatcha been eatin' for breakfast? The hearts of the men who done ya wrong? Fertilizer?"

"Nope. No more chemicals for me," I said. "Or human organs." *Weird.*

Rye laughed and turned to unpack his horse.

"Bax, Brand," I said. "I hope it's okay I'm here. I wanted to talk to y'all for a minute."

Brand hopped off his horse, and it struck me odd that he seemed so comfortable living the ranch life. The last time I'd checked, he was all corporate, CEO business guy.

"Of course it's o—"

Bax interrupted Brand in a clipped tone. "What is it you wanna talk about?"

"I, uh, just wanted to check in," I said. "I stopped by Merv's 'cause I promised I'd let her know when I got settled, but I thought maybe we should talk about Stu. Merv invited me to Sunday supper, but I wanted to make sure you were okay with that."

"Well," Bax drawled, "I'm sure you can see that I'm busy. You shoulda called first."

As Bax dismounted, Rye took his reins and said, "Would you look at that. Your calendar just opened up." The dead-eyed stare Bax shot him didn't faze Rye at all. "Brand and I are both capable of waterin' down horses. We can probably manage to feed 'em, too, and maybe even brush 'em without your supervision. Go talk to your damn brother."

Bax didn't respond, but as he passed Rye, he smacked Rye's hat off his head. Rye only laughed again as he bent and swiped it from the dirt.

Brand smiled, making a shooing motion with one hand, encouraging me to follow Bax as our oldest brother stomped to his house.

I followed after him like a little kid again, a little boy who wanted to be with his brothers, wanted to fit in with them and be as cool as they had been back then.

But when we climbed the porch stairs and Bax opened the kitchen door, I hesitated. The last time I had been in this house, the ogre had been here, too, and it wasn't the most pleasant memory.

The day after he'd broken my nose in the barn and knocked me out cold because I'd accidentally broken his shearing clippers, standing in this very kitchen, I'd hit the old man. Punched his ugly nose, too, and told him I was leaving.

He could find some other schmuck to work for free because I was done.

As the memory came back to me, I rubbed the dent he'd left on the bridge of my nose. His only reaction had been to spit at my feet, laugh at me, and he snarled, *"Good luck, asshole. Let's see how long you last without my food and my fuckin' hospitality. You'll be back."*

I hadn't even turned eighteen yet, but I never went back, and it had taken a whole bottle of Crown Royal that night to make me forget that I'd left Merv alone with that monster.

Somehow, I found places to crash, friends' couches, barns, and once I slept in the woods in an old bear den for three nights. I graduated high school, though my grades hadn't been anything to crow about, but at least I made it through on my own. I'd managed to find a job and was able to keep it, despite the fact that I showed up most days hungover. But Farmer John hated Noah Lee, so he hired me just to spite my "daddy." That was fine by me. I wanted Noah to feel the burn of not having his "good-for-nothin' son" there to do all the hard jobs he was too lazy to do.

I wanted Noah to fail miserably all by himself so that everyone in town would know it was his own damn fault. Not mine.

"Say what you came to say," Bax barked impatiently, and I crossed the threshold like it wasn't hard at all.

"I'm sorry."

"I'm sure you are," he said, "but your sorry don't really change much."

"I know that."

He turned and leaned against the kitchen counter, but instead of the old, yellowed Formica, it was a beautiful new granite stone, marbled with pitch black and glittering white veins. The cupboards were new too, traditional and crisp white on top, but the bottom cabinets and the new kitchen island in the middle of the room were a deep, navy blue.

"Do you though?" His hands gripped the edge of the granite, and his knuckles drained of color while he tried to pulverize it. "You show up here out of the fuckin' blue. We haven't heard from you in ages, and now you expect us to do… what? Just act like the last five years didn't happen?"

"No." I shook my head. "I don't expect anything from you. From any of you. Abey and Brand seem happy I'm back, and so does Merv, but I wasn't expectin' that. Shit, I didn't even hope for it. Hope is dangerous for me."

"Yeah, well, they're dipshits." He watched me shifting my feet on his shiny tile floor. "Who are you?"

"What?"

"Who are you?" he said again. "You're a stranger. You're not the Dixon I remember. You look different, but it's more than that. You used to blend in with the shadows, but now… I don't know. Now, you're here. You're takin' up space in my kitchen."

"Yeah," I agreed. He was right. I felt it, too, like I'd barely existed before, but now I took up space everywhere I went, and it was uncomfortable. I felt like I was in the way. In Bax's way. In Stu's way. In AJ's way.

I was standing in my own goddamn way.

"If you need me to say it again, I will: I'm not here to take Stu away from you."

"Oh, I know you're not." His bravado was painful to witness. I'd caused it. It was my fault he felt like he had to stand guard over his family, ever the noble knight.

"Brother, maybe you won't believe me, but I love you, and I'm so fuckin' grateful that you stepped up for Stu when I couldn't, but I had no right to ask you to do that."

"No, you didn't."

"But I'm not sorry I did because Stu has a father now. A *good* father. A better one than I could've been to him. He has opportunities in life, and he won't have to grow up lookin' over his shoulder, dreadin' poverty and hunger, pain or sorrow.

"And I'm not sorry because I look at you, at the life you've made for your family, and I'm so fuckin' proud of you."

Bax hung his head. He shook it.

"Fine. You can come to supper, but there are conditions."

CHAPTER FIFTEEN

AVERY JANE

FRIDAYS WERE EASY.

At least lately they had been, but I hadn't been sleeping well the last few weeks, and today I was so tired, I felt almost delirious. I'd already chugged one very large lavender London Fog from Coffee Shot and was planning to go back for another.

Usually, the end of the week was busy with bouquet creations for lovers to give one another over the weekend or center pieces to display at family dinners, but the last couple weeks had been slow, so instead I busied myself prepping recurring orders.

One large order would go to the Lee Family Inn, the new-ish and lavish B&B on the outskirts of town that Dixon's family owned and operated. During the holidays, I'd make bouquets for the inn with fall-colored chrysanthemums and Christmas poinsettias, but throughout the more mundane parts of the year, I made arrangements for them with dahlias and daisies, tulips, and roses, with native Wyoming plants as fillers.

I delivered the table topper to Cade Ranch for Everlea,

and she was pleased as punch with the plum-colored Asiatic lilies I'd chosen. But to rough them up a bit for the ranch setting, I'd used a rectangular, reclaimed wood box I'd picked up at a local farmers market, set low vases in the bottom, packed them in peat moss, and wove pincushion scabiosa pods and yellow billy buttons around the vases. A few black dahlias and white anemones finished the masculine look, and feathery wisps of dried pampas grass were the perfect finishing touch.

By the time I finished deliveries in town, it was noon, so I repacked my van and headed out to Lee Valley. The day was gloomy, rain had been forecasted, and the clouds certainly agreed. They'd been rolling toward Wisper since the morning.

I pulled up in front of the large cedar inn that had been built into the side of a mountain, and with its beautiful shingle-and-shake eaves, it was the picture of an expensive, rustic getaway. I was happy that I'd added the black dahlias to the bouquets for Lee Valley, too, because they would enhance the whole natural mountain vibe.

As I set about organizing the flowers by which floor of the inn they would go to, I slipped in my earbuds and jammed out to Madonna's *True Blue* album. If "True Blue" was playing and I wasn't happy, something was really wrong. And "Live to Tell" had been the song of my soul since I was twelve.

It was fitting that it popped up on my playlist now because the song had always reminded me of Dixon. All those stories he used to tell were his secret wishes and dreams wrapped up in dragons and queens and all their frocks and frills, and I used to be the keeper of those secrets.

Bopping along in my own little world, my whole body broke out in goosebumps when, without warning, someone plucked my right earbud out of my ear, and a deep voice cut through the music.

I yelped in surprise, and the arrangement I'd been holding slipped through my fingers, but before it splattered at my feet, big hands caught it and placed it back in the van with not a flower out of place.

"Sorry," Dixon said. "Didn't mean to startle you."

"Jeez, Dixon." Hand to my heart, I breathed, "You scared the crap out of me." He passed me the earbud. I took the other one out, tucked them into their box, and stowed them back in my pocket. I looked behind him and saw his car idling. "What're you doin' here?"

"I saw you drivin' over here. I was headed to your shop to change the locks on your back door, but I figured that'd be pretty dumb if you weren't there."

"Thanks, but there's nothin' wrong with the back door. You don't have to change the locks."

"I know. I checked it the other day, but with the break-in at your house, I thought it's probably a good idea to change it anyway."

"I've never given anyone a key to the back door though."

"Doesn't mean *someone* couldn't get ahold of your key and make a copy, especially if that someone has been snoopin' around in your house."

"Oh," I said, a little taken aback at the thought. He was right, but the possibility had never even crossed my mind.

"It's no problem," he said. "Won't take long."

"Okay. Thanks."

"Sure. So," he said, waving his hand toward the rest of the flowers in the back of my van. "What else is on your agenda today?"

"Oh, um, this is it. After I'm done here, I'm gonna head

over to Mountain Home. I promised someone a game of Go Fish."

Kicking the toe of his boot into the gravel and staring at the scattering rocks, he looked very lost on his family's land.

"What brings you out here?" I asked. It seemed today I would have to wring conversation out of him. "You said you had to work today."

He nodded. "Already did. Went in at four thirty. The boss gave me a key, if you can imagine that. Anyway, I was done with everything by ten. I've gotta run back over there this afternoon to help with a big delivery, but he told me to enjoy the rest of the day till then.

"I met my sister-in-law this mornin', Devo. Do you know her?"

"Yeah, she's a lot of fun."

"Yeah? I don't know about that. She kinda scares the shit out of me. She told me if I break her wife's heart again, she'll beat me up."

I laughed, trying to picture tiny Devo Mescal-Lee pulling Dixon's hair and pummeling him with her itty-bitty fists. I didn't doubt she'd get the job done though.

"Other than that, she seems cool."

"She is," I said. "I've met her at several Wisper events. You won't find anybody more dedicated to her community."

He nodded again and tucked his hands in his front pockets, then lifted his chin toward the inn. "It's crazy that's here now."

"It hadn't been built last time you were home?"

"No. That was almost five years ago. I came up once or twice to check on Stu, but I didn't talk to my family or look around much."

That had to have been hard, but I didn't say so, and neither did he.

I wasn't sure if he was uncomfortable around me today for some reason or if he just felt out of place here at Lee Valley, but I knew I could help.

"Have you seen inside? It really is lovely in there. People come from all over to stay at the inn. Your brothers and Bea are the bosses, but they have a few really great employees. And the rooms are downright luxurious."

"No," he said. "Haven't seen it."

Had he not been invited to? But maybe with him coming home unexpectedly, his family just hadn't thought to give him the tour yet. I could rectify that.

"C'mon. If you're not busy till later this afternoon, I could use your help with the flowers, and then you could come with me to Mountain Home for a few hours. I'd love the company."

He must've recognized the olive branch, because something in his aura eased, and his whole body relaxed right before my eyes. He smiled, and even though the dark clouds still loomed above us, it felt like the sun had come out just to shine down on me.

"Sure," he said. "Love to." He looked behind him at his still idling car. "Let me just park real quick."

With the El Camino locked in the little parking area on the north side of the inn, Dixon followed me to the entrance. His footsteps behind me sounded a bit tentative. There was that hint again, a hint of the angst I'd noticed inside him when he felt like he didn't belong somewhere. It was just a hush, but I heard it, just like I had the first night he came to my house.

Didn't he know? He had always belonged wherever I was, and he always would.

He rushed in front of me to open the heavy wooden door, and as we stepped inside, his eyes widened. "Wow."

"I know, right? It's really nice."

Following his line of sight, I tried to see the inn the same way he was seeing it for the first time.

The whole place had been built and lit expertly to seem open and bright during the day, and you couldn't help but notice how the outside world snuck in through big windows and doors. Nature whispered in an old language, its voice the rhythm of the sounds of our steps on the real, knotty wood floors. The coolness of colors and textures and the warmth and life force of live plants argued playfully, creating the feeling of home.

Elk antlers were the focus of the front room. Collected after their shed and hung above an overlarge fireplace, they were a reminder of how dangerous and untouchable the wild surrounding the inn could be. But my flowers and other décor lent beauty and familiarity to the danger and made the reception room, which also functioned as something like an old-fashioned parlor, feel rich and warm. And in the evenings, the lights darkened, shading corners and hushing conversations, and it transformed the whole place into a sexy, secluded hideaway.

A staircase curved behind the reception desk and opened up to the second floor, and it flowed perfectly, the polished brass banister earthy in a way but fancy at the same time. Dark, plush couches and chairs filled the first floor, and a local artist's paintings of the Tetons in each season highlighted the lushness of the inn and juxtaposed the ruggedness of the locale.

Big, wide front windows framed Dixon's family's wooded property. I'd heard locals saying recently that moose had been seen near the inn, and it was common knowledge that elk and deer played in the fields frequently. I tried to crane my neck and spot some through the windows but didn't see anything. They had probably already hunkered down before the storm.

Everything had been perfectly decorated and seemed a bit fancy for the area, if I was honest, but God knew we got enough big-spender tourists out this way. Dixon's brothers had figured out how to cater to every kind of vacationer. If you were looking for a more down-to-earth experience, you could rent a cabin and help at Abey's and Devo's veggie farm or take guided horseback tours of the land, but if you wanted the poshness of an all-inclusive inn and catered, five-star meals, you could pay the big bucks and stay at The Inn at Lee Valley.

Dixon looked a little like his head might be spinning, so I ushered him up the stairs to deliver the flowers and watched his hand slowly slide up the smooth banister as we climbed. And when I unlocked a room with the master keycard the desk clerk had handed me, like she did every week, Dixon's head snapped back.

"This is… I've never seen a nicer hotel room in my life. Who the hell stays here? Royalty?"

I laughed. "All kinds of people, I'd imagine. I don't usually see or talk to the guests, but I've caught a few here and there. And one time, a woman staying in this very room liked my flowers so much, she stopped by the shop and ordered more."

He smiled. "Of course she did. Your flowers are beautiful."

"How would you know?" I joked. "You bought bottom-of-the-barrel daisies."

He rolled his eyes. "Merv loved 'em."

"I'm sure she did. They came from you."

We finished the delivery, his eyes roving over every detail

of the inn while we worked, and then we returned the keycard and walked back out to my van.

"I'm damn proud of my family right now," he said quietly. "And way past impressed."

"How's it goin' with them?" I asked as I drove us out to Old Fish Creek Road to Highway 20, and then to the rehabilitation center on the opposite side of town.

The end of summer was in full swing, and cars and trucks passed us with their windows down, music blaring from within. Soon, the local ice cream truck would be making its rounds through town, its happy song tinkling on the warm air, hopefully before the big storm came knocking. When Nana Nelson's husband passed, she used part of his life insurance payout to buy the truck, and all the Wisper kiddos waited for her every Friday in front of their houses after school to get a frozen treat. I'd bought a Bomb Pop from her a time or two myself.

"Oh, yeah, it's..."

Dixon didn't finish his sentence, which told me enough.

"Not goin' well?"

"It's not bad. It's just that it's kind of overwhelmin', y'know?"

"How so?"

"Well, it's not just my son I wanna get to know. It's not just him I owe amends to." He sighed heavily and shrugged. "It's goin' better than I thought it would, though. They could've shut me out completely. Maybe they should've. I didn't even know about the inn until Abey mentioned it my first day back. Life went on without me. I knew it would. I *hoped* it would for Stu's sake, but it's just that I don't know where I fit anymore."

Finally, he'd said it out loud.

"It will take time," I said softly. "That's all."

It was clear when he spoke and the weight of a thousand burdens lowered his voice that he needed his family. "Yeah."

"Do you have plans to spend time with Stu yet? Are they… allowing that?"

"Bax is comin' around slowly. Merv invited me for Sunday supper, and he agreed. He has a lot of rules though. Which is fine. Of course it is, but I just hope I don't fuck it up."

"Rules?"

"Yeah, y'know, like 'Don't tell Stu you're his birth father.' 'Don't bring up rehab or drugs or jail.' Like I would with a five-year-old? And my favorite is 'Don't come around here expectin' everyone to forgive you.'"

"Oh, Dixon. I'm sorry. That must've been hard to hear, but you know your brother is hurt, right? He's tryin' to protect Stu, but he's protectin' his heart too."

"Yeah, I know," Dixon said as I pulled into Mountain Home's parking lot.

I shut off the van and turned toward him. "Tweedledum?"

Looking out his window, his eyes focused on the mountains, rising and falling over the many grand peaks. "Yeah?"

"It's gonna be okay. You got this. And *I'm* happy you're home. You fit with me."

CHAPTER SIXTEEN

DIXON

AVERY JANE HARLOWE was an angel from Heaven above.

I followed and watched as she flitted and danced from room to room in the retirement part of Mountain Home, saying hello to the residents and passing out loose flowers to brighten their day. I felt uncomfortable and unwelcome in a place of healing, but that wasn't a new feeling for me, and if AJ wanted to be here, there weren't a lot of other places I'd want to be.

She pulled a thick pair of wool socks from her bag and handed them to an old woman who accepted AJ's gift like the socks had been woven out of strands of gold.

"So your feet don't get so cold and achy," AJ said with a smile, and the woman looked like she might be holding back tears.

"Thank you, child. How thoughtful."

A man interrupted us in the doorway to the TV room.

"Avery Jane? Who's this? I thought you kicked your good-for-nothin' boyfriend to the curb."

AJ turned slowly, a mischievous grin growing on her lips. "Oh, you know I did, Callum. Why? You jealous?"

Callum blushed. "Well now, I'm just curious. You show up here with this man, and I gotta wonder."

"This is my friend, Dixon. He grew up in Wisper and just moved back. Dixon, this is Callum Craig. He broke a hip last month, but you'd never know by lookin' at him."

Callum nodded and looked me over, head to toe. "What is your occupation, young man?"

"M-my occupation?"

"What do you do for a livin'?"

The old Dixon snapped back, "I knew what you meant, old timer." Being hounded by old men tended to get my hackles up.

His only response was a lifted eyebrow and a pointed stare, but there was kindness in his eyes. He hadn't meant anything by his question.

"I've had a lot of jobs. I've worked sheep and cattle. I fix stuff. But my last job was fellin' lumber."

"Ah, a lumberjack."

Lumberjack didn't exactly describe the job I'd worked in the Cascades, but it was close enough, and I didn't imagine this man Callum actually cared about my job history. He just wanted to know if I was good enough, if I earned enough money to be good enough for AJ.

I wasn't, and I didn't.

"I've chopped down a few trees in my time," he said. "It's a good job. Satisfyin'. Why'd you quit?"

"Yes, sir, it is. I didn't quit so much as I left the PNW to come home."

"And why'd you come home?"

"Family. I-I have a son. He's here."

"Oh, well that's nice. A son is a good thing to have. I have two, and four grandsons to boot. Would you like to see pictures? I've got a ton."

"Sure," I said after AJ nodded and urged me to go with Callum.

"Avery Jane is a special woman," he said as we entered his room. There were pictures taped up all over the walls of people he wanted to be reminded of and drawings I imagined his grandsons had made for him with happy stick-figure families and dogs. "Have a seat."

He motioned to a loveseat in the corner opposite his mechanical hospital bed, so I sat and clasped my hands together over my knees. Talking to men older than me had never been comfortable. Noah Lee had ruined it for me. And besides my brothers, I'd never really known any other men well enough to care. But it seemed like Callum wanted to connect, and I knew my discomfort was something I should probably try to work through for Stu's sake.

"Yes, sir. She is special."

"You know her well?"

"I used to. We grew up together, but I've been gone a long time, so I guess we're gettin' to know each other again as adults."

"She comes here once or twice a week," he said. "I'm only here temporarily. In fact, I'm set to go home next week, but there are a lot of folks who live here and will die here. Avery's visits are a breath of fresh air. I have family who visit when they can, but not everyone is so lucky."

"I understand. She brightens my days too."

"Stella, the woman you just met, she tells me when Avery was datin' that fella from over east of Jackson, he didn't like her visitin'. She stopped comin' for a while there. You're not gonna be another one who tries to dull her shine, now are ya?"

"Oh, no sir," I said with a chuckle. "I wouldn't dare." I couldn't live with myself if I did.

"That's good then," he said, and he pulled a photo album from his bedside drawer. "Here it is. I have hundreds of pictures on my cell phone, but my wife made this album for me before she passed, so I like to keep it close."

"I'm sorry for your loss."

"Thank you."

He sat next to me on the couch slowly. It looked like sitting was still painful after his hip injury, but other than that, AJ was right. I never would've known he was experiencing pain.

"Gotta take it slow these days. The doctors want me to use pain medication, but I won't do it."

"Why not? It helps."

"Sure it does, but that stuff lulls you into a false sense of wellbeing, and the next thing you know, you're on your ass with another broken hip. Besides—" He flipped open the album, but then looked up at me, and there was a lifetime of wisdom in his eyes. "Stuff is dangerous. I have a feelin' you know a little about that?"

Breath rushed out of me, and he nodded. "I thought so."

"Yes, sir. I'm an addict. I've been in recovery more than four years now, but I'm still an addict."

"My son went through it after he broke his leg skiing. That's how I knew. He's in recovery, too, and somehow you remind me of him."

"And your son, he's…"

"He's sober and healthy, raisin' his family over in Boise. Here he is." Callum thumbed over a couple pages, then landed on one with a big eight-by-ten printed photograph stuck inside a thin, plastic jacket. He pointed to a middle-aged man who looked a little like him in the eyes and the shape of his jaw. “That’s my son, August. My wife always called him Auggie. And that woman there is his wife, Dina, and those are my grandsons, Griffin and Chase.” His finger lingered over the image of two boys maybe two years apart in age but almost identical, with black hair and brown eyes. “Those boys wouldn’t exist without NA and all the recoverin’ addicts Auggie met in the program. I’m grateful to men like you.”

“You are?”

“Sure. If it weren’t for you, my son wouldn’t have had anyone to turn to when he needed help and guidance.”

“Wow. I guess I never really thought about it like that.”

“Yeah. So, who helped you?”

“A lot of people. Avery Jane doesn’t know it, but she helped me. My brother, my friend Nesty, and a guy named Mo in California. He made a big impression on me. He showed me that sober life probably wouldn’t be a perfect life, but that it was worth fightin’ for all the same. And he encouraged me to connect with my family again when I was ready. It took me a few years, but I finally got there.”

“And your son?”

“Oh,” I breathed. “He’s… perfect. He’s funny and lovin’ and now that I can see him and hear his voice? Nothin’ in this world can compete. Not drugs, not alcohol, not anything.”

“Good,” Callum said. “Never forget that. You got a picture?”

“No, I don’t. All I’ve got is this.” I pulled the tattered piece of Stuart’s baby blanket from my pocket and held it in front of me like a photo. It had been that important to me, and when I looked at it in the darkest parts of my sobriety, I had imagined Stu’s face so many times.

“Well here,” Callum said. “Give me your phone.” He held his hand out till I dropped my cell into it, then he clicked it on and tapped around on the screen for a minute. And when he handed it back, Stu's face smiled out at me from a family picture on the Spitfire Ranch at Lee Valley website.

"How'd you—"

Callum winked. "Small town, sonny. And your mama goes to my church."

I laughed. Of course she did. Of course he knew who I was.

He smiled and nodded.

Inspecting Stu's silly grin in the photo, I widened two fingers over it to make it bigger. "How do I make it stay on the screen?"

"Take a screenshot, and then you can make that your background." When confusion showed on my face, Callum chuckled and took the phone out of my hand. "My other son works in the tech industry. He wouldn't allow me to be technologically illiterate, so I've gotten pretty handy with these things. I could write a book on your phone, edit it, and make a book cover. Could apply to run for office or play a game of Gin Rummy with someone in Belgium if I wanted to.

"There," he said, and he handed the phone back. "I put my number in too, so if you ever need anything or want someone to talk to, you can call me. I know I'm old, but I can connect you with Auggie if you're lookin' for sober friends."

I managed to thank him, but it was hard with the big lump blocking my throat. "That's… It's pretty cool of you. Thank you."

Callum was nothing like Noah Lee, and I felt foolish for worrying he would be.

WHEN WE LEFT the retirement home and walked through a corridor to the children's wing, I was quiet.

"You okay?" AJ asked, and she took hold of my hand as we strolled.

"Yeah. Just thinkin' about some things."

"What did you and Callum talk about? He loves to gab."

"Oh, nothin' really. Just family. Life in general. He showed me pictures of his kids and grandkids. He's a nice guy."

"He really is. He's a big flirt, too, but he's still very much in love with his wife. She passed last year."

"He told me. I was sorry to hear it."

"Dixon," AJ said, and she stopped in the middle of the hallway and stood in front of me, still holding my hand. "If you want to talk, I'm here, okay? I know you're feelin' out of sorts today, but—"

"I'm fine," I said, swiping a loose lock of her hair away from her face. Her skin was fresh and clean. Her lips, bare and the prettiest pink color like the softest, most delicate rose, blushed a little darker when I touched her. "I promise. It's just that I don't talk to a lot of older men. My history with father figures isn't the best, so I'm uncomfortable around them. But Callum wasn't like that at all. He was easy to talk to, and I guess he's got me rethinkin' some of my relationships over the years."

"Oh," she said, surprised, "that's really nice."

"I guess I'm still learnin' how to relate to people, y'know? I've spent a lot of time alone."

She nodded as expectant thunder rumbled outside. "When we have time, I'd love for you to tell me about it."

"Not much to tell," I said, shrugging. "Chopped down a bunch of trees and ate a lot of cold SpaghettiOs. C'mon." I squeezed her hand. "Let's go make some kids laugh."

"Okay. You have some jokes you can tell 'em?"

"No," I said, stopping dead in my tracks when she started back down the hallway. "I thought *you* did."

"I got nothin'. We usually play Go Fish or War with a deck of cards, and some of the kids like to brush and braid my hair or just sit and tell me about their day. It doesn't really matter. They just like to know someone's there."

"And you're sure it's okay that I'm here? I'm not— I don't have— I mean, their parents might not want them talkin' to an ex-junkie."

"The children's parents have to sign a waiver to allow them to interact with volunteers. If they don't, then those kids stay in their rooms or are taken to another part of the building while I visit. I've met most of the parents, though, and they consent. Plus, my mom's best friend, Cela, is the director of Mountain Home, and I already texted her to let her know you were with me. She's fine with it. She knows your mom."

I laughed as AJ pressed a button on the wall and pushed the door open when it buzzed and unlocked.

"Of course she does," I said. "It seems everybody in this town knows Merv."

CHAPTER SEVENTEEN

AVERY JANE

"ONCE UPON A TIME, THERE WAS A ROGUE," Dixon said to a group of kids sitting in wheelchairs and on couches in the day room, and some on the floor with their legs criss-crossed. Dressed in their hospital gowns and robes, sticky footed socks, and various casts and healing implements, their rapt attention stayed focused on him as he spoke in his deep voice.

The day had grown darker. Rain pounded outside, and fat streams of it ran down the window behind Dixon seated in a chair at the back of the room. All the kids had turned to face him so they could watch as he told a story he was making up on the spot. They didn't seem to care that his jeans had been worn through at the knees or that his hair hadn't seen a pair of scissors for far too long.

"What's a rogue?" Jarod Keller asked.

He'd been rehabbing from a surgery to correct a severe scoliosis curve in his spine and still had external fixators sticking out of his shirt. He always wanted to hug me when I visited, but I was afraid to hurt him or mess up his hardware, so instead, with his mom's permission, I gave him a gentle side hug and a secret piece of chocolate when the other kids weren't looking.

Dixon cleared his throat. "A rogue was someone in olden times who was dishonest or up to no good, and this particular rogue happened to be the son of a very important man in their little town."

Sunday Marten raised her hand. "What's the son's name?"

"Don't ask stupid questions," fourteen-year-old Carter Billings said. "He'll get to that part if y'all let him tell his story."

"Thanks, man," Dixon said to Carter, "but there are no stupid questions. His name was… Augustus. Augustus Quail." Dixon smiled at Callum, who had leaned against the doorjamb to listen, and went on. "He was known around his town for stealin' things. All the shop owners closed their doors and locked 'em up tight when Augustus was near. They had all decided he was a good-for-nothin' teenager.

"He stole food and clothes from the locals, and then he would disappear for a few days. No one knew where he went, but they just figured he'd gone to sell all the things he'd stolen."

Carter scoffed. "Didn't they have cops and sheriffs in this town?"

"They did," Dixon answered, "but the cops weren't fast enough for Augustus. He was young and spry and too quick for anyone to catch. Plus, he was a master woodsman. When he was a little boy, his dad taught him, so he knew the land and could hide like a mountain lion. Nobody ever saw him runnin' away, and when he came back after a few days, he didn't have any of the things he'd stolen, so the cops could never prove it was him who stole all the stuff."

"Nobody had a Ring camera?" Sunday asked.

Dixon laughed, and the smile on his face took my breath

away. I'd forgotten how happy weaving tales made him, how it lit up his eyes.

"What's your name?" he asked her.

"Sunday Marten," she said, smiling up at him, and if I wasn't wrong, a little bit smitten. "I'm eleven."

"Naw, Sunday, this was old times. Before the internet and cell phones. No cameras."

"Um," Cela winced next to me and nudged my arm with her elbow. Her name tag and the keys hanging from a lanyard around her neck jangled, but she adjusted them. "Do you know where this story's goin'? 'Cause right now we're gettin' dangerously close to teachin' the kids how to be felons."

"Have some faith," I whispered. "All of Dixon's stories have happy endings. You just have to wait for it."

"Okay," she said, but she didn't sound as sure as I was that Dixon would be teaching the kids some kind of life lesson at the end, or he'd make them howl with laughter. Whichever he chose, his story would be good for their souls, and they'd tell the tale over and over to their families and the nurses on the night shift.

"Now, Mr. Quail, Augustus's father, was one of those shop owners. His wife, Mrs. Quail, made the best bread in all the land. It was soft and smelled so warm and sweet that people would come from miles away to buy some for their families. She was always makin' bread; she baked in the mornin', in the heat of the day, and at night. She even woke up at midnight sometimes to bake her bread. She knew how hungry people could be, and she wanted to be able to feed them.

"But Augustus's father watched over her carefully and kept track of all her ingredients. He was a miser—"

Sunday made a face. "What's a miser?"

"A miser," Dixon said, "is someone who likes to make

money but doesn't share it. Like Scrooge. You know who Mr. Scrooge is, right?"

The kids nodded.

"Good, so Augustus's dad was a miser, and he didn't give the bread away to anyone. People had to pay a pretty penny for it. But Augustus's mama was really smart. She knew how greedy her husband had become, and it broke her heart because she knew some people couldn't afford to buy her bread. So do you know what she did?"

Quiet as mice, the children shook their heads, waiting for Dixon to reveal his secrets.

Clearly but quietly, like he was letting the kids in on the secret, he said, "She dug a hole in the back of her kitchen that led out to the woods, but she hid it behind a window curtain and a wooden bread rack her husband had made for her. So, when Augustus needed to disappear, he had an escape route, and then she changed her recipe. She taught herself how to make even more delicious bread with less ingredients. She could make twice as much as before, and Augustus's father was none the wiser."

Carter rolled his eyes. "But *why* was he stealin' bread? And you said he stole clothes too."

"I did," Dixon said, a mischievous smile growing behind his eyes. "Augustus stole clothes and shoes, bread and milk. He even stole two chickens once from a local farmer."

The kids giggled, probably imagining a boy stealing chickens and trying to run away with them.

Dixon straightened in his chair. Here came the crux of his story.

"In the forest, a mile outside of town, there lived a group of people—men and women, old folks, and children with red cheeks, cold from the blowin' wind, and all of 'em were hungry.

"They were kind and hardworkin' folks, but they weren't from Augustus's town. They weren't even from the same country, and they didn't speak a lick of English, so nobody would hire them or help them.

"But Augustus did. He ran into them one day on his way home after school. He couldn't understand them. He didn't even know what language they spoke, but he watched them cut down trees to make shelters for their families and forage nuts and berries from the forest floor, and they weaved beautiful baskets out of tree branches, but there weren't many options for meat and bread. And their clothes had so many holes that you could see right through 'em!

"So, for months, Augustus had been stealin' to feed and clothe the forest people. They traded with him, and Augustus passed on the beautiful baskets they gave him to all the townsfolk he'd stolen from. Everyone asked and begged to know where the baskets had come from because they were of the highest quality and so pretty, but no one knew. Augustus never spilled the beans.

"Now, he knew it was wrong to steal. He wasn't really a rogue. He was just a boy, but he was a boy who knew right from wrong, and he knew it was wrong to let those people starve when he could do somethin' to help. His daddy didn't remember, but Augustus had asked him to help in the very beginning. You know what his dad said?"

The kids shook their heads.

"Mr. Quail told Augustus that givin' the foreigners help was a copout, and they needed to work harder to provide for themselves. He wasn't about to just hand his hard-earned money over to lazy people."

"Then what happened?" Jarod asked.

"One day, Augustus stole a pair of pants from a local clothes maker, and he ran to his mama's bakery. He stuffed two loaves of bread in his shirt and climbed down the hole in the floor. But this time, his dad saw and followed him.

"When he got to the end of the tunnel next to a big oak tree, the old man squinted against the bright sunlight, but he saw the path his son had taken and his footprints in the dirt, so he followed again.

"He knew he was close when he heard strange, foreign voices, so he hid behind the base of a wide cedar tree." Dixon lifted and wove his long arms into the air, and the kids' eyes followed. "Branches swayed high in the forest canopy, creakin' and whooshin' in the wind. But then Augustus's father heard his son's voice, and he could tell Augustus was scared."

I could've dropped a thumb tack and every single person in the room would've heard its quiet ping on the floor. Even Cela had gone quiet beside me. Callum tossed me a wink and a smile, enjoying watching Dixon tell his story.

Thunder rumbled again outside, and suddenly, Dixon jumped out of his seat, his arms now spread wide, and the kids stared up at him expectantly. "Mr. Quail leapt out from behind his tree, expectin' to fight these foreigners and protect his son… but what he found instead rendered him speechless and made shame course through his heart."

Dixon closed his eyes, dropped his arms to his sides, and hung his head, and in unison, every kid in the room begged, "What did he find?"

Dixon nodded, ready to deliver a heartwarming finish, and he looked up solemnly. "Mr. Quail found Augustus holding a small child, skinny as a stick and weak from hunger and cold. The little boy's mother *begged* Augustus, but he had no idea what she was askin' of him.

"But Augustus's father knew." Dixon puffed up his chest

and deepened his voice. "'Give me the boy,' he told his son, 'and run ahead. Fetch the doctor.'

"Augustus was surprised to see his father in the woods, and even though he was afraid of bein' punished for stealin', he hoped his father would show compassion. 'They can't pay,' Augustus told his dad. 'They have no work. No money.'

"'That matters not,' his father said. 'Go on now, son, and be quick. We won't be far behind.'

"Augustus ran as fast as he could, but this time, he didn't take the long and windin' secret path. He ran straight through the forest until he hit the town border, then he yelled and called loudly for the doctor. People in the little village peeked out of their windows at Augustus, and then they began to emerge, gossiping with each other about the unruly teen and what he might be up to this time.

"But after a short while, behind Augustus, his father and the forest people appeared from the thick of the trees, and Mr. Quail commanded, 'We need clean water and food. Bring everything you have.'

"Well," Dixon said, "the townsfolk all scurried about, ransackin' their kitchens for food and fillin' jugs with water from the town well, because Augustus's father was a miser, yes, but he loved his town. He wanted to protect his neighbors and make sure they were fed, just like Augustus, but now he knew he'd made a mistake. So when Mr. Quail spoke, his neighbors listened, and they could hear the regret in his voice.

"Soon, the town meetin' hall was filled with the most delicious meats, cheeses, and breads, and everyone's cups overflowed with fresh water."

Quietly, Dixon sat, and he crossed his arms and leaned back in his chair. "The end."

"What?" Carter blurted. "The end? That's a crock! What about the sick kid?"

"Did Augustus get in trouble?" Sunday asked.

Dixon smirked, looking around at all the inquisitive faces still focused on him. "You tell me. What do you think happened next?"

"He probably went to jail," Carter said.

Sunday shook her head definitively. "No, he was the town hero. They wouldn't put him in jail. His dad would apologize to Augustus, and he'd tell his son that seein' the sick boy reminded him that love matters more than money. The neighbors would have a party for Augustus, and the forest people would all move to town. They'd build them a big mansion, and everyone would live happily ever after."

Dixon just smiled, letting the kids dream up their own ever afters.

"Yeah," Jarod added. "And the forest people knew how to make different kinds of bread 'cause they were from a different country, so I bet they taught Augustus's mom how to make their bread, and then the head of the forest people and Augustus's dad went into business together and became the richest bread kings in all the land."

From the back corner of the room, thirteen-year-old Tiffany Eddison raised her voice a little, which was a welcome surprise since she normally spoke in whispers and barely at all. "I think Augustus married the forest people's princess."

"He's a teenager," Carter pointed out, rolling his eyes.

"So." Tiffany's face turned red. "Teenagers fall in love all the time. Haven't you ever heard of *Romeo and Juliet*?"

And now Carter was blushing, and he stiffened and turned to stare at a wall.

"Y'all think about it," Dixon said, "and maybe I'll stop by

soon so you can tell me what you came up with. Write it down so you don't forget."

"Okay!" Sunday jumped up from her spot on the floor, and she rushed to Cela and me standing near the door. "Can Mr. Dixon come back next week, Cela?"

"Sure, honey, if he wants to." Cela looked across the room at Dixon.

He shrugged before he high-fived Jarod. "I'm down."

CHAPTER EIGHTEEN

DIXON

"THAT WAS GENIUS," AJ said, "makin' the kids come up with their own ending."

"I don't know about genius, but I know how hard bein' stuck in a hospital is, how boring and lonely. This way, they have somethin' extra to focus on if they want to. And maybe some of the kids will start to imagine other stories."

Like Stu.

Being around other kids made me ache to see him again. What was he thinking about right now, right this very minute? Was he home from school? Did Bax and Bea allow him a popsicle, or were they more the "apples are a good after school snack" kind of people?

"I'll drop you back at your car," AJ said as she drove through town. Rain still fell, but it had quieted to a mist. "Thanks for goin' with me. I think the children really enjoyed story time."

"Yeah," I said, thinking I'd really enjoyed it too. Maybe AJ was right. Maybe I should start writing my stories down. I mean, I didn't have any expectations that I'd become some kind of bestselling author, but what could it hurt to jot down the crap running amok in my head?

I thought about it while we drove. AJ was quiet, too, and she had this small, serene smile on her face the whole way. She turned on her van's radio halfway to Lee Valley, and old eighties pop songs played in the background.

When she pulled up behind my El Camino, I asked, "If you were gonna write some stories down, what would you use? Your phone? Plain ol' paper?"

Turning slowly to face me, she judged the look in my eyes and spoke carefully, like she didn't want to spook me out of my plan. "I'd use my laptop. There's a free document program you could use. I'll show you."

"I don't have a laptop."

"You can use my old one. It still works. I bought a new one because it came out in a pretty pink color and has a bigger screen, but the old one is tried and true."

"I can't take your—"

"Dixon, it's a used laptop, not a car, and if you don't take it, it'll just collect dust on the shelf in my closet. It's a gift. Please accept it."

"Okay," I said. "If you insist. Thanks."

The smile lighting her eyes was magnificent, and the dimples I still remembered showed around her mouth. "You're welcome. Now, get to work. I'll text you this weekend."

"Yes, ma'am," I said as I opened my door. "Oh, but if I don't get back to you right away, forgive me. I'm startin' my second job at the animal clinic tomorrow mornin'. They didn't tell me the hours, so I don't know how long I'll be. And then Sunday is supper with my family over at Bax's house." Which got me thinking. "Do you wanna come with?"

"To dinner? With your family?"

"Yeah," I said. Having her support would make things less daunting. Her laugh comforted me and made me remember who I used to be.

"Thanks for the invite, Dixon," she said. "But I think it's probably best if you go on your own. It's your first chance to start to get to know your son, and your family has missed you. They won't want to share your attention with me."

"Oh, yeah. I guess you're right." But damn, when I pictured showing up with her next to me, I envisioned good vibes and a successful dinner. And when I thought about showing up alone, my mind ran wild with the unknown.

"Raincheck?" she said, and I nodded once and closed my door.

"GOOD TO MEET YOU," a tall man with a wonky accent said when I arrived at All Animals Veterinary Clinic the next morning.

We shook hands. "I'm Doc V and this is Dr. Masterson." He motioned to the far side of the surgery prep room, where a woman wrestled with a young Dalmatian. The dog wiggled and fought, tossing his head this way and that, trying to get free from the leash she'd just managed to secure around his neck.

"Hi," she called over her shoulder. "I'm so sorry. I hate to do this to you on your first day, but can you take this dog, please? I have surgery scheduled in five minutes, and I can't get him calmed down."

This was the exact reason I'd applied for the part-time job when I saw a notice about it on a bulletin board in the local coffee shop. The ad had called the position "Animal tech and wrangler." I wasn't sure about the tech part, but I had the wrangler part down pat.

"No worries." I crossed the room and took the thin rope leash from her hand.

"Thank you," she breathed, exasperated. "I'm Oly. I go by Dr. Masterson with the clients, but we're pretty laid back behind the scenes."

She seemed familiar to me. I probably went to school with her, but she was a few years older than me, and it wasn't like my memory of those years was crystal sharp.

I nodded and stepped closer to the pup, my eyes on his and my posture relaxed but commanding. Raising my hand in the air, I gave him the non-verbal command to sit that I'd learned from the Coulters in California. The dog didn't know the commands, but he recognized my firm direction, and he sat.

"Whoa. How'd you do that?" Dr. Masterson asked. "I've been tryin' to get him to do that for thirty minutes!"

Doc V approached us with his hands on his hips. "I think Mr. Lee must be one of those, em, what do you call them… dog talkers?"

"It's just Dixon," I mumbled. Being called Mr. Lee, even though technically and legally it was my name, raised the hair on the nape of my neck.

"Dog *whisperer*," Dr. Masterson said. "And yeah, I think you're right. Oh my God, I'm so glad you're here. Okay, Luuk will walk you through what we need you to do. I have one spay before Beanie's surgery in an hour. If you could have him calm and cool by then, I'd be in your debt, and I'll buy you lunch."

"You don't have to do that. I love dogs. It's no problem, really."

"No, no," she said. "Lunch is on me. It's your first day. It's an All Animals tradition."

"Come with me." Doc V clapped me on the shoulder, then led Beanie and me through a door at the back of the room which opened up to long rows of various sized kennels. "Our office manager isn't here today. It's her birthday, so she took the day off. She'll go over all of this with you next Saturday, but I'll get you started."

"Thanks."

"Where are you from? I know a few Lees; we go out to Spitfire Ranch to treat their cows and occasionally a lamb or a horse. You're not one of those Lees, are you?"

"I am."

"Oh, wonderful. So you know animals."

"Yeah. I haven't worked a ranch in a long time though."

Doc V waved away my comment. "You never forget this stuff. I grew up on a dairy farm in the Netherlands, but I hadn't been around cows for many years when I was going through vet school, but the information came ruching back at me when I needed it."

"*Rushing* back at you?"

"Isn't that what I said?"

I shook my head, trying not to laugh. The dude was a hoot.

He chuckled at his mistake. "*Rush*-ing. Got it." He tapped his temple and smiled, and then he began to tell me the day's schedule and what he would be needing from me.

ON THE OFF CHANCE SHE might be up, I texted AJ late that night while I lay in bed *not* sleeping.

Did you know that some dogs are left-handed? Or I guess I should say left-pawed

Almost immediately, she texted back.

TWEEDLEDEE

😲 I did not. How was your first day?

Good. I like the doctors. I didn't meet my direct boss. Doc V said it's her birthday today so she got the day off

Yes, that's Yola. Manny's wife? He ordered her a big bouquet to celebrate. Calla lilies are her faves. I dropped them off this morning

Sometimes I forget just how small this small town is

I love it. Can you imagine me delivering flowers in a big city? I'd never know who the recipient was, if they enjoyed their arrangement. Because Wisper is so small, I get to know my customers and learn which flowers will really make them smile and appreciate their bouquets

The thought of AJ mulling over which type of rose to put into a bouquet, which color, how many, made me smile. She had always been a giving person. She'd given me peace when we were kids, and that only seemed to have intensified now as adults.

No, I can't imagine. But I bet your beautiful soul would shine no matter where you were

. . .

She began to reply; three little blinking dots appeared on my phone's screen, but then they disappeared. A few seconds later the phone rang, and the blurry photo I'd taken of AJ yesterday appeared beneath "Tweedledee."

I kept reminding myself to snap some photos of Stu tomorrow so I wouldn't forget when I was at the ranch. Having a picture of my kid on my phone seemed like the most important thing in my world aside from actually talking to him, though, so I knew it wouldn't slip my mind.

I answered her call with a jittery stomach and a smile I couldn't quite quit. "Hi."

"Hi," she said, and the warm sound of her voice sent a shot of dopamine straight through me. "I know you've had a long day, but would you like to come over for tea again? I'd love to hear about the animals."

"Can't sleep?"

"Am I that obvious?"

"Be there in five."

CHAPTER NINETEEN

DIXON

THE WALK to AJ's place was as known to me as breathing, and I grinned like a goof as I hurried over there, like somebody lit a fire in my pants. I didn't want to show up too soon, or she'd think I jogged there, but I also didn't want to make her wait.

The image of her standing in her doorway, welcoming me into her home, had become my favorite part of the day. I envisioned it while I walked and thought about all the animals I'd met in the day and how stoked I was to be a part of the All Animals team.

It was a job I could be proud of, a job Stu could be proud of. What kid didn't like animals? And it felt really good to be considered part of a team. I'd never really felt that in a work situation, and I was unusually excited to meet the other team members. Granted, I was only a small part, but they were good people. They cared about the animals they treated, and I was proud to be part of that.

I wanted to kiss AJ for asking about my day. There wasn't one person in my life who bothered. That wasn't exactly true. Abey had tried to connect, but it wasn't an easy connection.

There were just too many years between us, still so much she didn't know about me. The ambiguity was my fault, I knew, but I wasn't ready. I couldn't even imagine sitting down with my sister, or any of my siblings for that matter, and spilling my guts. I would, in time, but I got the feeling that they didn't know what to say to me, and I had the suspicion that they were wary of saying anything in case it might set me off, that anything they had to say might drive me back to drugs.

For AJ to care enough about me to *not* be scared of my reaction and ask about such a mundane thing seemed huge to me. It had been so long since I'd let anyone care for me at all, and AJ made me realize more than ever what a mistake that had been.

So, when I stepped onto her porch and she answered her door in pink pajamas, mint green fuzzy slippers with pink bows, and her hair up in a knot on her head, I couldn't help myself.

Wrapping my arms around her, I drew her into them and leaned down to kiss her soft petal lips. It was just a quick peck, but she rested her head against my chest and let me hug her silently, and the sound of her quiet breath and the steady pulse of her heartbeat was like a drug.

But to compare her to some dirty, life-threatening substance that had the power to rip families apart and make liars and thieves out of honest people seemed gross and insufficient.

AJ was so much more than that. She was the strength of the sun when it beat down on a sapling in the dirt, giving its power to the tree, telling the small, unprotected thing it was okay to thrive, to grow and be seen. She was the love behind everyday words and actions that allowed the people around her to feel secure and brave.

She made me feel brave.

"I thought about you today," I said, hugging harder and pulling her closer.

She wrapped her arms around me and clasped her hands together behind my back. "You did?"

"Yeah. The first dog I worked with was a Dalmatian, and he reminded me of your old dog, Miggie. Remember her?"

AJ laughed against my chest. "Oh God, I miss that dog. Remember she used to dig up the wild thyme Gran planted, and she'd eat it with a side of cat poop from the neighbor's yard, and then she'd come home smellin' like an overripe garbage disposal? Her breath!"

Chuckling, I said, "I remember, and then your mama used to make us try to brush her teeth, but we thought your toothpaste would make her breath smell better than the beef-flavored dog toothpaste. She ate the whole tube of Aim and barfed all over your bedroom floor."

Laughing softly, AJ pulled back and looked up at me, so I released my hold around her, but she took my hand and dragged me inside and to her couch. A mug with a snapshot of AVery Pretty Petal's storefront printed on it sat on her coffee table, the peppermint tea bag dunked into the steaming water and the tag hanging from its string over the edge.

"You're too good to me," I said as I sat, then lifted the mug for a sip.

Fancy Kitty jumped onto the back of the couch to sniff and check me out, and then she perched behind my head and began to lick her ginger paws and start her nightly cleaning ritual.

"No I'm not," AJ replied. "I'm perfect for you."

We both paused. I knew what she meant, but to hear her say it like that…

"So," she went on like she hadn't said anything, "what kind of animals did you get to play with today?"

I pretended she hadn't said anything either and counted off the different species of animals on my fingers. "Dogs, cats, two ferrets, a horse, and a llama."

"Really? They threw you right in there, didn't they? A llama on your first day? I've heard they can be pretty temperamental."

I laughed. "You ain't kiddin'. That thing hated me. It was kind of a ding to my ego. I pride myself on bein' able to relate to animals."

To prove my point, Fancy stood and stretched, digging her sharp claws into the back of AJ's couch, and then her paws began to knead my shoulder. She climbed over me and laid on my chest, looking up and right into my eyes.

Scratching behind her ear, I said, "It's always come so easy to me, but this llama today? No go. I think he knew we were there to rid him of his most prized jewels. He spat at me the minute he saw me, and things only got worse from there. And that green stuff they spit smells like death. Miraculously, he missed me. Even the vet was surprised. He said llamas usually have pretty good aim."

AJ made an "ew" face, but then laughed. "You were lucky."

"I dunno about luck," I said, "but I've still got good reflexes."

I pushed my hair behind my ear, and AJ's eyes followed my hand. "What are the tattoos on your fingers?"

Splaying my fingers, I looked at the markings. They weren't the most sophisticated tattoos, but they meant a lot. I lifted my hand and held up four fingers.

"A number for every time I quit drugs." Tucking those fingers to my hand, I held up my thumb with the X. "And the X is for this time. The last time." I put it on my thumb because that was what I used to push the plunger down on the needle every time I shot up. If there was ever a time I thought about doing it again, I'd see the X. It stood for Stu. It stood for the end of a really shitty time in my life. It stood for me because I'd made the decision to stop and to place value on myself again.

AJ smiled softly and swiped her own mug off the coffee table and sipped it, bunching her knees up in front of her, but then she extended her legs, and her slipper rubbed against my thigh.

Fancy jumped down and ran off when I set my tea on the table and lifted AJ's legs. When I set them in my lap, she tried to pull her feet away, but I held her ankles and wouldn't let her.

"How was your day?" I asked, sliding her slippers off her feet and letting them thunk on the floor in front of the couch.

She set down her mug and wiggled her toes, which not surprisingly had been painted a bubblegum pink color. Quietly, she sighed and tucked a throw pillow behind her neck, then reclined against the arm of the couch.

When I began to rub and dig my thumbs into the high arch of her foot, she moaned softly. "Long, which is kind of unusual for a Saturday in late summer or early fall. Usually, people are too busy with the new school year or with the harvest to remember to order flowers for their loved ones, but I got slammed. I made seven arrangements, took almost twice that number of orders for next week, and at one point the shop had so many customers waiting, they had to line up out the door. Poor Gran's tuckered out. She was my helper.

"I've got an online ordering portal, but most local folks just stop in when they're out runnin' errands."

Working a stubborn knot of muscle on the rise of her arch, I rubbed it out over and again until it released.

"That feels amazing," she said, and she closed her eyes.

"Sounds like a successful day though."

"Oh yeah. I'm not complainin'. Today's sales will pad my bottom line and allow me to run more ads. Soon, I'll have to hire help. I always thought the shop would stay local and small, but with online orders and the ease of makin' websites nowadays, we're growin' without me even really havin' to try.

"Gran's been retired for years, but she loves hangin' out so she can get all the town gossip. She always offers to help, and so does Mama when she's not workin', but I can't rely on them. Gran's got bad knees, and my mom has zero creative bones in her body. I have to instruct her and tell her where to place every single flower or else her bouquets look like a tangled, messy pile of flower vomit. She tries, but…

"Someday, I'd like to open a second store. Maybe in Jackson. I'd need several employees to pull that off, but we're not quite there yet, you know?"

I watched her mouth as she talked, stealing long, wanting glances since she couldn't see me. I wanted so badly to kiss her again.

She moaned louder when my hands slid higher and wrapped around her ankles. And when they moved even higher and slipped beneath her silky pajama bottoms, she sighed and scooted closer to me. Her pillow fell to the floor, and her hair splayed out beneath her on the couch cushion like silk.

"It's been a long time since anyone touched me like this, Dixon. I-I think maybe you should stop."

"Why's that?" I asked, scooting closer to her, too, and I turned and lifted her foot to my mouth.

When I kissed the tip of her big toe, she gasped and her eyes popped open. "Because you said you only wanna be friends, but that's not what I want, and you touchin' me like this isn't makin' it easier to not throw myself at you again."

I wasn't sure when or why that had changed, but it wasn't what I wanted either. In her quiet house with not so much as a clock ticking, the connection we'd always had sparked and flashed between us. Since the day I'd stumbled into her shop, it had been morphing and changing into something I had no right to expect.

Quietly, I said, "Maybe I want you to." *Maybe I want you to plaster yourself all over me. Maybe I want your full, lush ass in my hands, your legs hooked over my shoulders, and your fingers streaking my back with scratches.*

"You do?"

I nodded. I couldn't speak. The want I felt for her was so big, it clogged my throat and made my heart race like a jackrabbit trying to escape a cougar's snapping jaws.

The happy, calming sound of her voice was doing something to me, and how had I never noticed the sexy timbre and the squeaky rasp? It had always been that way, I finally realized, kind of a husky, beckoning sound, and now I wanted to hear it when she came and called my name.

She stared at my face, probably trying not to get whiplash, but I watched her reacting to my touch, watched her breasts rise and fall with her breath, watched her hands grip the couch. She licked her lips, and her pink tongue left behind a silky, wet sheen that made the pout of her bottom lip irresistible, and that was the last straw. I needed that plump skin between my teeth.

Carefully, I inched closer, sliding my hands even higher.

I had been wrong before. AJ *was* a drug. She was a comforting ease, and every touch of my skin on hers made me remember the past. It became clearer and clearer, but the bad, painful memories weren't flooding my mind like they usually did.

No, AJ made me remember laughing with her in the forest. She made me remember the simple happiness of long summer days under the sun, reading together as she lay next to me in the dirt or propped against the base of a tree, peeking over my shoulder to get lost in whatever fantasy I'd borrowed from the library, and Smartie wars when we kept count of how many we tossed that landed in each other's mouths.

Her mouth now was the portal to remembering who I used to be, and I wanted so goddamn badly to remember the person who hadn't injected filth into his veins or lied to the people he loved. I wanted to be worthy of my son, and even though I was sober and should've been able to hold my head high, I couldn't.

AJ's touch on my skin or the taste of her tongue in my mouth couldn't make my neck any stronger, but I wished for it.

Her eyes didn't stray from mine, and slowly, she unbuttoned her pajama shirt. The fabric slipped over her skin like water over a stone at the edge of a brook and revealed to me something I hadn't realized I'd been longing for.

Connection, touch, and need. But not chemical need. No, this was about instinctual need, a base desire.

But only AJ would do. It was why I'd been dreaming about her before I came home. Somehow, somewhere deep inside, I knew I needed her in my life.

I hadn't been with a woman since Kel, and sadly, no matter how hard I tried, I couldn't recall the act that had created the best thing in my life. We had been high that night. We got high every night back then, and all those nights bled into days in my mind.

It was just another reason I wanted to remember who I'd

been before the drugs. Another reason I wasn't good enough for my son.

Only AJ had the power to make me forget. She could blur out the ugly with her flowers, her gentle acceptance, and her beautifully brilliant smile.

"Please," I whispered. My hand wandered up her leg and over her soft stomach.

She nodded and reached for me, and her legs settled beneath me as I crawled over her.

Regarding me for a long moment, her eyes caressing the long strands of my hair as it fell between us, finally she asked, "What's changed?"

"I'm not sure, but I need you. I want you. I need my face buried between your thighs, and I wanna know the taste of you."

She blushed and lowered her gaze, but I fit my finger beneath her chin and lifted her eyes back to mine. "But can I ask, why do *you* want *me*? I don't have much to give you."

She breathed a laugh, and the sound was sex and home and the answer to a question I'd never bothered to ask.

"I've always wanted you," she whispered. "You have to know that."

"I *don't* know that."

"Well, now you do. Kiss me. Touch me. Take what you need from me. Everything I have to give is yours, even if it's just for tonight."

CHAPTER TWENTY

AVERY JANE

"YOU'RE SHAKIN'." Dixon's whole body vibrated as I led him to my bed. "Are you nervous?"

Unbuttoning his jeans, I bit into my bottom lip while I imagined what I might find beneath. I pushed them down his thighs and to the floor, and when he sat on the edge of my bed, I stepped between his spread legs.

"A little," he whispered. "But I don't think that's what's makin' me shake."

"Then what is?"

His hand slipped up my back as he looked up at me, and I inched closer as he settled it gently between my shoulder blades.

"I want you so much I can barely catch my breath."

Pushing my fingers through his hair, I scraped my nails over his scalp, and he moaned and breathed out his anxiety. I pulled his mouth to my breast, and his tongue peeked out for a taste.

Slowly, I slid my fingers beneath the waistband of my pajamas and my underwear, and I pushed them over my hips and let the fabric fall and pool around my feet. Dixon's hand roughed over my skin when I climbed up and straddled his thighs.

"AJ…"

"Yes?"

"I-I don't know if this is—"

"It's what we need," I whispered and smoothed his hair away from his face. The tangles I'd created fell behind his shoulders, which led my curiosity to his chest. I grabbed the hem of his T-shirt and lifted it, and his bare chest beneath was strong and cut.

"It's irresponsible. I don't have a condom and I can't risk—"

"In the drawer." Casting my eyes toward my bedside table, I blushed. I hoped he wouldn't judge me for being prepared. Cody had chastised me once for it, but then he never bothered to bring condoms, and then he'd get mad at me when I wouldn't sleep with him.

And call me a hopeless romantic, but if Dixon and I had to stop now, I thought I might cry. The build up to us being together like this had been going on for far too long. If I was honest with myself, it had been building for years.

Dixon leaned to open the drawer, and my eyes followed the long line of his neck as he stretched. He pulled out a condom packet and straightened, and I gripped his erection in the tight cage of my palm. I'd been trying really hard not to focus on his cock and the way it throbbed and pulsed in anticipation, but now I stared. And I was *not* disappointed.

His eyes rolled closed, his jaw clenched, and it seemed like he stopped breathing.

"Please?" I said softly. "Let me love you."

The intensity of his gaze when he opened his eyes almost scared me. He hadn't moved. He still held the condom trapped between two fingers, so I pulled it free and tore it open, and when I rolled it into place, he shuddered.

"Like this?" he asked, looking between us at my extremely expectant body—nipples pebbled and as hard as stone, skin tight, and goosebumps broken out everywhere. "You deserve more than some quick f—"

"You can have me however you want me," I said, and I meant it, "but we're already here. I'm ready, and *I* want *you*." Twining my fingers through his, I led our hands beneath me and let him feel how wet I already was for him. His arousing foot massage had done the trick.

I rubbed our hands through my slick wetness, until the slippery glide took on a rhythm, and then I untangled my fingers from his and held steady with my hands on his shoulders.

Reaching forward, I touched my lips to his tentatively and whispered, "Please don't make me beg," as I began to ride his hand, my hips surging and retreating slowly, and I savored every sensation his rough skin on mine caused.

I nipped his bottom lip between my teeth, and he groaned and opened his mouth. He tilted his head and inhaled as I exhaled. It felt like every breath I'd ever taken was for him.

"Avery Jane," he said, "I-I want this more than I can say, but I'm not— You deserve better than me. You deserve *good* things."

But his fingers rubbed me faster.

Peppering greedy kisses along his jaw, I whispered, "I deserve *you*. Someday you'll see that me deservin' good things is the same thing. Stop tryin' to talk me out of this."

That stopped the delicious rubbing, and his gaze held mine for a long moment.

"You're smart and beautiful," he said, touching one finger to my bottom lip. "This smile and these carin' eyes, they should be focused on somebody else. I'm scarred and sorry and broken. You deserve better."

"I don't care about scars."

"You should. They remember all the bad shit I've done. If you look close enough, they'll tell you a story about a worthless man who was so scared of who he had become that he ran from his home, and he hid and cowered away while the rest of the world went on with life and faced their problems. I carry so much pain, AJ. I don't want it to infect you."

"Skin does not have a memory, Dixon. It's not your skin that remembers the pain. Those scars have completely forgotten you. They have no idea where they came from, and it's a good thing because you can't change your skin, but you can change your heart and your mind."

A tear fell from the corner of his eye. He didn't acknowledge it. Instead, his hands gripped my hips harder. He kissed me again, guiding me lower and meeting me halfway, then entered my body slowly, as if he were afraid to break or scar me too.

The connection was immediate, like coming home again, and I imagined I could see inside him, that I could see the deep lake of pain and regret he held in his heart. The lake churned and surged, and I wanted to ride it, to surf and conquer it.

He deserved placid waters.

The shaking got worse. His whole body quaked with it, and I was shaking now, too, silently willing him to move inside me, but I didn't want to rush him.

"No," he said gruffly. "*Not* like this."

Hope crashed into the pit of my stomach.

"I understand," I mumbled, and the anticipation I'd been feeling about where we'd been headed splintered apart inside me. "If you're not ready, it's o—"

But the words in my mouth died before they could reach my lips because Dixon twisted and took us down to my bed. Still inside me, the lower half of his body remained unmoving, but he leaned on one hand and used his other to swipe my hair behind my shoulders. His steely blue eyes took a careful inventory of my body, starting with my lips and slowly moving down the length of my neck.

When he leaned lower and his mouth opened over my breast, I felt his breath on my skin, and my nipples rose even higher and peaked for him. I moaned and arched up to feel his body against mine.

Finally, he thrust inside me slowly.

Whispering, he said, "I wanna fuck you proper, wanna feel every inch of you against every inch of me."

Breath eased out of my lungs in a moan, and my eyes fell shut.

He was big. He filled me fully, but the *way* he filled me, every curve and corner of him smoothing every edge and hardness inside me, made me wild. I rolled my hips and tried desperately to pull him in deeper.

The moonlight outside my window brightened our skin and made it glow, but shadows still lurked and lingered in the corners of my room. They darkened his hair. The soft strands brushed over my skin while he sucked my nipple into his mouth, tugging it gently with his teeth, but as soon as he'd gotten a taste of me, he stopped.

Looking into my eyes, he pulled out and his hard, wet cock slapped against my inner thigh.

"What?" I asked. *Oh God, please don't stop.*

He shook his head and moved down my body slowly, so slowly that I began to beg while he kissed every inch of me, just like he'd promised.

"*Please*, Dixon," I pleaded, but he wouldn't answer.

Instead, he spread my legs wider and settled between them, groaning softly, Then he opened his mouth.

The first soft lick of his tongue between my legs made me gasp. The second had me digging my nails into his shoulders, and the third made me groan and push up on my heels. He growled and followed my body, then devoured me like I was his last meal.

Squeezing his head between my thighs harder and harder while his tongue dealt faster and punishing pressure to my clit, my hands gripped his hair and I rolled my hips wildly against his face, watching his head surge between my legs and his fingers dig deeper into my skin.

And when he dragged them over my hip and slid two inside me while he sucked my clit into his mouth, it didn't take more than a handful of pumps before I was coming, giving in to the pleasure and calling out the release of all the doubt I'd been feeling about him wanting me like this.

I didn't have time to think about it, though, because he pulled his fingers free from my body and licked them, but then he crawled up, planted both hands on the bed beside my arms, and his cock glided smoothly inside me.

The rough sound in the back of his throat when the after-shocks from my orgasm gripped him tightly was feral and possessing, but in the best way.

And then he began to *fuck* me.

My bed frame squeaked in protest. It hadn't seen action for a long time, and the headboard began to bang against the wall with every powerful thrust of his hips, as if he could inject every piece of himself into me. Wrapping my arms around his shoulders, I held on for the ride.

The vulnerability etched across his face, lining the edges of his eyes, mesmerized me, and I traced them with careful fingers. He leaned into my touch but never looked away, not even when my hands snaked beneath his arms and my fingernails dug into his ribs because I was so close to coming again.

I wanted to hold out for him, but he noticed the pull of my body on his, and he hissed and fucked me harder. Faster. Wilder.

My breasts bounced and rubbed against his heaving chest, and my mouth popped open, but no sound came out because bliss had overtaken my ability to speak. Pleasure rushed through me in waves, like a steady, rhythmic pulse of some far-off sea in my dreams crashing against a distant shore.

My eyes rolled closed, my thighs clutching Dixon's hips between them to hold him where I needed him to ride out my waves. But that just made him fuck faster, and my orgasm rose higher and higher until I was coming all over again.

"AJ," he breathed into my mouth. "Look at me." When I did and the blue fire of his eyes burned right through me, he whispered, "I'm afraid."

"There's no safer place for you than inside me," I promised breathlessly, tucking wild strands of his hair behind his ears. "We can be afraid together. Let go. You deserve to feel good. To be loved. Come inside me."

He washed our fear clean as he captured my mouth again with his eager lips and tongue and his breath rushed in. I inhaled as he came, smoothing my hands over the wide plane of his back and the slightly raised edges of forgotten scars there, listening to his cry into the night, hoping he would never let me go.

CHAPTER TWENTY-ONE

DIXON

BEFORE ANYONE ELSE SHOWED UP, I clocked an hour on the rowing machine at the community center, the repetitive, full-body push and pull easing the adrenaline rushing through me every time I thought about last night.

Those thirty or sixty minutes every morning were the only time I could guarantee solitude so that I could center myself and gauge the strength of my mind.

I was grateful my boss had offered me the use of the small gym. Some guys I knew from rehab became militant about working out, like they replaced addiction to drugs and alcohol with an addiction to running or lifting weights, but I understood because the difference in how I felt all day after a workout compared to a day without was night and day.

After that and ten minutes under a perfectly functioning showerhead raining the hottest water my skin could stand, my morning meeting went well.

Theo was there, but he didn't lead the group. An older cowboy, Charlie, ran things. He was cool. He told me he was an artist, and for some reason, I found myself actually talking to him. I blurted that I was thinking about writing a book, and he thought it was the best idea since sliced bread, so he pulled up some kids' books online, and we sat and studied their cover designs for a while after everyone else had left.

It was AJ's magic at work. She had me feeling happy and light, which was a welcome change. Being weighed down with misery and self-loathing was exhausting.

To be connected to her the way we were last night… I had no words for the feeling. It amazed me how easily she fit into my fucked-up existence, and there were only tiny moments of doubt when I worried I would let her down or hurt her.

It wasn't my intention. I wanted to be a light to her like she'd always been to me.

Hours later, she was still on my mind, and I relived our red-hot night together the entire drive to Lee Valley—the curved swell of AJ's hips under my hands, the way she'd laughed when my fingers traced her ribs, and the delicate feel of the petal-soft skin between her legs, like the most fragile flower in one of her bouquets, wet with dew and sweet, but if I wasn't careful, my fumbling fingers could crush and ruin it.

Before fear and whispers of old memories could set in, I was at the ranch, pulling up in front of my brother's house.

The clock on my dash flashed 5:30. I was too early for dinner. I wasn't sure how I'd gotten the time wrong, but I figured I could use the next hour to prepare myself for the onslaught of questions my family would soon start lobbing at me and for the stab to my heart I knew I'd feel when I saw my son, so I started counting my way through some breathing exercises and tried to center positivity in the forefront of my mind.

It only took a few minutes for me to realize it wasn't working and that my hands had started to sweat and my heart was racing again. It only got more intense when Stu slammed open the door, jumped onto the porch, and then rushed at my car.

Bax wasn't with him, but when I climbed out of the El Camino and shut the door, I saw my brother watching us through the kitchen window over the sink.

"Hi, Uncle Dixon!" Stu flung himself at me and hugged me, his little Wranglers and U-Dub T-shirt with the telltale bucking bronco on the front making him look like a miniature cowboy. He was even wearing little cowboy boots, but his were newer and a lot nicer than mine. "Are you here for supper?"

"Yeah," I said, trying not to smile too much, but it was the first time I'd touched him since I left him. "I'm a little early. Is that cool?"

"Totally cool, dude," he said and he released me, but he grabbed hold of my hand and dragged me inside. "My mama made a puppatizer. It's this cream-cheesy thing. Do you like cheese? I love it."

His hand, so little and warm, fit inside mine perfectly. I marveled at the fit, at the way I'd fucked up everything else in my life, but this, Stu's hand in mine, still worked. It was still pure.

"Oh, you mean an appetizer? Yeah, I could chow down on some cheese."

My son smiled blindly up at me, and I tried not to let them in, but thoughts of all the drugs and the wasted time swirled around in my head. Despite all the shit I'd put him through, he was innocent and perfect, and I was the exact opposite.

That awareness felt like a punch to my solar plexus, and for a second, I worried the pain would squeeze my heart until it gave up the ghost, but at least this time, crossing the threshold into the house I grew up in didn't even register. But once it did, I realized that it was just a house. The fears and memories that had painted this place in darkness were just that: fears and memories in my head.

I could choose to let them take up space, to grow darker and dominate the first chance I had to get to know Stu and color our future memories, or not.

Today, in the moment, I chose… not.

"Dixon." My brother turned and leaned against the kitchen counter as Stu reached for a ball of cream cheese in a clear plastic bowl on the island. It looked like it might have bits of ham in it and tiny, round green onion slices. "Here." Bax snagged the bowl out of Stu's reach and used a butter knife to scoop a chunk of the cheeseball onto a paper plate, then dumped a handful of crackers next to it and handed it to Stu.

Stu's eyes flared. He plopped the plate down on the kitchen table in the corner and hummed his anticipation as he dug a cracker into the cheese and shoveled a huge bite into his mouth.

"Looks like he's not a picky eater," I said because nothing else was coming to mind. The awkwardness between Bax and me could probably be felt in Idaho, like some ambiguous shifting of a tectonic plate.

"Kid eats every dang thing he sees," Bax said, smiling at Stu, but then he cleared his throat and looked away. "Merv will be here soon. Bea's upstairs with Athena. They'll be down in a minute. Roxi has to work tonight so Abey can have it off, but Brand's on his way."

"Cool."

With a mouthful of cream cheese and crumbling butter crackers, Stu asked, "What's for dinner, Daddy?"

Bax looked at me, probably trying to gauge my reaction

to hearing my kid call my brother "Daddy," but I worked hard not to react.

"Burgers. I've got the grill heatin' up out back."

"Did you remember to get pickles at the store?"

"Sure did. The sweet ones you like."

Stu pumped his fist in the air and shoved more cheeseball in his mouth. "Yes!"

Bax chuckled. "Pretty easy to please him since he's so food motivated."

I laughed, too, because his comment reminded me of Zephyr and Tilly when they were pups and how easy it had been to get them to do whatever I wanted if I had a piece of chicken in my hand.

When Stu had his fill of cheese and crackers, he pulled me to the living room to show me his collection of toy trucks and tractors. He had miniatures of Bax's, Brand's, and Abey's trucks, and so many tractors that he had to use a huge plastic bin to house them when he wasn't playing with them.

"I'm gonna run this place when I'm big," he said, pushing a blue truck around the floor, "like my daddy. Do you work on a ranch too? How come you don't work here? Uncle Brand works here. How come I didn't know you before? Did you like fishin' when you were little like me?"

As I sat on the floor and crisscrossed my legs, I couldn't see him, but I felt Bax monitoring our conversation from the kitchen.

"I lived in California. Do you know where that is?"

Living was the wrong way to describe what I'd been doing all those years, but it was the easiest explanation for a five-year-old.

Stu shook his head, making *vroom vroom* sounds as his truck climbed the side of the couch.

"It's kind of far away, and then I lived in Alaska."

"Oh, I know Alaska. That's where the ice road truckers live."

"Do they?"

"Yeah, haven't you ever seen that show?"

"No."

"It's really good. Aunt Roxi and Aunt Devo like it. We watch it together."

"That's nice. Sounds like you have a pretty cool family."

He nodded and traded out his blue truck for a white one. "Where else did you live?"

"The Pacific Northwest, in Oregon."

"Is that a different country?"

"No. There's only one state between here and there. It's got lots of trees, and you can see the ocean from some parts of Oregon. Have you ever seen the ocean?"

"Athena says I have 'cause we went to Florida when I was little, but I don't 'member. But we have a big lake here, and me and my daddy go fishin' all the time. At least when it's not winter."

"The Pacific Ocean is much bigger than Lee Lake," I said, "and some of the fish you can catch are huge too. When I lived in Alaska, I worked on a fishin' boat, and we caught a few."

As soon as I uttered the words "fishing," Stu froze and looked at me with wonder, but then a tirade of new questions came at me in fast succession.

"You worked on a fishin' boat? Was it a big boat or a little one? Did you catch lobsters too? What's the biggest fish you ever caught? Did you ever fall in the water? Did they make you wear one of those orange vests? Did you sleep on the boat?"

The screen door squeaked open and clapped closed in the kitchen, and then Abey's voice filled the living room.

"Whoa. Slow down, Stu. You're gonna break Dixon's brain."

Devo, with her shrewd brown eyes and short dark hair that curved up under her ears, followed after Abey and plopped down on the couch. She held out her hand until Stu slapped her a high five.

"This is my Aunt Devo."

"Uncle Dixon and I met the other day," Devo said. "'Sup?"

"Hey."

"But I would've known who he was even if we hadn't met."

"How?" Stu asked.

Devo laughed. "It's the eyes. His look just like your—" She stopped herself before she said "like yours," and cleared her throat softly. "His eyes look just like your grandma's."

I nodded, acknowledging that she'd stopped herself from inadvertently telling Stu I was his real dad.

"Sorry I haven't been around much," she said to me. "I'm usually at the community center every day, but I've been workin' on a project in Jackson this week. We're settin' up another donation drop center there."

Stu parked his truck next to the bin, and then the TV behind us playing a cartoon at a low volume drew his attention.

"But I'll be there tomorrow. How are you likin' it?"

Abey sat next to Devo and smiled at me as she slipped her arm behind Devo's shoulders.

"It's been good…"

We talked for a while. I felt a little guarded because Devo was unapologetically direct and sarcastic, but the way she looked at my sister made me like her easily. She looked at Abey the same way I'd found myself looking at AJ, stealing glances when she wasn't aware of my stare. And the love written across Devo's face? It was epic and whole, and it made me so happy that Abey had found the kind of love she'd been dreaming about her whole life, the kind of love Noah Lee didn't think she deserved or would ever find.

But she had, and it was the best Fuck You to that man. For a second, I wished he was still alive so Abey could have the satisfaction of seeing the shock on his face when she leaned down to kiss her wife like she just had.

He probably would've choked on air and kicked the bucket all over again.

"Kids?" Merv's voice filled the house when she arrived. Bax followed her into the living room, and Brand arrived with some kind of ambrosia salad his wife had made for us even though she had to work. And then Bea and Athena came down the stairs, talking about clothes or shoes or something.

But Athena was not the same kid I'd known when I'd beat feet out of town. She was a young woman now, tall like her dad and beautiful like her mama, Candy.

In fact, the resemblance literally took my breath away, and when Athena said my name and came at me with open arms for a hug, all I could do was stutter a quiet hello.

"Hi, Uncle Dixon. Mama would be glad you came home," she whispered as she hugged me. "I am too."

"Thanks," I mumbled, reaching quickly over her shoulder to wipe a tear out of the corner of my eye.

Candy wasn't the reason I'd become an addict, but her death was the excuse I used to flee my family and all the pain it held for me at the time.

"God, you look just like her," I said as she stepped back and wrapped her arm around Stu's shoulder. Everyone stared at me like I had cheeseball all over my face.

Athena beamed at the compliment. "And you look nothin' like you used to."

Looking down at myself, I dusted off the front of my second-hand T-shirt, thinking maybe I should've dressed a little nicer.

Too late now.

"The grill should be ready by now," Bea said, cutting in and interrupting the awkwardness. "What's say we move this party to the backyard?"

CHAPTER TWENTY-TWO

DIXON

"SO, Dixon, where the hell have you been?"

Devo was the complete opposite of Bea. Although they were both outspoken, Devo shined a light on the awkwardness, and her question turned all heads in my brother's backyard in my direction again.

My mama's stare and her blatant need to know was the most intense.

"When Brand found me, I was in California near a little town called Mad River. After that, I wandered for a bit, but then I headed up to Alaska to work on my friend's uncle's fishin' boat. I stayed there almost two years, then I landed in Oregon. Worked a farm for half a year or so and then for a guy in the Cascades. He let me stay in a cabin he's got up there."

"You've been busy," Brand said.

"Alone?" Merv asked, her voice so full of pity, I could almost taste it.

"Yeah."

"Were you lonely?" Athena asked.

Shrugging, I said, "Sometimes."

"I like bein' alone sometimes too," Stu said as we all sat around the table and Bax turned to tend the burger patties he'd just dropped onto the grill. "'Cause then I don't have to share my toys." Climbing into Bea's lap, he dipped a baby carrot into a puddle of ranch on her plate. When he bit down on it, the *snap* was loud, and before he'd finished chewing, he shoved a short stack of sweet pickles into his mouth. "But don't you have a friend?"

"I do, actually," I said, shading my eyes from the sun's glare peeking through some trees as it set in the west. "I have a friend in California, Ernesto, but everybody calls him Nesty. And I have a friend right here in Wisper, AJ, and I made a new friend in Oregon. His name's Murdoch. He's a moose."

Stu snorted. He hopped down and skipped over to me, then crawled into my lap.

A kind of euphoria rushed around inside me, like a warm wind kicking up a dust devil. It was the most natural thing in the world to hold my son, like I'd been doing it his whole life. But I hadn't been. Tears threatened, but I sucked in a big breath and held it as he wiggled to get comfortable and turned to look at me.

It felt like my family held its collective breath, too, every single one of them waiting to see how I'd react.

"Your best friend's a moose?" Stu asked.

I nodded. I didn't dare speak in case all kinds of confessions spilled out of my mouth.

"That's weird. What did you do? How do you *know* he's your friend? And how do you know his name is Murdoch? Did he tell you?"

"No, he didn't tell me. I guessed while we took walks together," I said carefully, judging my own words, but I had it under control. "Climbed to the top of the mountain and yelled out so we could hear the echo."

"Mooses can't yell."

"No." I smiled at his no-nonsense view of the world. "You're right about that. He bellowed. I yelled. And I told him about you."

Or maybe only slightly under control.

"Me? But you didn't even know me."

"I did. You're part of my family, and I told him about my family and how much I loved y'all and missed you."

"You missed me?"

Bax turned, spatula in hand, and watched my face as I decided how to answer my son. Bea watched closely, too, but I didn't blame them or hold any anger at their overprotectiveness because they were doing what I'd asked them to, both of them ready to jump in if I said anything or did anything that might hurt Stu.

"Yeah, I missed you, all of you, and I wondered what you were up to. If you were happy and got to play a lot and have fun. And I wondered if Granny made you her famous custard pie. If your mama tickled you and let you stay up late sometimes to watch a movie."

Looking at Bea, a guilty smile grew on Stu's face. "She does."

And in that moment, I knew.

I knew I couldn't tell him the truth, 'cause if I did, his whole world would crumble. His memories of Bea and Bax and Athena would change. What if he became angry like I had that no one ever told him the truth about his real daddy?

What if the truth led him to drugs?

Standing and gently removing his little arm he'd wrapped around my shoulder, I carried him back to Bea and set him in her lap while she stared up at me.

My skin lost its connection to his, and it felt like the fabric of my soul ripped free from my bones.

"I'll, uh, I'll be right back. I need to use the john."

Bea nodded silently, and I turned and walked away as fast as I could, listening to my sister and mama calling my name and their worried voices fading behind me.

IN THE BATHROOM, I turned on the faucet, let the water run, and slid down the door.

What the fuck are you even doin' here? You can't do this. You don't have shit to give your kid. You don't know how to be a fuckin' father. You're stupid and worthless and—

Something shiny and brilliant caught my eye, and I focused on the empty toilet paper holder and forced myself to count to ten. Someone had meant to put on a new roll but must've forgotten because it sat on the sink, still rolled tightly. But that gleaming silver bar led my eyes around the bathroom until I realized that the whole thing had been renovated.

The scuffed and stained ceramic tub—the one Noah Lee had almost drowned me in because I'd come home with dirt on my face after playing all day when I was ten and it irritated him—had been replaced by a modern clawfoot, and all the fixtures were new too. The showerhead up top looked like one of those fancy rainfall doodads, and even the toilet was new. It had more buttons on it than my cell phone.

My phone.

I pulled it from my back pocket and clicked it on with my thumb. Stu's and my family's faces appeared, but I opened my contacts to avoid their happy smiles.

There was something shiny and new in my life, too, and right now I needed her.

Please come to my brother's house

It only took AJ two minutes to text back. I counted.

What happened? What's wrong?

I can't do this, AJ. Not alone. Please.

TWEEDLEDEE

On my way

CHAPTER TWENTY-THREE

AVERY JANE

DIXON TEXTED that I should meet him by the old barn, the one he'd worked in with his dad. The one he hated.

His SOS text had felt different than when he first invited me to dinner with his family. I knew he wouldn't have sent it if he didn't really need me. For him to show vulnerability like that told me he wasn't in the best place.

I walked the perimeter of the rundown structure but didn't see Dixon anywhere. The big sliding door to the barn had been left open, so I slipped inside silently and looked around at abandoned farm machinery and too many cobwebs. There were lifetimes of history steeped into these walls. The sun filtered through weathered boards on the second floor, and dust motes floated in streaks of warm, late afternoon light.

Calling out quietly, "Dixon? Where are you?" my heart raced and fear seeped in beneath my skin. I wasn't afraid of Dixon but of the pain I knew would be trying to change him back to the same angry teenager who'd wanted to burn this place down.

He didn't answer, so I poked around more, trying not to trip over useless remnants of Dixon's old life. It was funny, but I thought I could still hear the bleating of the sheep from his childhood.

Finally, there was nowhere left to look but up in the hay loft, so I climbed an old ladder, hoping it wouldn't disintegrate beneath my feet, and when I got to the top, I found him in a ball on the dusty floor, with a full bottle of cheap whiskey near his head, still sealed.

"Dixon! Are you hurt?"

Rushing to him, I knelt in front of him, looking everywhere for an injury or something to explain why he looked like a memory of himself, coiled up like one of those tiny, empty shells on the beach at the lake.

He was in some kind of trance or meditation, but when he finally noticed me beside him, he sat up and reached for me, his grip on my arms so tight that I winced as he pulled me close and hugged me.

"Thank you," he whispered. "It hurts so fuckin' bad, and I don't think there's a drug on this planet that can take the pain away."

"What hurts?" I begged. "Tell me."

"Stu. He's perfect and happy and I can't fuck that up. I-I can't tell him the truth because what if I do and he turns out like me? I never should've come home. I was right to stay away." He looked around the barn, probably seeing memories of things I could never imagine. His eyes landed on the bottle, and then I heard Noah Lee's voice coming out of Dixon. "I'm not good enough. I can't do this. I can't do this. I can't—" He stopped and looked at me. "Take me to the bus station? I can go back to Oregon. I can probably get my old job back. It'll be better for everyone if I'm not here. Better for Stu—"

Leaning back and balancing on the balls of my feet, I scolded him. "Stop this *right now*."

The stunned expression on his face would've been funny if he weren't in the middle of a panic attack.

"I'm sorry I yelled at you," I said, "but I needed a way to stop this descent into lies you seem to be determined to drown in." Smoothing away the surprise from his face with my thumbs, I held him between my hands and spoke softly. "You *are* good enough. You were right to come back, and you *can* do this. You said you want to be in Stu's life. You can't do that if you're hundreds of miles away in the forest somewhere with no cell signal. That kid needs his dad. Now, I don't know if it's better if he knows who you are or not, but he *deserves* to know you.

"Just like I do. You are worth knowin'. You are special and loved, and Stuart deserves to hear your stories, and he needs to know that when life gets hard, there are ways through. *You* can teach him that."

Dixon pulled me close again and touched his lips to mine. "I didn't drink it. I hid the bottle in here years ago. I just wanted to look at it. There's some kind of fucked-up curiosity inside me. I just wanted to know if it still had the same hold on me it used to… but I didn't drink it."

"I know you didn't."

His eyes, so tender and open, searched my face. His hands clutched at my hips, and he held me there, in his broken embrace. "Where have you been all my life?"

"I've been here, waitin' on you to get a clue."

He laughed then, a deep, booming mouthful of mirth that filled me up like Christmas dinner.

"I'm sorry you had to wait so long, Tweedledee," he said, and he kissed me. "I won't ever make you wait again."

"MISS AVERY!" Stu screeched and bounced in his mama's lap like a Yorkshire terrier when he saw me, walking hand in hand through the grass with his "uncle" across his back yard. But then confusion stopped him. "Did somebody order flowers?"

"Hi, everyone. No, Stu, no one ordered flowers, but your uncle Dixon's my friend. He invited me. I hope that's okay?"

"The more the merrier," Sheriff Abey said, smiling at me across the big, cedar outdoor table.

"Thanks."

Dixon's mama, on the other hand, looked concerned that I'd shown up and maybe a little annoyed, but I didn't think she'd dare say anything. We knew each other from my friendship with her son and from my shop, but we certainly weren't besties.

No one else mentioned my sudden appearance, and Bax seemed fine with it. "You like your burger still mooin' or charred?" he asked.

"Slightly charred, please. Thank you."

He nodded and got to work loading up a plate with a burger, potato salad, and half an ear of corn on the cob he'd grilled. When he handed it to me, he said, "I'll have you know that beef was raised right here on Spitfire Ranch. It's the best burger you'll ever eat."

Dixon's other brother, Brand, laughed. "Humility, Bax. We've talked about this."

"What?" Bax said with his hands on his hips. His black apron, which said "Stand back. Good-lookin' is cookin'" bunched up when he shrugged. "I'm not sayin' anything that ain't true." And then he grabbed another full plate and handed it to Dixon.

Dixon passed the mustard to me but not the ketchup, and he smirked when he noticed my surprise that he'd remembered how much I'd always hated the slimy, red gloop.

"I haven't forgotten anything, AJ. Things might've been muddy and hard to see for a while, but everything's clearin' up now."

LATER THAT NIGHT, Dixon followed me back to my place and parked behind me.

He was exhausted after dinner and two more hours of small talk and missed opportunities to say what he needed to say to everyone.

I wasn't sure exactly what he wanted to talk to his family about, if it was something that they should all hear or something specifically intended for Bax's ears or their mama's, but it seemed obvious to me every time Dixon inhaled deeply and leaned forward slightly in his chair, but the moment would pass, and he became more disappointed and quiet as the night wore on.

It wasn't the right time, not with Stu there, but as each chance to unburden himself dissolved into the night air, I watched as the weight of his secrets became heavier.

It scared me because those secrets held the pain he'd been running from most of his life.

Stu didn't seem to notice, and when he wasn't kicking my butt in multiple games of War with a deck of cards from a stash in a weatherproof box on the patio, he held my hand and dragged me around his yard, pointing to flowers and plants and grilling me on their names.

Dixon walked behind me now, up the stone path to my front door, silent as a mouse. I didn't know what to say, if I should say anything at all or just let him be, but when he reached for my hand and pulled me to face him on the threshold, I knew words weren't going to be necessary.

Lifting his hands to my face, he held it, then softly let them ease around my head. He tugged my ponytail free and stuffed the elastic band in my front pocket, then pulled his fingers through my messy hair, watching as the strands untangled and fell behind my shoulders.

"I love your hair," he whispered. "It's so soft. Makes me remember good times."

And when his eyes landed back on mine and he leaned down to kiss me, words ceased to exist at all.

Fancy rubbed against our legs, hoping for some attention, but when she realized she wouldn't get it, she darted off into my yard and probably climbed her favorite cottonwood.

Dixon's kiss was soft and precious. His lips lingered a centimeter from mine while he breathed me in, lifted me up, wrapped my legs around him, and carried me inside. He shut the door behind us with the heel of his boot.

We didn't make it to my bedroom. He sat on my couch with me straddling his lap, and I listened to the squeaky resonance of crickets rubbing their legs together outside like bows on tiny violin strings while he pulled his shirt over his head.

Slowly and cautiously, my lips met his chest and a two-inch scar beneath his right clavicle that looked like it had been sliced into him with a knife. I licked it like I could still taste the blood it had bled, and Dixon moaned, but his body became a rigid plank under me.

"Am I hurtin' you?"

Shaking his head, he whispered, "You could never."

He lifted my T-shirt and tossed it, then reached behind me to unhook my bra. When it fell, he set it on the arm of the couch while I unbuttoned his jeans. But instead of taking them off, he lifted his hips and reached in his back pocket for his wallet. He pulled it free, opened it, and tugged out a condom packet.

"It's not too forward of me?"

I shook my head. "I've waited a long time to be with you like this. I would've done it in the barn earlier, if the situation had been different."

He smiled, but he whispered, "Not *that* barn."

"No, you're right. Not that barn."

He unzipped my jeans and slid his hand beneath my underwear, watching my face as his fingers slipped between my thighs. My hands gripped his biceps and my eyes rolled closed as he began to rub and slide through the slick he found there.

And when he dipped one long finger inside me, I moaned loudly and my head fell back, my hair tickling my shoulder blades, swaying to the rhythm of his slow pumping.

His muscles hardened as he leaned forward and took my nipple with his teeth. He bit down gently and then sucked and licked the sting away, and I rode his hand, using my knees on the couch for leverage.

Words failed me again as he released my breast and relaxed back against the cushions, watching me take pleasure from his body, studying me like he'd never seen a woman getting off before.

He cupped his hand and pushed another finger inside me, and then his thumb smeared my wetness around until he found my clit and rubbed over it slowly in circles.

My heart began to race, pleasure bloomed and spiked in my core as he pumped faster and rubbed roughly. His cock grew harder in his jeans and pulsed with need.

I gasped and held my breath when I came, trying not to be loud because I was sure Mama and Gran were next door, watching their Sunday night movie and eating cherry pie with vanilla ice cream.

Dixon leaned forward, looking up at me, and he captured my mouth with his for a kiss, but then he lifted me and stood. He pushed at the coffee table with his foot so we had more room, and while I found my bearings and stood tall, he dropped to his knees and yanked my jeans down my legs.

I gasped and gripped his shoulders when he lifted my feet, one by one, to remove my socks and shoes, and then I was completely naked in my living room, waiting for him to shed his jeans and boots too.

He stood, his cock sprang free from his boxers when he lowered them, and my mouth watered to taste him. The condom lay still sealed in its little, square wrapper on the couch, but I wasn't ready for that yet.

My pale hands were a stark contrast to his tanned skin and more scars I now noticed that marred him here and there. The longer line over his ribs looked similar to the cut I'd kissed earlier, and I wondered if he really had been in a knife fight.

I didn't ask. Instead, I pushed his naked body until he fell back onto the couch. I knelt between his legs, and he gripped the cushions beside him as I opened my mouth.

His cock was hard as wood and pointing directly at my lips. When I parted them, he filled my mouth completely and slid to the back of my throat easily, and then his hands tangled in my hair again as I began to suck. My tongue lapped and massaged, and I dragged it up his length, hollowing my cheeks and sucking harder.

Dixon panted, thrusting his hips against my face, so I gripped them to hold him still.

He whispered, "Sorry, but your mouth feels so fuckin' good wrapped around me like that."

I nodded and my hair fell down over the sides of his

thighs as I sucked even harder, and then he was groaning and hissing and straining to hold back.

He said nothing, but he slid his arms beneath mine and lifted me up. In a flash, the condom was on, and he plopped me in his lap and glided inside me.

Squeaking my surprise, I yelped and laughed at the sound, but then I was moaning and panting, too, and I fucked him greedily, taking from him what I needed.

Need had been building inside me for years, and he was the only man in the world who could release it all.

Like I was the lock, and he was the key.

The acknowledgment of that fact felt like relief, and more than anything, I wanted him to open me up and consume everything I had become. I wanted him to want me and love me as much as I'd loved him when we were kids.

I had no idea about his life before he'd come home. I didn't know if he'd had relationships or someone to ease his own thirsts the same way he was quenching mine, but none of it mattered to me.

All that mattered was his skin on mine, his hot hands gripping my hips and guiding me to slow down so we could savor each other. I wanted to make this last, to never forget how full he filled me.

Because another fact remained: Dixon Lee was a runner, and if he got a hint of how much I wanted him, it might scare him away.

I didn't want to do that. He had so much to wade through with his family and Stu. Making that harder for him by muddying things with words like need and love seemed like the wrong thing to do…

But that was what I was feeling.

Snapping his hips beneath me, he skimmed his rough palms up my ribcage and dug his fingertips into my back. I imagined I heard reverence in his voice when he moaned my name and his eyes fell shut.

Before I could stop myself, I whispered, "How is it you're here, and it's like you never left? How is it you're still so deep inside me, reaching places I never even knew needed you?"

Either he felt the same way, too, or my words had ruined everything because he fucked faster, his hands now pushing me down to take him deeper. He ground his cock inside me until I was coming so hard that tears leaked out of my eyes. The whole world blurred as my body became a ramrod, and Dixon bucked into my orgasm like it was a storm he wanted to get swept up in.

When he came and pulled me down on top of him, I nuzzled his neck, resting my head on his shoulder, and we lay together, catching our breath and just existing. For a moment, with his fingers dragging through my hair lightly, life felt like a dizzy dream.

Suddenly, the crashing sound of breaking glass shattered our euphoria, and in an instant, the throw blanket on the back of my couch covered me, hiding me from view. I gripped the soft edge, trying to understand why Dixon moved me off him and rushed toward the broken living room window, stepping on shards of glass with bare feet as he searched the darkness outside for the person who'd just chucked a brick through it.

The brick that now lay on my floor. A word had been carved into it: WHORE.

CHAPTER TWENTY-FOUR

DIXON

THAT FUCKING douchebag was lucky I was bare-assed when he decided to make his presence known.

He got away, but not before I caught a glimpse of his profile and the hook of his nose. I wouldn't forget his face.

Roxi arrived before my sister, gun drawn while she searched the Harlowes' property, but she came up empty and met me, now dressed in only my jeans, on AJ's porch.

"I didn't find anyone," Roxi said, holstering her gun while she took in an eyeful of my bare chest and arms. "Listen, I know we don't really know each other, and I don't mean to be invasive or insensitive, but are you sure you should be involved in this… I mean with Avery, if this guy is causin' problems?"

"Why? Because I'm an addict, I can't handle some joker tryin' to scare my—"

"No, not because you can't handle it. The look in your eyes right now tells me you know exactly how to handle this asshole, and *that's* what I'm worried about."

"Have I broken a law, Deputy?"

Concern settled into the lines around her eyes. "No."

"Do you have reason to think I will?"

"Nothin' concrete," she said, "no."

"Then do your job and write up your report or whatever you need to do. AJ will need that when I take her to file a restraining order tomorrow."

To her credit, Roxi didn't react. She nodded and patted my shoulder as she passed me and walked inside to talk to AJ, but I felt like a prick for speaking to her like that. I knew she hadn't meant anything and she was worried about her husband's brother, but it rankled because she was right.

I did know exactly how to handle this fucking guy, Cody Mahone, if he ever showed his face again. But the *way* I wanted to handle him wouldn't help me with my family and could land me in my sister's jail cell.

So, what? Was I just supposed to stand around and let him harass AJ? She was terrified that he'd been watching us, that the pervert had the balls to stand outside her house and peer in through a tiny crack in the curtains while we were… making love. Or fucking. Or whatever the hell had just happened between us.

Whatever it was, I felt things I never imagined I could. Any memories I had of sex had been twisted and tainted by drugs and highs, but tonight had been like watching morning fog being burned away by the sun.

The way I had begun to feel about AJ was becoming clearer and clearer.

And I wanted more.

But the way I *needed* her scared me to death.

When Abey arrived, she asked the same questions Roxi had: Should I really be involved in this? Maybe I should cool it with AJ while she gets her drama worked out.

But there was no fucking way I would leave her to deal with her ex by herself.

Abey and Roxi finally left, and so did AJ's mama and Gran, and I snagged some old remnants of wood stacked up next to Gran's garage to board up AJ's window while she swept up the glass. The cuts on my feet were nothing. I didn't even feel them, but clotted blood wet the bottom of my socks.

I banged the last nail into the wood with AJ's pink-handled hammer and turned to look at her sitting on her couch with her arms wrapped around her knees, like she was freezing cold in the middle of August, but she'd already turned off the air; the huge, gaping chasm on her wall let the summer heat in too fast to keep up.

I said, "Tomorrow—"

She sighed. "I will go to the station and find out exactly what I'll need in order to file a restraining order. I promise."

"Damn right you will," I said, "and I'll be right there with you."

CHAPTER TWENTY-FIVE

AVERY JANE

WISPER'S COURTHOUSE wasn't even a mile from my cottage

It was more an honorary courthouse used for traffic and parking ticket disputes and occasional squabbles between farmers, so Deputy Roxi suggested that I should turn in my paperwork at the Teton County Circuit Courthouse in Jackson instead because it would ensure faster results.

Dixon insisted on driving me Tuesday morning after I'd had a chance to fill out the forms and get copies of the police reports, so I sat in his El Camino, gazing out my window and sipping the London Fog he picked up for me from Coffee Shot. I'd never told him my favorite drink, but somehow, he knew.

"I'm sorry about the car. I know it's a hunk of junk."

"It's fine," I said, trying not to fidget. The cuticle around my thumb had just stopped bleeding. "I know you'll fix it up and make it nice again."

"Yeah, although, I was thinkin' eventually I might like to buy somethin' that's a little safer in winter, in case, y'know, I'm drivin' Stu somewhere."

"Good idea."

"My boss offered me the use of one of the center's trucks, but I wouldn't feel right drivin' it outside of work hours." He looked at me. "Are you nervous? How do you feel about what we're doin' today?"

"I'm nervous, yes." Halfheartedly, I shrugged. "I don't think it's gonna help the situation, but I know it's a step I need to take."

"Why wouldn't it help?" Dixon asked, sipping his own decaf London Fog, though I had a feeling it was a little too sweet for him because his face scrunched up into a grimace every time he took a drink.

"Just 'cause Cody has money. His family has money. They're pretty well known around here. For all I know, the judge who presides over the temporary protection order hearing might even know them. Then all we've done is wasted our time and your gas."

And possibly enraged an already pissed-off control freak.

"It's not a waste, AJ. Just filin' the papers and showin' up proves somethin' to authorities. I've known a few guys who had protection orders against them, and if they cared about their lives at all or their freedom, they were scared of 'em. Cody won't wanna spend time in a jail cell, and if his parents are as affluent as you say, then they won't want that either. It'd be an embarrassment."

"True. Hopefully that's enough to stop him."

Dixon nodded as he pulled into the parking lot behind the courthouse and parked. "I haven't been to Jackson in a long time. The last time I was here…"

His voice trailed off into silence, so I asked, "The last time you were here, what?"

"It's nothin'. A guy I used to know died."

"He died? Dixon, that's not nothin'."

Looking out his window, he rushed through an explanation. "He was high. He broke into a jewelry store after hours. He'd just gotten out of jail on bond, and he wanted to get one of those fancy rodeo buckles for his brother." He waved his hand in the air, wiping away the sad memory of his friend. "It's a long story. Anyway, he got caught that night. He had a gun and fired at the sheriff. The sheriff fired back, and Ty died."

His hand on his thigh clenched tightly into a fist, so tightly that I thought his knuckles might snap. Dixon sharing with me calmed my nerves. Every time I thought he couldn't be any more vulnerable, he proved me wrong.

Reaching to cover his hand with mine, I squeezed gently. "I'm so sorry for your loss."

"Thank you," he whispered, but then he shifted in his seat and took a deep breath, clearing the memory completely from his mind. "You ready then?"

"As I'll ever be. Let's do this."

DROPPING off the protection order packet took less than five minutes.

The statements from Dixon's sister and Deputy Roxi were enough to give the judge cause to grant me a temporary order. I got lucky with a female judge, and she called me into her chambers to ask one question: "Do you know who you're filing a restraining order against?"

Of course I knew, but what she meant was did I understand the implications of accusing a Mahone of wrongdoing? I did understand. And I knew it might come back to bite me in the ass, but I also knew my life was more important than my store or my house.

As soon as I entered the courthouse, the gravity of my surroundings made it clear to me that I couldn't downplay Cody's behavior anymore. Too many women had crossed the same threshold I had, and some of them weren't alive anymore to tell their tales.

If for no other reason than those women and their families, I needed to stand my ground, to fight fire with fire, and hope that justice would prevail. But there were lots of other reasons too. Mama and Gran were the most important. How long until Cody decided to hurt them to get to me?

Our safety was the most important thing, so I chose to move forward.

The judge read over my paperwork with focused interest, and I thought I discerned a little bit of satisfaction in her expression. Maybe she knew what dicks the Mahones could be. I had no clue if Cody had ever had a restraining order issued against him before, but this wasn't the first time the Mahone name had come up in a court of law. Of that, I was sure. They had lawyers on their payroll for all kinds of things. I'd always had the feeling that they weren't exactly law-abiding people, but of course I knew nothing about that and couldn't prove anything.

Now all I could do was wait for my petition to be processed. The judge told her clerk to schedule the hearing for seventy-two hours, to give them time to notify Cody, because he would be required to be present for her ruling. If he didn't show, the judge might grant the order of protection by default. But I knew he'd be there, with probably no less than three lawyers to represent him, but the only representation I'd have would be little ol' me, myself, and I. There was no way I could afford a lawyer.

And there was no way for me to be sure about what

would happen next, but I had to believe the law and truth would be on my side.

Dixon had talked to his sister, who said she'd stand up for me in court. But even if Abey hadn't offered, I wouldn't be alone because Mama and Gran promised to go with me too. Dixon said he'd be there but that he wouldn't go into the courtroom because he thought that his history and his rap sheet could hurt my petition.

So, Friday morning, I hung a "Sorry, we're closed" sign in the front window of the shop, and we all headed to Jackson. Dixon rode with Abey in her cruiser, and I rode with Mama and Gran. When we met in the parking lot, he took hold of my hand and accompanied us to the entrance. Before the rest of us walked through the doors, he placed a chaste kiss on my cheek and said, "You got this."

Mama clucked her tongue in disproval, but quietly. I knew she worried about me, and she hadn't really had the time to get to know Dixon again, but I also knew that when she did, she'd change her tune.

I felt confident about the entire situation… until we entered the courtroom and I saw Cody with *four* lawyers and his mother in tow.

It was all just a show for the judge, but I didn't think she was too impressed, because the first words she said after she sat and opened a file folder with my petition inside were, "I think one lawyer would have been sufficient."

Cody looked more than confident he'd get out of this. He smirked across the aisle at me while his lawyers sized me up, whispering to one another.

The judge read my petition aloud and asked Cody to explain himself. He didn't say a word. One of his lawyers, a middle-aged man with a Jell-O jaw and bad hair plugs, answered every question.

Finally, Judge Petersen asked, "Are you unable to speak for yourself, Mr. Mahone? Because I'm not asking for legal mumbo jumbo. What I want to hear is your side of the story."

The lumpy lawyer nodded, and Cody smiled and broke into a deluge of charismatic chatter about who his parents were and how upstanding his family had always been in the Wyoming community, but none of it explained or confirmed anything. I wasn't surprised about that; like, had I really expected him to tell the truth?

"So then," Judge Petersen inquired, "how do you explain Ms. Harlowe's complaints that you've been paying her uninvited visits, that you broke into her home and threw a brick through her window, you're stalking her, and that your behavior is escalating to the point she feels unsafe?"

"Wasn't me," Cody said. "I'm not the only man she's dated. In fact, her current flavor of the month is waitin' outside as we speak. Who's to say that guy isn't the one causin' her troubles? He looks like a low life to me. Maybe he threw the brick through her window."

"Excuse me." Abey, dressed in her sheriff uniform and badge, had been standing at attention silently behind everyone with her hands folded together behind her back, but now she interrupted and stepped forward. The judge nodded at her to continue.

"Deputy Sheriff Abey Lee of Wisper, Wyoming, for the record. My brother, Dixon Lee, is the man outside. He's a friend to Ms. Harlowe, and he's been there to help her clean up after Mr. Mahone's *visits*. I can assure the court that he was not the individual who broke into Ms. Harlowe's residence when she wasn't home, and he didn't throw the brick through her window because he was a guest at her residence when it happened. He identified Mr. Mahone last Sunday evening after the incident when my deputy showed him a picture of Mr. Mahone."

The judge turned her head slowly, looking at Cody pointedly.

He shrugged indifferently. "Like I said, wasn't me. I just have one of those faces. Everybody thinks they remember me."

God, the audacity of this man! Lying right to a judge's face?

Cody's mama had been listening closely. I thought her ears perked up when Cody mentioned Dixon, but she never tried to utter a word. Her face looked like it had been superglued into a disapproving expression, until Judge Petersen asked Cody to provide proof of where he was last Sunday night.

"At home," he said easily. "Sundays are for family at the Mahone household."

Cody's mama's face fell, like she knew her son was lying, but still she said nothing, until the judge addressed her directly.

"Can you corroborate your son's whereabouts this past Sunday night, Mrs. Mahone?"

Deadpan and with no more life on her face than a corpse's, she replied, "Of course I can."

The judge saw through Mrs. Mahone's lie, though, and all the contempt she seemed to have for the entire situation. So, much to her and Cody's lawyers' dismay, Judge Petersen issued me the order of protection.

"If you, Cody Dennis Mahone, knowingly come within three-hundred feet of Ms. Harlowe, you will be arrested. Which means, if you see her, turn around and walk away. You may not commit any further acts of stalking. Stay away from Ms. Harlowe's home, her place of business, or any other location you are aware that she frequents. Do not intimidate, threaten, or otherwise interfere with Ms. Harlowe, her family or household members, or her friends.

"You may not contact Ms. Harlowe, her family or household members or her friends through telephone calls, mail, e-mail, texting, social media, or any other form of communication."

She paused, her eyebrows raising slightly, but then asked, "Have I made myself clear? Do you understand the conditions and restrictions of the protection order?"

The dead-eye stare Cody focused on Judge Petersen made the hair on the back of my neck stand up, but she wasn't intimidated in the least.

"Mr. Mahone, I need a verbal response to my question."

"Yes, *ma'am*," Cody seethed. "Heard you loud and clear."

"Good. Then we're done here for today."

Cody pushed back from his table and stood before the judge had even finished speaking. His lawyers followed him out of the courtroom, but his mama lingered for a few seconds. She looked at me like she wanted to say something, but then she shook her head and walked away.

Mama and Gran crowded around me, hugging me and soothing my anxiety about being near Cody again. Abey shook the judge's hand. They spoke in hushed tones across the room, but as Gran tried to squeeze the breath right out of my lungs, I thought I heard Judge Petersen say something to the effect of, "I may get flack for this, but it was worth it."

CHAPTER TWENTY-SIX

DIXON

A MAN who resembled Cody Mahone in stature—and there was something in his eyes—stood by a black Escalade, smoking Camels. Who the fuck still smoked Camels nowadays? I knew they were Camels because the smell wafted on the lazy summer breeze right to my nose, and flashbacks of my old man hit me like some kind of horror-movie montage. They were the same brand Noah Lee had smoked most of his life.

The guy watched me while I sat in my car waiting for AJ to finish inside, and when I got out to stretch and pace, he smirked and flicked a cigarette butt at my car.

My guess was that he was Cody's brother or possibly a cousin or something, but he was failing at intimidating me. I'd met plenty of guys like him over the years—the lowest man on the family totem pole, who they really only relied on for muscle. His opinion didn't matter to the higher ups. Kind of like mine.

He didn't count in the overall picture of the Mahone family, but *I* didn't discount him because, while I was fairly certain he had no clout, he definitely knew how to scrap. His stance and the restless look in his eyes alone told me that much. He might as well have been flexing his biceps and slamming his fist into his palm, like some moron from a mafia movie.

Before anything could come of his intimidation tactics, and after he'd flicked no less than half a pack of smokes at my bumper, Cody Mahone himself came fuming out of the small courthouse. A gaggle of lawyers followed behind him, arguing about an appeal, and an older woman lagged behind them all. She walked with grace, like a dancer might, but it felt forced. I wasn't sure if that was to give her flowy skirt a chance to billow around her legs or if she thought someone important might be watching and she wanted to appear above the rest of us, but her eyes never left mine as she climbed into the Escalade.

When her door had fully shielded her from my view, she snapped, "Get in the truck, Justin. *Now*."

Muscle man jumped into the passenger seat next to Cody behind the wheel, and they peeled out of there, their tires smoking on the pavement behind them.

One of the lawyers, whose gray, pinstriped suit didn't seem to really fit his lank frame, yanked his tie loose and shook his head silently as he walked to his older-model sedan parked a few spots away, sneering at the disappearing Escalade. He might have been hired to represent Cody Mahone, but it was clear he didn't like the son of a bitch.

When the lot was empty, AJ, her gran, and her mama rounded the side of the building, and as soon as she saw me, she smiled and ran to me, her pretty, blue dress flowing out behind her, and she launched herself into my arms.

"Things went well then?" I asked, holding her up while she wrapped her legs around my hips.

"Very well," she said, and she kissed my cheek.

"Good. I'm glad it's done." I returned her smile, thinking I'd never seen anything more beautiful and hopeful than the woman in my arms.

But I had a sinking feeling it wasn't over.

When was life ever that easy?

ON THE WAY back to Wisper, Doc V from All Animals called to make sure I'd be there early tomorrow morning because they had a mastiff scheduled for a dental cleaning and would need help handling him.

Apparently, the guy who started the clinic, Dr. Prittchard, who I still remembered from my fleece farm days, had finally retired, so Doc V and Dr. Masterson had bought the business from him. He was the guy they usually relied on to handle difficult cases, but with him gone, I was their only hope.

Doc V also asked if I'd be interested in going with him sometimes because there were plenty of cattle and horse calls he could use some extra muscle on. I said yes and assured him I'd be there in the morning. It felt kind of nice to be relied on. It made me proud that the docs had faith in me.

AJ's mama and Gran wanted to stay in Jackson for a little shopping, so she rode with Abey and me. We dropped her at her store, and as Abey drove around the block to park behind the sheriff's station, my phone rang again. I recognized the number even though it wasn't one I'd entered into my contacts yet.

In fact, it was the only number other than my mama's old landline that I knew by heart.

"Bax, is everything okay?"

Abey shut off her truck and turned toward me. "What's goin' on?"

I shrugged.

"We have a situation," Bax said.

"What's that?"

"I, uh, well Bea and me, we need you to come out to the house."

"Is Stu okay?"

"What happened?" Abey asked. "What's wrong with Stuey?"

Bax must've heard the panic in our voices. "No, no, he's fine. Everyone's fine, but Merv went to Idaho Falls for the night with her friend."

"Merv has a friend?" The statement felt like an oxymoron to me.

"Yeah. Clay, he's her… boyfriend."

"*Boy*friend?" 'Merv has a boyfriend' was the last thing I ever thought I'd hear.

"Yeah, he's a dude and he's her friend. Pretty sure he's in love with her, but she says her 'heart's not up for grabs but ain't nothin' wrong with a woman enjoyin' a man's company now and again for dinner and a movie.'

"It's old news," Bax said. "Get over it. But Rye's out of town for a couple days. Brand's gotta be out with the herd since Rye's gone 'cause we've got multiple heifers due or in labor, everybody else is workin', and we need… We need a babysitter. I dunno. Shit. I told Bea this wasn't a good idea, but she's relentless. Anyway, are you busy?"

"You want me to come and stay with Stu while you're gone… alone? You trust me to do that?"

"No, I don't fuckin' trust you, but Bea does. And Stu asks about you every five minutes. You said you wanna be in his life, so be in it. You're either in or you're out. If you're out, then fuck off. He doesn't need the confusion, but if you're in, then… well, then get your ass to my house by six. Athena has a barrel racin' thing that's supposed to run late.

"And Stu will..." Bax cleared his throat. "He'll have more fun here. With you."

Whoa. Hell must be really fuckin' cold right now.

"I'll be there."

"Good."

Abey whispered, "What's goin' on?"

I shook my head. I couldn't believe what I'd just heard. Bax wanted my help. *Needed* my help. And with my kid?

Confusion was giving me a headache though. Was it a good idea? I wanted to run to Stu and tell him the truth, but at the same time, the possibility of him finding out that I was really his dad made me sweat. I felt like I might barf all over my sister's fancy truck.

Did I have what it took to be a good influence?

But Bax had one more warning left to give me. "But lemme just say it again: You are not to tell Stuart who you are. Do you understand? He's not ready. It's not the time. I-I just need— Tonight, I just need a babysitter."

TWEEDLEDEE

How was the rest of your day?

Unbelievable. Yours?

Mine was plain ol' fine. Selling flowers.
Making the big bucks.

Why unbelievable?

Bax asked me to babysit Stu this evening. I'm getting ready now

Dixon! That's amazing. I'm so excited for you

Thanks. Just be on standby in case I need help figuring out how to entertain a five-year old

You got it

If all goes well, we should celebrate. I'd like to take you to dinner tomorrow night if you're not busy

You're asking me on a date?

I guess I am. Yeah

D: Is that a yes?

Yes, I will most definitely go on a date with you

Good. I mean thanks or you know, whatever a guy's supposed to say after the woman he wants says yes

You want me?

I do

And PS, I miss you

CLOUD NINE DIDN'T EVEN DESCRIBE how high and happy I felt; it was more like cloud seventy-seven.

Spending the evening with Stu *and* going on a date with AJ? I had to be the luckiest fucker on the planet.

My excitement wavered a bit when I walked out of Mrs. Ellison's house and a big, black SUV sped around the corner. I didn't get a good look at the driver's face or the license plates, but I texted my sister anyway, to let her know to be on the lookout in case it was Cody Mahone or his low man, Justin.

Abey texted back, "10–4," and I knew she'd have things under control.

I left too early for my babysitting gig, so I stopped off at the cemetery to pay a visit to my old friend, Candy. She had always been the one person I couldn't wait to share good news with.

When I got there and found her headstone, I could tell Athena and Stu had been there. Dried flowers lay at the edge of the stone, and two toy Matchbox trucks sat next to them. I wondered if AJ had made the bouquet for Athena.

Stu would've been told that the baby Candy had been carrying, who'd died when his mama died, was his brother, so it seemed fitting for Stu to leave toys for Bax Jr., or "Duo" as the headstone read. I had a faint memory of my brother calling his unborn son Duo, but I'd completely forgotten about it until this moment, when I saw it carved into a thick slab of granite.

The loss of that little boy and his mama had ruined my brother. I felt a pang of guilt and shame, remembering my desperate belief that replacing Duo with Stu was a good idea.

But I couldn't bring myself to be too sorry about it, because even though Stu hadn't replaced Duo in Bax's and

Athena's hearts, my little boy's presence had brought much-needed light back into their lives.

Was it wrong of me to bring Candy good news when she couldn't experience it for herself?

I wasn't sure, but my friend, the woman who'd loved me and supported me even though she knew what a fuck-up I'd been, would want to hear that I was happier than I'd ever been and that I was falling in l—

Falling in love? Or was I flat-out, crazy in love with AJ already? How long had it been? Two weeks?

That felt reckless and irresponsible, which was exactly the way my family would have described me five years ago. Were Abey and Roxi right that I shouldn't be caught up in AJ's life?

AA and NA would both dictate that I should slow down. Unexpected complications were well known for derailing a recovering addict's sobriety journey.

"But she's so much more than that," I told the headstone. "You remember her, right? My little flower girl? If you knew her now, though, Candy, you'd understand. Actually, she reminds me of you. She seems to like me despite my past and all the stupid shit I've pulled."

A warm afternoon wind tugged at my T-shirt, so I straightened it, hung my sunglasses from the neck, and ran my hands through my hair.

"I dunno why I'm here. I guess I… I guess I wanted to tell you I was home and that I still remember all the things you wanted for me in my life. It took me way too long, but I'm gettin' there.

"And I wanted to tell you I'm sorry. You were a friend to me when no one else in the world wanted anything to do with me, and what did I do with that? I convinced myself I was in love with you because you were the only person who gave a shit. And then you died and I didn't save you.

"Yeah, yeah, I know. I tried. There was nothin' more I could've done. I know all the bullshit the therapists have to say about it, but I failed you. It's still carved into my heart just like your name in this stone."

Nudging Candy's and Duo's headstone with the tip of my boot, I admitted, "I wish I could've saved you the same way you saved me. You died not knowin' that the unconditional love you gave me would lead me back home years later. And everything that happened led me to leave Stuart with Bax, and I think it was the best decision I've ever made.

"You should see him, Candy. He looks just like me, but Stu's perfect and beautiful and funny."

It was downright ridiculous, but I could've sworn I heard Candy's voice in the air. It whispered through the boughs of the nearby trees, getting caught up in patchy swaths of sunlight. I closed my eyes and breathed, trying to remember all the good things she used to tell me I was capable of.

Maybe after all these years, she was right.

CHAPTER TWENTY-SEVEN

AVERY JANE

EVEN THROUGH TEXTS, Dixon's anxiety about doing and saying the right things around Stu was palpable.

Should I tuck in my shirt?

Is it ok to tell Stu jokes? Wait, forget that. All the jokes I know are about alcoholics or junkies

Maybe you should come watch Stu. I'm gonna fuck this up and then Bax will never let me see him again

Snap out of this, Dixon! You are NOT going to fuck it up. Just breathe and try to believe in yourself. I believe in you 🩶

Thank you

But are you sure?

Yes, I'm sure. Now go play with your son. Talk to him. Ask him to tell you a story

Dixon's multiple and recurring messages slowed me down a bit, trying to catch up on my online orders, but when my phone stopped chiming every two minutes and I finally finished, I closed the shop and headed home.

The window guys had emailed and said they'd be out Friday morning to replace the one Cody had broken. That made me breathe a sigh of relief. Something about that broken window still felt unsettling to me.

God, what a creep! Just knowing Cody had been watching Dixon and me having sex made me want to throw up. The night had been intimate and perfect, and Cody had to go and screw it up. Although, I hoped he got a good look at what Dixon was working with because if he had, he was definitely suffering from penis envy.

Thinking about Cody suffering put a smile on my face. I popped in my earbuds, Madonna's rich voice filled my head, and I hummed along to "Holiday" as I walked home. Gran and Mama were still in Jackson, drowning themselves in summer sales, and I'd left the van parked in front of Gran's house, but walking seemed like a great idea. It would give me time to clear my head and allow me to reset so I'd be ready for my date tomorrow night.

But fate had different plans.

As I passed Coffee Shot and the quaint, locally-owned shops along Main Street, I began to hear whispers. They eked their way past the music, even though the people gossiping tried to talk quietly.

Ramona Wheeler, a teller at the bank, whispered in Jethro Leavitt's ear, "That Dixon Lee is nothin' but a bad omen. Mark my words. You remember all the trouble he used to get up to?"

"Oh, I remember," Jethro said. "Put his poor mama to

shame, and his daddy probably died with a bad taste in his mouth."

"Yeah," Ramona agreed, scoffing and shaking her head as she pretended to peruse the cookbooks in Your Local Bookie's window, "and then he knocks some girl up down in California or somewhere, and he abandons the child here with his family? Shame, shame."

Jethro tutted and leaned in again to gossip some more, but I shut out the sound of his voice. Those people didn't know Dixon. Not like I did. They had no idea the circumstances and hardships he'd had to survive in his life.

How dare they judge him like that?

They both noticed me at the same time, and their heads turned in my direction, but neither seemed to care that I might've overheard them.

I had always been a wallflower in town. I was quiet and usually kept to myself, so when I saw Marial and Betty Johnson with their heads together, I smiled and said a soft hello, but as I passed them halfway between the bookstore and Henly's, my name came out of their mouths in hushed judgment, and I couldn't help my reaction. I gasped and stopped in my tracks, looking back at them. They shut up quickly, but they both stood there staring.

"What?" I said. "What gossip could you possibly have about me? What have I ever done to you?"

Marial had the grace to smile sheepishly, embarrassed she'd been caught talking nonsense, but Betty just turned and walked away, her usual air of conceit wafting out behind her like a bad stench. Her husband's cattle farm had been the most successful in the area until Spitfire Ranch took away that distinction, and Betty's demeanor turned from stuck-up to flat-out jealous, so it didn't surprise me to find her talking about a member of the family who owned the rival business.

But it was wrong and harmful. What if Stu heard the gossip?

Heads turned all down Main Street, as far as my voice would carry, so I yelled, “You should all be ashamed of yourselves, talkin’ dirty about a man who’s fightin’ tooth and nail to redeem his bad deeds. Are all of you so righteous?

“Jethro, I’ve caught you more than once drunk and passed out in the alley behind my shop, and I helped you. Got you coffee and sobered you up before you went home to face your wife. And Ramona, I know it was you who took a Sharpie to the ads the community center put up for the LGBTQ support meetin’ over at Ace’s House. I saw you do it! Shame, shame on *you*!”

Turning on my heel, I huffed and stormed away, feeling somewhat vindicated, but then it occurred to me the reason they’d been talking about me, so I turned right back around.

“Y’all have no right to talk about who I spend my time with. None at all. So I fell in love with a man you don’t approve of. Why do you even care? You’re all a bunch of jerks, and you have nothin’ better to do than—”

The door to Henly’s popped open, and a fast hand grabbed me by my arm and yanked me inside.

“Hush, Avery Jane,” Mr. Henly whispered, the skin around his eyes and mouth crinkling with pity. “You’re just makin’ it worse.”

“Makin’ it worse?” I repeated, while my heart tried desperately to beat right out of my chest. “How am I doin’ that?”

“Just let them chew their cud. They’ll get over it and move onto the next thing quicker if you leave it alone.”

“They don’t have any right to talk about me like that. I’ve never done a bad thing to any one of them! What are they sayin’ about me?”

"Oh, you know." He waved his hand toward the door. "People 'round here have long memories. They remember all the trouble your boyfriend got up to when he was young, but they also remember—"

Mr. Henly stopped and clapped his hand over his mouth, but I pulled it away.

"You better start talkin', Mr. Henly. I'm your best customer, but I will order my candy online if you don't fess up right this minute."

He winced and looked at the floor, but then his old, brown eyes landed on mine. "They also remember your… your daddy. They remember how he treated your mama when he was drunk, and they're sayin' you're gonna end up just like her. Alone and… miserable."

CHAPTER TWENTY-EIGHT

DIXON

WHEN I ARRIVED at the ranch, my brother, Bea, and my son met me in front of the house, Stuey sporting a blue and white Spitfire Ranch trucker cap way too big for him.

I flicked the brim and patted his head. "What's up, kid?"

He smiled, but then Bax's stern face crowded mine.

"Bedtime is 8:30. Bea made dinner for y'all. It's in the fridge. Think you can manage to microwave it?"

"'Course."

"And no TV. Stu lost his TV privileges this mornin' when he decided to replace the truth about who broke the gear shift on the skid steer with a fantastical story about an invisible monster who goes around bustin' up farm equipment." Under his breath, Bax added, "Makin' shit up like somebody else I know.

"He wants you to take him fishin'. You've got about an hour and a half left of daylight, two at most, so you better get to it, but take a flashlight just in case. Stu knows where everything is, and there's bait in the fridge in the garage. And keep your phone on you. I better be able to get ahold of you if I need to."

"10–4," I said, and I saluted Commander in Chief Bax.

Stu giggled, but Bax scoffed.

"Don't be a tool, Dixon. I don't have to do this."

Bea stepped in finally. "C'mon, husband. Let's get goin'. Athena's textin' up a storm, wonderin' where we are. The boys will be fine." She flashed me a soft smile as she pushed Bax toward his truck.

"You have nothin' to worry about," I called after him. "I got this."

Bax stopped and turned, his eyebrows ticked up with doubt.

Okay, so maybe I couldn't blame him for worrying, but I felt confident and grounded. I knew I could return Stu to Bax in the same condition I'd found him.

"Bax, you promised you'd try," Bea said. "Let's go."

"Fine," Bax retorted, but I could see the worry lingering in his eyes. "We'll be back around ten, maybe ten-thirty."

Reluctantly, Bax backed up and drove off, with Bea waving out the window to Stu. Stu waved back, then grabbed my hand and dragged me inside.

He tossed his hat onto the couch. "C'mon. I need to get my fishin' pole. It's in my room, but Daddy cuts the hook off so you gotta tie it back on for me. I'm not good at that part yet."

As I followed my son up the stairs, his little feet pounding the wood, I realized I'd never seen his room, and it nearly knocked me sideways when he ran into the same one I'd slept in as a boy.

It was different now, of course, and had been repainted a dark, dusky blue color, with hunter green accents. The walls used to be a sickly-sweet robin's-egg blue that Merv had picked out when Bax and Brand were babies, and I'd shared the room with them both when I came along. Bax got the single and Brand and I shared bunkbeds so Abey, the only girl in our family, could have her own space for all the dolls Noah Lee bought her that she never played with.

When we were really little, though, she used to sneak into our room when our parents were asleep, and the four of us would pull our blankets to the floor and sleep huddled up together.

Even then we knew a monster lurked down the hall. It took a few more years for me to realize that our dad, or at least the man claiming to be mine, was the monster.

Stu threw open the closet door and disappeared inside for a few seconds, and I looked around.

Crayons and pencils littered his desk, and wadded-up pieces of paper had been discarded on top and on the floor surrounding a black, plastic wastepaper basket, the waxy, unfinished drawings on them hinting at Stu's imagination and all the stories living in his head.

His bed had been made, probably by Bea or Bax, and it was the epitome of what I'd expect to find in a little boy's room, with green-and-blue plaid sheets and comforter, and his white pillowcases coordinated with green fish on them, so that even when he slept, he could dream about fishing.

"I like your room," I said.

"Thanks. Mama let me pick out the sheets and stuff."

"You chose well. Y'know, your dad, Uncle Brand, and I used to share this room when we were your age."

"I know. Daddy told me. Here it is!" He hopped out of the closet, holding a kid-sized fishing pole, which was also dark blue. "My dad says I'm too little for a big pole. He says it'd probably knock me over and the hook would get stuck in my britches, whatever that means."

I laughed, remembering Bax saying the same thing to me when he and Brand had taken me fishing on our lake. They fashioned a pole more my size out of a tree branch and taught me on that. They'd also taught me to swim and ride a bike and a horse. When I was little, my big brothers were my whole world.

When my chuckles died down, I said, "He just means that you wouldn't be able to control the pole very well, and the hook would probably get caught in your pants."

"Oh, that makes more sense, but I'll be bigger soon, and then I'm gettin' a bigger pole than his. It's in the garage. C'mon. Let's go get it so you can borrow it."

"Comin'."

We raced back down the stairs and ransacked the garage until we found Bax's pole, and I pulled a Styrofoam container from the old fridge tucked in the corner, filled with wet dirt and earthworms.

And then I saw it—Bax's four-wheeler.

Oh man. I'd wanted to ride this thing my whole life. When I was down and out once, I considered stealing it to sell for dope money. For many reasons, I was glad now I hadn't. While Stu rummaged through Bax's bigger tackle box, searching out fancy lures for fish we'd probably never catch, I ran my hand over the four wheeler's handlebars and gas throttle.

Memories of the past played in my head. At one point in time, all four of us had our own four-wheelers. We rode every chance we got, and Abey and I tried like hell to keep up with Bax and Brand and their friends. My bike broke down. It wasn't as nice as my siblings'. Bax tried to fix it, but it needed a specific part. He'd gone to our dad and asked him to buy the part. Noah Lee never bought it, and my bike sat on the side of the house, collecting rust for years until the prick had it hauled away with some other junk.

In my delinquent years, many times, I fantasized riding

Bax's bike off a cliff. That would show them all, and I'd take the shiny prize with me. Something stopped me from following through, and it wasn't until I got sober that I realized the love and respect I had for my brother was the thing that had kept me alive.

"Hey, Stu, this thing still run?"

Looking over his shoulder, an excited glint lit behind his eyes. "Yeah. You thinkin' what I'm thinkin'?"

"I'm thinkin' if we ride to the lake instead of walkin', we'd have more time to fish before the sun goes down. Is that what you're thinkin'?"

"Yes!"

"You got a helmet?"

"Oh man. You're gonna make me wear that dumb thing?"

"You better believe I am."

Dejectedly, he walked to Bax's work bench and pulled an electric blue helmet down. The name "Stu Man" had been stuck on the back with white mailbox-letter stickers. Before he slipped it on his head, he said, "Fine. Happy now?"

"Yes. Your head and all the stuff inside it are really important. By the way, I heard you like to tell stories. That true?"

"I guess so."

"Your dad said you told a good one this mornin'."

Stuey twisted his lips, giving away his guilt. "That story got me grounded from TV."

"Maybe you can tell it to me while we fish."

"Okay," he said, nodding and smiling.

I hit the button on the wall to open the garage door, and evening light flooded in and washed away the dark. "Alright then. Hop on, Stu Man."

THE RIDE WAS AWESOME.

I smiled the whole damn way to the lake, with Stu in front of me, clutching the handles and helping me steer while the wind whipped at us. Although, I didn't go nearly as fast as I wanted to. My cargo was way too precious for speed racing, but the trees still blurred slightly. The warm summer air molded and rushed around us, and I didn't think I'd ever felt anything so perfect.

We parked a few yards from the lake near a little fishing dock someone had recently built that jutted over the edge of the water near where the lakebed had always dropped off, offering deeper fishing, and Stu hopped off the bike easily.

We didn't always have trout here. They started populating when I was a teenager, swimming in from the creek that fed Lee Lake, but we'd always had bluegill and largemouth bass. I was excited to get my hands on a couple trout so I could cook them up and eat the suckers. I hadn't had fresh lake trout since the Cascades. Maybe AJ and I could grill them. I noticed a grill tucked against the side of her house, hidden under a waterproof tarp, when I boarded up her window.

Stu looked up at me as we walked, shading his eyes from the late sun with his little hand. "You're my dad, aren't you?"

"Wh-what?"

My legs stopped working, and they felt like they might buckle beneath me. Instinctively, I leaned on Bax's fishing pole for support but felt it bend and realized quickly that it wouldn't hold me up.

Shit. Fuck.

Had I said something?

Curious blue eyes, carbon copies of mine, stared back at me carefully while I tried to process what he'd just asked. *Bax is gonna fuckin' kill you, Dixon, you idiot!*

"Why would you ask that?"

Stu was too young to figure it out on his own. I must've said something. I promised Bax I wouldn't, but maybe it slipped out? The secret ate at me every single minute of every single day, so it wouldn't have surprised me, but the anger I felt at myself for breaking the biggest promise I'd ever made roared inside me.

Bax would never forgive me now.

"Stu? What would make you ask me that?"

He shrugged and slipped his hand inside mine, like he might find comfort in my touch. Was this what comfort looked like to a little boy?

Kneeling in the dirt in front of him, I took the fishing pole out of his hand, laid both on the ground beside him, and set Bax's tackle box next to them. "Stuart, I really need you tell me why you asked. It's important."

His voice came out a whisper, like he might be afraid that admitting the truth would get him into trouble. "I heard it."

"You didn't do anything wrong," I assured him. "And it's okay for you to ask, but I really need to know where you heard it."

"At school."

"A kid at school told you I was your dad?"

He nodded, watching my face as if he expected answers to show on my skin.

The truth itched beneath it, desperate to be freed, but the promise I'd made to my brother couldn't be rescinded. If I broke it now, with everything bad that had happened flowing between Bax and me like a rabid river rushing down a mountain after a storm, he'd never forgive me. He might have, if we had more time, maybe come around to forgiving me for all the shit I'd pulled in the past.

But if I told Stu the truth now, my brother would never accept another sorry from my mouth.

I looked at my son, at the faint freckles popping on his cheeks and the way the fine, sun-lightened baby hairs around his temples curled a little in the heat, and the decision seemed easier than breathing.

I couldn't lie to him. Not to Stu. I would never forgive *myself* for that.

I cleared my throat. "And if I were, y'know, your… dad? How would you feel about that?"

He thought for a minute, and the contemplation in his eyes was so serious, but absolutely adorable. We might've looked like twins, but right then, Bax was written all over Stu's face.

"Could I have two dads?" he asked, innocence radiating out of him like sunshine. "My daddy would be sad if he couldn't be my daddy anymore, but I don't want you to be sad either."

"I would never take you away from your daddy, kid." Resting my hands lightly over his shoulders, I promised, "Not ever. I swear it to you."

Stuey nodded and reached up to hold onto my shoulders, too, huddling us together like conspirators.

"But I *am* your dad."

The rush of endorphins when I said it, the release of the secret I thought I would carry to my grave, threatened to take me out. My heart thudded behind my ribs painfully, and for a second, I worried all the shit I'd crammed into my body for so long had weakened it. My hand twitched toward my phone in my pocket to call Bax, so I could admit to him that I was just as afraid as he was for Stu to know the truth. I'd dragged Bax into my mess, and now, part of me wanted my big brother here to help me.

But no. This secret, this release of truth felt right. It needed to come from me, and I knew that if I confessed it to my son with anything less than total confidence and conviction, he would doubt it for the rest of his life.

He would doubt me.

"I was there the day you were born," I said. "I was the first person to hold you. I was the guy who got to check to make sure you had ten fingers and ten toes. It's a pretty important job."

"Who's my real mama?" he asked, his eyes roaming my face. They reflected the lake's crystal waters and held more emotional intelligence than I'd ever had in my life, and I wondered if he'd been born with it, or if it was something he'd learned.

Sadness rushed to the forefront of my mind from the dark corners where it had set up permanent residence when I thought my friend's name. "Her name was Kel. Kellie. She's in Heaven. Do you know what that is?"

"Yeah. That's where my pawpaw and my brother Duo are. Is she with them?"

"I suspect she is."

"Good," he said. "I'm glad she's not alone."

"Me too. But you're not… mad that I didn't tell you the truth?"

"No. I don't think so, but Dad—"

Just hearing it come out of his mouth, hearing my son call me "Dad" knocked me on my ass, and I sat in the dirt, looking up at the little wonder in front of me, studying my reaction.

He stepped closer and crouched, then crawled into my lap. I looked out at the lake, breathing in the scent of my son's shampoo, watching as the water trapped the last of the sun's rays beneath its smooth, sparkling surface before the mountain's shade darkened everything and dragged us into the night. The new inn sat off in the distance behind a brush of trees, the waning light glinting off its windows. I hoped no one was watching while I tried to memorize how light Stu felt in my arms and the sweet way he smelled while I waited for him to finish his question.

"But Dad, where were you? Why weren't you here when I was growin' up? Is it because my real mama went to Heaven and you were sad?"

Squeezing my arms around him carefully, I let the warmth of his skin seep into mine. I had never really allowed myself to believe this moment was possible, and now that it was happening, I felt utterly unprepared, but so fucking thankful that I wasn't sure I could contain it.

I didn't know if I could be that strong.

When I could speak, I said quietly, "That's part of it. But your mama and I were sick. Really sick, and neither one of us knew how to take care of you. That's why I brought you to your daddy. I knew he could love you and make sure you didn't get sick too."

"Did you have the chicken pox?"

"No," I answered, trying not to laugh, but it was just so perfect that he couldn't yet imagine anything worse than chicken pox.

"Oh, 'cause Sydney at school had the chicken pox, and her mama wouldn't let her play with anybody or come to school for a whole week! That's bonkers."

"No, luckily, we didn't catch chicken pox, but we were sick with somethin' else. It's really serious and scary, and I didn't want you to be around that. Besides, I had a lot I needed to learn before I could be your dad."

He'd been playing with the cuff of my T-shirt and its frayed edge, but he looked up and trained his eyes on me, and suddenly, I felt all thirty-six of my years. Every single decision I'd ever made, or failed to make, hovered over my head like baseball-size hail ready to fall.

"I thought all dads are born knowin' how to be good."

"No, sometimes they aren't so they have to learn."

"Did you have to go to dad school?"

"Kind of but it's not like your school. I didn't have to go to a classroom."

"Did you have a teacher?"

I thought about it. Yeah, I did have teachers. Many of them. Brenda and Brooks Coulter, Mo, even Nesty. Every person I'd ever met had taught me something important, something I would use in order to be a good dad to my son.

And AJ had helped me believe I could be.

"Yeah, I've had a lot of teachers. Some really good ones who taught me how to do good things, and some not-so-good ones who taught me what *not* to do. But do you know who my favorite teacher is?"

Stuey shook his head.

"You," I said, smiling, because if he'd never been born, I wouldn't have come home. I wouldn't have fought so goddamn hard to deserve this precious life. And I wouldn't be in this moment now, clearheaded and holding my son, loving him.

He giggled. "I'm not a teacher."

"You are. You might not know it, but you taught me more than any other teacher I've ever had. It's because of you that I didn't go to Heaven with your mama, Kel. And it's because of you that I'm happy and have love in my life.

"You taught me *how* to love."

"*I* love you," he whispered, reaching up to pat my cheek. "And I don't care if you're my uncle or my dad."

Covering his hand with mine, I held it in place, hoping the

stubble beneath wasn't too scratchy as I fought hard to hold back tears. "I love you too, kid, more than I'll ever be able to explain. I know you can't understand it yet, but it's why I stayed away. And I know I probably don't deserve it, but I hope someday you can forgive me, because your love is the most important thing in my life."

"But you have lots of people who love you," he said. "Granny, Athena, my mama and daddy, Uncle Brand, and Aunt Abey. And your friend, Avery. She loves you too. Do you love her?"

"How do you know AJ loves me?"

He rolled his eyes dramatically, like it was old news. "She's always smilin' at ya, and she gets them googly eyes whenever you talk."

"She does?"

"Yep. That's a green flag."

"A green— How do you know what a green flag is?"

"Sydney at school. When she came back after the chicken pox, she said she loves me. She said her mom told her she thinks I'm a cute little thing and that it's a green flag that I come from a good family, and that my dad is hot."

I snorted. I couldn't help myself. "She thinks Bax is hot?"

"No, she thinks *you* are, but I don't understand. It's hot today, but the day she said that, it was a lot cooler."

Laughing, I said, "It means Sydney's mama thinks your dad is handsome, but she meant *me*? How'd she know who I was?"

He shrugged. "Lots of people talk about you."

Oh, I bet they do.

"So just now, when you asked if I was your dad, you already knew?"

He nodded. "I've had my sup-pishons."

"Suspicions."

“That’s what I said.”

Thank fuck. My brother can’t kill me. It’s not my fault! For once in my life, somebody else gets the blame.

Although, that didn’t convince me at all that Bax still wouldn’t murder me and dump my body in this very lake.

CHAPTER TWENTY-NINE

DIXON

BAX BELLOWED into his cell phone, "You did WHAT?"

When we got back to the house, I heated up Stu's dinner and sat him at the table with a glass of milk. That seemed like a fatherly thing to do.

And then I hid in the laundry room so Stu couldn't hear me and called Bax.

"Dixon, I warned you. I fuckin' warned you!"

"Bax," I whispered into my cell, "you're not hearin' me. He already knew. *He* brought it up. All I did was confirm the truth. Did you want me to lie to him?"

"Oh, that's *all* you've done? Right. Just don't say another word till we get there. Jesus fuckin' Christ. We're leavin' the fairgrounds now."

It probably should've taken Bax and Bea a lot longer to get home, but thirty minutes later, their truck skidded to a stop in front of the house. Bax's door sounded like it might fall completely off the frame when he slammed it shut. And I heard Bea pleading with him to "stay calm" before the screen door clacked against the wall when he threw it open.

"Stuey." His eyes zeroed in on Stu, and he swept across

the room, lifted Stu straight out of his chair, and hugged him so hard, I didn't think Stu could get a full breath.

"Daddy? I thought I wouldn't see you till tomorrow. Where's Athena?"

"She's still at the fairgrounds. Shaylene's mama will drive her home later. Are you okay, buddy? You're not upset?"

"No. Why?" Stu pulled away and patted Bax's cheek. "I'm okay, Daddy. How'd Athena and Tulsa do? I can't wait to see 'em do the barrels at the rodeo."

Bax didn't say anything, and he sat with Stu in his arms, like letting go might be physically impossible. Bea took the chair next to them, and then everyone looked at me, standing in front of their fridge like a deer in headlights.

"I didn't say a word. I swear. He asked me."

"Stuey, honey," Bea said, caressing her hand over Stu's messy helmet hair, and she smoothed away a streak of dirt on his cheek with her thumb, "how did you find out about Uncle Dixon?"

He shrugged, looking just a little bit guilty.

"Stu, we need to know."

He sighed. "Sydney's mama said my daddy was hot. And Mrs. McNamara at school agreed, and she said 'That Bax Lee sure is one fine cowboy.'"

Bea's face turned purple. "She said *what*?"

"That's what Sydney said, a-and then Sydney's mama said, 'No, not Bax. I meant Dixon. He's Stu's real dad.'" Poor Stu looked perplexed, like he couldn't figure out why his family was so upset about something another five-year-old had said. "Sydney told me at recess."

Bea looked like she might be ready to murder both women. "Oh my God! I'm callin' the principal right now."

"Bea, just wait," Bax said. He pulled Stu's face back to his. "What else did you hear?"

"Well, after dinner the other night, when Avery came over?" Bax nodded. "That night, you were readin' me my book before bed, Mama. 'Member? But I had to potty, and on my way back, I heard daddy talkin' on his phone in your bedroom. You were talkin' to Uncle Rye, Daddy, and you said Uncle Dixon's name, and then you said, 'He better not try to take Stu away from us.' And then you said, 'Oh, shut up, Rye. God, your sunshiny dispolition pisses me off.'"

Bea corrected him before she realized what she was correcting or that he'd cussed. "Dis*position*."

Stu nodded. "That's what I said."

"I'm sorry we didn't tell you the truth," Bax said. "Grown-ups always say stuff like this, but we really were tryin' to protect you."

"It's not right to lie, Daddy. You told me that."

"No, you're right. It's not okay to lie. It's also not very nice to eavesdrop."

"What's that mean?"

"It means listenin' to people when they're havin' a private conversation."

"Oh." Stu looked at the floor. "Am I in trouble?"

Bax and Bea shook their heads. "No, Stuey," Bea said, "you're not in trouble, but do you have any questions about what you and Dixon talked about? What did he tell you?"

Stu looked at the ceiling and tapped his index finger against his chin, and I tried not to laugh, but he was just so damn cute that I had to fight it hard.

"He said that he was there when I was born. Did you know I was born in California? And he said he was sick and couldn't take care of me so he brought me to you so I wouldn't get the chicken pox."

"Um, Stu," I hedged. "That's not exactly what I said."

"Oh, and he said my real mama's name is Kel and that

she's in Heaven with Pawpaw and Duo. Isn't that nice, Daddy? They'll never be lonely."

Bax was speechless. He looked from Stu to Bea and back at Stu. "That's a nice way to think about it." Reaching for Bea's hand, they held onto each other, and in that moment, I missed AJ so much that I physically ached for her.

Since I'd come home, she'd been there for me countless times, just like Bea was for Bax. AJ was my person. She wasn't just a light in my life. She was the sun in my universe, and her warmth and the connection she had to the earth beneath my feet were the foundation I was just now realizing we might be able to build a future on. A sturdy one. A happy one.

Stu nodded, smiling brightly, and then he looked at me. "Do you have a picture of Mama Kel?"

"No," I said, "I'm sorry, but I-I don't. I don't have many things from back then. I had pictures on my old phone, but I lost it a long time ago."

"It's okay," Bax said. "We do. When we couldn't find you, we had someone dig a little into Kel's background, and we found her senior picture from high school. But Stu, you don't have any other questions for Mama or Daddy? Or Uncle Dixon?"

"No, well maybe one. What should I call you?"

All eyes landed on me again. I had no idea how to answer, but Bea saved me.

"What would you like to call him?"

"Mama," Stu griped, "you can't put me on the spot like that. I dunno. It needs to come to me organally."

A snort burst out of Bax's nose, and Bea corrected Stu again. "Organically."

"That's what I said."

Bea stood and scooped him out of Bax's arms. I wanted to

hug him and ask for more time. I wasn't ready for the night to end, but she carried him upstairs to get ready for bed, which left Bax and me alone.

When they were out of hearing range, he said quietly, "I've a been a little worried about the gossip around town gettin' back to Stu." He sighed heavily. "But I wanted to strangle you tonight."

"I know."

"I've wanted to strangle you for a long damn time."

"I know that too."

He crossed the distance between us and stood in front of me. "But right now, for some goddamn reason, I need to hug you." He didn't wait for my response. He wrapped his arms around me, patting my back like guys do, but then it became a real hug, and he held onto me like he loved me.

"I'm sorry," I said. "I can't imagine what I've put y'all through, but Stu forgot to tell you the second most important thing I said tonight. The first was that I love him, but the second is that I'm so damn lucky that you're my family and that bringin' him to you was the best decision I've ever made.

"I stand by it, brother. You saved me. You saved him, and I'll never know how to make you understand how much that means to me."

"That little boy," Bax said, and he tried to clear the lump out of his throat, but didn't quite manage it, "he saved *me* when I didn't know how to let go of the past. He gave me a future to look forward to. Bea and Stu both did. Athena too. They all saved me, and he… Stuey, he's—"

"He's your son," I said, hugging my brother harder. "He's *our* son, and nothin' will ever change that."

DRESSED IN SOFT, white pajamas with brown cows all over them, Stu climbed into his bed and smiled up at me and Bax on either side. He stuffed his bare feet under his bed sheet and rubbed them over the mattress.

Bea walked into Stu's bedroom, carrying a manila folder, and when she stood at the foot of the bed, she pulled out a piece of paper and handed it to me.

I smiled when I saw Kel's young face looking back at me. Kellie Gale. She had been a whirlwind of a woman, and she'd never know the gift she'd given me. Memories swirled around my head of the silver lunch car diner by the park we used to go to get high. We'd sip milkshakes and talk about our lives before the drugs. Mostly I talked about my brothers and sister, but Kel had big dreams, and she could talk for hours about wanting to be a journalist someday.

"She wanted to be on TV," I told Stu as I handed him the paper. "She wanted to be the person who said, 'We have breaking news tonight.'"

He took the paper from my hand and studied the person looking back at him.

"She's pretty."

"Yeah," I agreed. "And she loved you."

Nodding, he folded the paper and stuck it beneath his pillow. Bea turned to leave the room, but Stu said, "Mama, where you goin'? Aren't you gonna read me a story tonight?"

She stopped in the doorway. "Oh, well, it's really late, and I'm kinda tired. I thought maybe tonight Dixon could tell you a story. I've heard he's really good at it."

Stu propped himself up on his elbows. "You are?" he asked. "Like me?"

I shrugged and sat on the edge of his bed. "I dunno if I'm any good at it. I'll let you be the judge of that, but yeah, I like tellin' stories."

Bax and Bea took turns kissing Stu's forehead, and then they left the room quietly, and I relaxed back against Stu's headboard. He lay down and turned toward me, waiting patiently with his hands tucked up beneath his cheek.

"Is it okay if I call you Deedee?" he asked.

"Deedee?"

"Yeah, D.D. for Daddy Dixon."

"Sure, kid," I said, trying not to die right there on the spot from too much happiness. "You can call me whatever you like."

"Okay. Good. Now, tell me a story, Deedee."

"Alright, bossy." I cleared my throat and hiked his blanket a little higher so he wouldn't get cold. "Once upon a time, there was a prince…"

CHAPTER THIRTY

AVERY JANE

"YOU WANT TO HAVE A PICNIC?" Mrs. Ellison asked, exasperated with me and my late-night request. "On my front lawn. At nine o'clock at night?"

"Yes, ma'am. Well, it's not a picnic really, just snacks and tea. But Dixon has somethin' to celebrate."

I'd never known him to be more excited about anything than he was earlier today when he told me about getting to spend the evening hanging out with Stu. I wanted to mark the occasion somehow, so he'd never forget how he felt tonight. And if I was honest, our date tomorrow felt like years too long to see him again, so when he texted to tell me he was on his way home and would call me soon, I threw some stuff together and rushed to meet him.

"He has to work early tomorrow mornin'," I told Mrs. Ellison, "so I wanted to meet him here and tell him congrats. We won't be long, and we'll be quiet, promise."

With her hands planted firmly on her hips, she stared me down. "No shenanigans?"

"No, ma'am. No shenanigans."

"Very well then." She turned and walked back into her

house, and I breathed a sigh of relief and got busy setting up beneath the oak tree in her yard.

The picnic set I'd won at a white elephant Christmas party two years ago, thrown by José and Daisy from the local diner, was perfect for the occasion, with plates, silverware, and a water-repellent blanket. I arranged everything on top of the blanket, opened the tote bag I'd lugged from my house, and pulled out cut up veggies, salami, and a Thermos filled with iced black-currant tea I'd ordered for Dixon. I tried it earlier in the day. It was delicious, even without caffeine and sugar, so I hoped he'd like it too.

He pulled up five minutes later and parked by the curb, but it took him a minute to see me. His door creaked and the metal groaned as he closed it. When he finally spotted me cross-legged on the blanket, he paused, his jingling keys dangling from his hand.

The moonlight highlighted his brilliant smile, and his boots pounded the grass as he rushed to me and swept me up into his arms. He hugged me tight and whispered, "He knows. My son knows who I am, and he loves me."

I gasped and hugged him back as tightly as I could. "What? You told him? I'm so proud of you!"

He shook his head, and his lips rasped against my neck and made me shiver.

"No. I didn't tell him, but he already knew. He heard it at school. Some nosy moms were talkin' about me, but when he asked tonight, I told him the truth. Bax was pissed, but Stu explained, and my brother actually hugged me. He told me he was glad I'd come home and that he was workin' on tryin' to forgive and trust me."

I wasn't about to tell Dixon all the gossip I'd heard around town. At least the gossip Stu overheard had created a positive outcome.

Dixon set me on my feet and held me at arm's length, his crystal eyes alight with happiness. "What is all this?"

"It's a picnic. I couldn't wait till tomorrow night to celebrate. But now we have even more reason. I know you work in the mornin'. I do too, so it's just some snacks and tea."

He lifted me again, wrapped my legs around his waist, and I hung on to his shoulders as he brushed my hair away from my face, held it between his hands, and kissed me.

"Thank you." He sat on my blanket with me still attached to his body and kissed me deeper.

It didn't take long until I was panting and gasping for air. Reluctantly, I pulled away. "Let's eat. I promised Mrs. Ellison no shenanigans, and if you keep kissin' me like that, I will break my promise, and your sister will probably have to arrest us for indecent exposure."

He smirked. "Oh, I got some shenanigans for you, baby girl, right here in my jeans."

I swatted his shoulder and climbed off him. "Are you hungry?"

Mischief played on his curving lips. "Starved."

"You're a little flirty when you're happy," I said, blushing and handing him the Thermos. He unscrewed the cap and sniffed, then took a long pull. His eyebrows rose with curiosity. "It's black currant tea. Naturally decaffeinated. Do you like it?"

"It's really good."

I nodded, pleased with my choice. "So, tell me more. What else did you and Stu talk about?"

Chewing on a carrot stick, Dixon's eyes slid to the side while he thought. "Well, he asked about his mama. Bax and Bea had a picture of her that I'd never even seen from when she was in high school. I guess they did some investigatin' so they'd be prepared when Stu was ready. He said she was pretty, and he tucked the picture under his pillow. Kel would've loved that."

"Was he sad that she's gone?"

"No, I don't think so. I mean, I don't think he fully understands, y'know?"

"Probably not. I remember my mom tellin' me my dad was gone when I was little. As far as I know, he's not dead, but I took it to mean that he was. I believed it until I was six or seven, when I heard my mom and Gran in the kitchen one day, mad because my dad had stopped sending child support. I think kids believe whatever's easiest to explain."

"Yeah, but not Stu. He heard the gossip, and instead of shruggin' it off, he confronted me about it. I wonder how long he's been chewin' on this."

"I told you he's a great kid. Really smart." Bumping my shoulder against Dixon's, I said, "Like his dad."

He scoffed and bumped back. "Oh yeah, I'm a regular Einstein. It was really smart of me to become an addict and abandon my kid."

"Don't talk about yourself like that. Why do you do that?"

His eyes slid to mine. He plucked at the grass beside the blanket, and then he turned to face me. "Because it's true."

"It's not. Why can't you see what I see when I look at you?"

"What do you see?" he asked, brushing his hands together, and blades of grass fell into his lap.

I faced him, too, crossing my legs in front of me again and straightening my spine. "I see a beautiful man who was smart enough to stay away from the people and the things he knew would hurt him until he was ready to face them. I see someone who can adapt and learn what he needs to survive."

Dixon took another swig of the tea and handed the Thermos to me.

"And," I said, nodding at the Thermos, "I see a man who knows his limits and what's good for him."

"It took a very long time for me to learn those things about myself, AJ. Probably a lot longer than most other people."

"Would you like to know how long I wasted with that jerk, Cody? I thought I had limits and knew what was good for me, too, but he weaseled his way into my life and I let him. Gran and Mama kept tellin' me to cut him loose, but I wouldn't listen."

"I'm sorry you had to go through that," Dixon said, "but you finally did listen. I didn't. I can't even begin to remember how many times my family begged me to change my life, but I was stupid, and I thought I knew better."

Grabbing his hand, I held it to my heart. "Not stupid, Dixon. Sick."

He rolled his eyes and pulled his hand away. "Yeah. That's what they tell me in NA. 'You were sick. Addiction is a disease,' and I know it's true, but sometimes it feels like an excuse, and I'm so fuckin' tired of excusin' all the bad shit I've done. I'm tired of my mama excusin' it, and it really pisses me off when I hear people talkin' like I didn't have a choice 'cause I was"—he raised his hands in the air and mimicked quotations with two fingers—"'sick.'"

He turned away and fell back onto the grass. "I did have a choice, Avery Jane. I chose wrong and look what it cost me. I'll never get any of it back. I'll never know what Stu's first word sounded like. I didn't get to hear his first laugh or feel his first hug."

"You're right," I said. "Addiction stole those things from you, just like cancer steals and so do all kinds of other illnesses."

"Goddammit. Now you're doin' it too."

"What am I doin'?"

"Makin' excuses for me. You sound just like my mother." He turned his head slowly, the blue of his eyes lit by the moon and trained right on mine. "You're such a dreamer. But tell me this: if your daddy came back, would you forgive him? He's a drunk, right? That's what your mama used to say."

"I-I—"

He sat up. "Not so forgivin' now, are ya?"

DOC V ASKED Dixon to accompany him on a few farm calls the next day after his shift at the vet clinic, and Dixon said he'd be too late and too dirty for dinner, so he postponed our date.

I was disappointed, but I also knew I'd hit a nerve last night, so maybe it would be better to give him some time to process what we'd talked about. I needed to process it too.

Was he right that I was ready to forgive all the things Dixon had done wrong, but not my own father? Why was that?

Mama left for work in the early, Saturday morning fog. I thought about catching her before she left and asking about my father. She rarely brought him up, and I'd long ago stopped asking. To her, my dad was old, tired news, but he kept coming up for me. And why suddenly did I want to know? Just to convince myself I was different than she had been? Who exactly was I trying to convince? Me or everybody else in town?

Or both?

Gran rode with me in the flower van to AVery Pretty Petal, and we got to work setting up for the day. I had a few orders waiting and started prepping flowers for three arrangements. She hummed while she dusted, shuffling on her feet so she didn't have to bend her knees too much.

"Avery Jane, there's somethin' I wanna talk to you about."

"What's that?"

"Well, first, I wanna tell you that I approve of Dixon. I know, I know, you don't need my approval, but I'm givin' it anyway. I've always liked him. I know your mama has doubts because Dixon's had some hardships and issues in his life. She worries for you because she loves you, and her history with your daddy probably makes that worse. But it's easy to see Dixon really cares for you, and if you trust him and believe in him, then I do too. You've got good sense."

"Thank you, Gran, but am I wrong to believe so fully in him? You can tell me the truth. I'll hear you this time. Am I makin' a mistake, believin' in someone who has proven time and again that he can be untrustworthy? He's never given *me* a reason not to trust him, but am I bein' naïve?"

"I think you're bein' who you've always been, someone who sees good in others. And there *is* good in Dixon. Maybe he just doesn't see it in himself yet.

"But I won't lie and tell you I'm not glad he's back. I am. I'm happy you two have reconnected. The friendship you had when you were kids brought me joy and kept me laughin'. He's good for your soul. And I really like that he pushed you to get that restraining order."

"Me too," I said, turning to unlock the register before we opened. "I'm glad it's done."

"But I want you to be careful," Gran said.

"Careful? About what?"

She paused, the duster still lifted in the air above some dried flower arrangements that sold well to younger customers who didn't want the responsibility of fresh flowers but still wanted the beauty. "Your heart has always been set on Dixon Lee, Avery, but the things he's struggled with aren't safe for you."

"Safe? I don't understand, Gran."

"Drugs. Alcohol. All that anger he used to carry around. You have addiction in your history too—your daddy. I just want you to be careful about what you give to Dixon. Things could get dark really fast down that road."

"But dark how? Mama never talks about my father. You know, I heard people talkin' about it yesterday. Gossipin' about me and Dixon, and Mr. Henly said they all think I'll end up just like her."

"Those assholes! Tell me who it was, and I'll rough 'em up for ya."

"Oh Gran," I laughed, rounding the counter, and I took the duster from her hand and set it on the table. Hugging her, I said, "Thank you for lookin' out for me. I don't know what I'd do without you in my life. I love you, and I'm not worried about turnin' out like you or Mama. I'd be proud to be as strong as either of you."

She smiled, and her green eyes twinkled with love. "When I say dark, I just mean addiction. It's not somethin' everyone can control, and it can get out of hand quickly. But like I said, you've always had good sense, and I don't think I have to worry about you like that.

"I just want you to be happy. You're such a solitary person. It scares me when people come into your life that you'll lose yourself."

"Like I did with Cody?"

Gran didn't have to say it, but she smiled gently and nodded anyway.

"Please don't worry about that. There's a huge difference

between Dixon and Cody Mahone. Dixon is a giver. Cody was a taker. I won't lose myself because Dixon would never let me get lost. I have no doubt that he'd disappear before that could happen."

"You're not worried about that? Him leavin'?"

I shook my head. "If you'd asked me yesterday, I might've said yes. But now?" Now that Stuart knew Dixon was his dad. "Now, no. But he said somethin' that's got me all tied in knots."

"What's that?"

"He thinks I forgive his mistakes too easily. He asked, if my dad came back, would I forgive him just as easily."

Carefully, Gran asked, "Would you?"

"No." I didn't even have to think about it. "No, I wouldn't forgive him. My entire life, I've struggled with feelin' good enough. It affected the way I see myself. Like, with friends. I wanted them to like me. I was desperate for them to like me. But when they did, it was me who let the friendship fade. Because I didn't feel good enough to have them as a friend. I tell myself they're better off without me."

"Honey, I didn't know you felt like that."

I shrugged. "You and Mama had enough on your plates. I didn't want to make you worry, and I guess I've always felt like my feelings didn't matter as much as other people's. And that's exactly why I wouldn't forgive my father, even if he came crawling back on his hands and knees.

"No kid deserves to feel like they don't matter."

"You matter to me," Gran said. "I love you. You're important in my life. There's not a minute of my day that I'm not thinkin' about you or wishin' good things for you."

Hugging her again, I said, "I know, Gran. I love you too. And maybe if I hadn't known how much you and Mama loved me, things would've been darker for me. Thankfully, we'll never have to find out."

Gran nodded again. She picked up the duster and shook it in the air. Dust motes floated down all around her. "Well, that's that. I've said what I wanted to about Dixon. Now, that *Cody* is another story. Don't think he's done with you. I saw it in his eyes at the courthouse. You just be careful, Avery. Hear me?"

"Yes, ma'am."

CHAPTER THIRTY-ONE

DIXON

KNOCKING SOFTLY on AJ's front door, I held the bouquet I'd driven all the way to Jackson and back for in my shitty car, missing her the whole way and wishing she was with me.

When she opened it, I pushed the frilly bunch toward her and said, "I'm sorry."

I felt pretty clever, giving flowers to a floral artist, and that was an apt title. AJ was indeed an artist. And I would bet money she didn't receive them often, which was why I had to go to Jackson. I couldn't very well show up at the local florist's house with a cheap handful of half-dead carnations from the Stop and Go. If I had, something told me she would've slammed the door in my face.

Old country music played in her house—Shania Twain, if I wasn't wrong—and she'd tied her hair back with what looked like the torn sleeve of a T-shirt, like a headband. The knees of her peach sweatpants were dirty, her tank top damp with sweat down the middle, and her feet bare. Her porch light cast a warm glow over her face and created shadows everywhere else.

"Thank you," she said, taking the flowers from my hand,

the tissue paper wrapped around them crinkling quietly. “They’re gorgeous. Where’d you get them?”

“King’s Floral in Jackson. They said they knew you, and the woman behind the counter made this specially for you.”

“Was it Kim?” she asked, and a gust of wind flowed from behind her, whipping through her hair.

I shrugged. “Dunno, but she had hair dyed the color of a purple crayon.” Looking past her shoulder, I asked, “The window guys haven’t replaced your window yet?”

AJ smiled, and her hazel eyes warmed. “That’s Kim King. She’s a sweetheart. Come in.” She stepped back to allow me in, spun on her foot, and I followed her to the kitchen. “The contractor cancelled, said he’d be here first thing Monday mornin’.”

“You know Brand owns a construction company, right? I could ask him if he—”

“Thank you. I appreciate the offer. If they cancel again, I can ask Brand for a recommendation, but I’d prefer to take care of it on my own.” She leaned against the kitchen counter, still facing away from me, and tapped her phone on the counter. The music stopped, and she sighed. “I’m sorry. I must look like hell. I’ve been cleanin’ for hours.” Pulling a glass vase from a low cabinet, she went on. “I clean when I’m upset or tryin’ to make heads or tails of things.”

I sat at her kitchen island and set my phone and keys on top. “I upset you.”

It wasn’t a question. I knew it was the truth, and it had been eating at me for days.

“I’m sorry about that. I was unkind.”

“No, you weren’t unkind.” She filled the vase three-quarters with water from the tap. “It’s not just our conversation the other night botherin’ me, but what you said was true, and I’ve spent the last couple days thinkin’ about it.”

"AJ?"

She plopped the flowers into the water and fluffed them a bit, watching as they fell into place, pruning a few loose leaves with her fingers, and then she turned to face me. "What?"

"You're doin' it again."

"I'm not," she argued, showing the first hint of anger I'd seen in her since I'd come back to town. I hated that I'd made her mad, but I liked that she was showing me how she really felt. "I'm tellin' you what's been goin' through my mind. You were right about my father. So, I've put some thought to what it might take for me to get over his absence in my life and let the anger and disappointment and… *Ugh*." She sighed heavily, and her shoulders slumped forward. "Goddammit, what you said made me realize how utterly abandoned I've felt my whole life."

"I didn't mean to make you—"

"You didn't *make* me feel anything, Dixon. You simply asked a question, but now that you have, it's got me lookin' at things from a new angle. I've had to admit to myself that I've made a lot of choices in my life based on that feeling of abandonment.

"But some good came from it, too," she said, "because now I know that I don't like feelin' that way. I don't want to feel like I'm not worth loving, and if forgiving my deadbeat dad will cure me of that awful ache in my heart, then I want to do that."

Slowly, she crossed her kitchen, and when she stood in front of me, I angled my chair to face her head on.

"New rule," she said as she climbed over me and straddled my lap, resting her arms over my shoulders. "I won't let you off the hook so easily when I think you've done somethin' wrong, and you will try to accept that what I say is true, even if you don't believe it. And especially if it's somethin' positive about you. Deal?"

I saw forgiveness shining in her eyes. When I walked in tonight, I wasn't sure I'd find it. Apologizing for something I'd recently said or done was a new thing for me, but living one more minute with AJ pissed at me was unacceptable. And it hurt.

"Deal?" she said again.

"Deal." I smirked. "You're a little feisty when you're mad."

"You ain't seen nothin' yet."

"You gonna show me more, little dragon?" Running my hands up her ribcage, I molded them over her breasts and then pushed her tank beneath them. They popped free because she hadn't worn a bra while she cleaned, and my dick jumped to attention under my jeans.

"Dixon, I'm a dirty, sweaty Dumpster fire. I'm covered in grime and multi-purpose cleaner."

Looking up at her, I asked, "Did you douse your tits with bleach?"

She swatted the back of my head and laughed. "No!"

"Good, then I want 'em in my mouth." I proved it when I leaned forward and wrapped my lips around one.

AJ groaned and arched in my arms, but I held her up, and her hair brushed over my forearms behind her. She slid a hand up and pulled off her headband, then let it fall to the floor.

"Why do we always end up like this? With me straddlin' you?"

Tightening my hands around her hips, I squeezed, feeling like I could eat her alive.

It was the reason we'd argued the other night, but something about the way she always forgave me for things I didn't deserve to be forgiven for—the way she believed in me—settled something inside me. I felt whole in a way I never thought I'd experience.

"You want me some other way?"

"Yes," she said. "I want you to stop bein' so careful with me. I won't break. I want you to show me how you really feel, and I want you to know that I'm okay with it."

She climbed down, pulled off her tank, and held out her hand. I whipped my T-shirt over my head, tossed it, and accepted that hand, letting her drag me through her living room. Before she could lead me to her bed, I stopped her behind the couch, and she turned slowly.

I didn't speak, but I bent her forward over the back of the couch. She let her arms fall limp but then gripped the cushions hard when I shoved my hand inside her sweats. I worked it beneath her thin panties, cupped her pussy, and she moaned loudly.

She pressed her ass back against my erection, and I began to pump and rub my hips lazily, working myself up into a frenzy with the friction from my jeans.

I hardened like bone just watching her become pliant for me like she was. She wanted to be *fucked.* She wanted to know the storm inside me, and I wanted to show it to her. I wanted her to feel it.

Pulling away, I gripped the top of her sweats and underwear in both hands and shoved them down her legs. She worked them off with her feet as I spread her thighs and trailed my fingers slowly toward her pussy. I dragged them between her lips, her breath sped, and she tried to fuck my hand.

"Hold on, baby girl," I breathed, listening to the shake in my voice and letting myself give into the want I felt for her, the wild, ragged need she'd awoken in me.

Unzipping my jeans, I remembered my wallet in my back pocket and grappled for it as they fell down my thighs. As soon as my cock was unbound, it sought her body like she was the only light in the dark. I let it slip between her ass cheeks so she could feel me pulse and jerk as I ripped open a condom packet. Without Shania's dulcet tones filling the silence, the sound cracked through AJ's living room loud as thunder.

She moaned again and clenched her cheeks. They squeezed the life out of my dick, and pre-come seeped out and coated her soft skin. I'd never seen anyone sexier than AJ, bent over and ready to take me, and seeing my cum marring the perfect, rounded globes of her ass made saliva pool in my mouth, but it also urged me to get the damn condom on.

When it was in place, I whispered, "Spread for me."

Wordlessly, she opened her legs wider. I swooped my hips back, letting my cock drag over her ass, and I slipped inside her pussy, her wet, sweaty body easing the glide.

"Yes." She begged, "*More*."

She moaned and began to move and suck me in, but I thrust my cock as far inside her as I could. Her ass slapped against my stomach, her feet lifted off the ground, and I held her where I wanted her with one hand on her back and the other pressed between her and the couch so I could rub her clit and make her wild while I fucked her.

She wanted hard, and that was what she got. I entered her over and over again relentlessly. Wrapping my hands around her full hips, every thrust was euphoric, and I had to fight hard against the urge to come.

I let it all go: the constant awareness of my family's disappointment in the back of my mind. The disappointment I had in myself, the anger, the sadness of a life abandoned, and the surprising joy I'd felt at finding it again. But mostly, the fear that I'd fuck this all up. All of it dissipated from the prison inside my head as I fucked AJ, but this time, I didn't feel guilty about the pleasure.

This time, I let myself drown in it.

Sweat coated my skin. It dripped down my neck and chest while I worked her, and I was mesmerized by the sight of it glistening on her ass. Rubbing it into her skin with my thumbs, I gripped her hips harder, held on for dear life, and *pounded* inside her.

My balls slapped against her thighs, the wet heat of our bodies fused us together, and I watched our sweat catch and glisten in my pubic hair.

She slid her hand beneath her, reached between her thighs with greedy fingers, and let them slip around my balls. She cupped them in her hand and squeezed, and breath froze in my lungs.

"Avery Jane Harlow, stop that right now or I'm gonna c—"

She squeezed harder. Cum shot out of me and filled up the condom, and I shouted my release, almost falling on top of her when the sudden orgasm rushed through me.

"I'm sorry," I said, panting and trying to catch my breath. I caressed her low back with relaxed hands, but then pulled out, holding the condom in place between the V of two fingers.

"Sorry? What for?" she asked, pushing with her hands on the couch and trying to touch her toes to the floor.

"You didn't come."

"No, but that was—"

"Fuck that," I growled, and pulled her up by her shoulders and flipped her. "That ain't who I am."

She squeaked her surprise when I lifted her and set her

bare ass on the back of the couch. Her eyes, wide open and curious, held mine as I leaned in to steal a kiss, and I guided her back down and left her laid out over a throw pillow. Her head hit the cushion again, but this time she watched as I hooked her legs over my shoulders and descended.

"Who's that?" she asked, her voice all husk and heat.

"Someone who leaves his woman unsatisfied."

"Ohh," she moaned when I sucked her swollen sex, savoring her tangy sweetness in the back of my throat. I watched her eyes roll and her lids fall closed in ecstasy, and she slid her fingers into my hair, pressing her pink fingernails into my skull, moving me where she needed me most.

Sounds of slippery sex and sucking filled her living room as I slid three fingers inside her and curved them.

It was overwhelming, the way we fit together, the real, visceral connection. There was no high making me feel bolder than I really was or more effective than I surely had been. No, this was simpler. Better.

There was nothing shrouding or hiding AJ from me or me from her. The light on the ceiling fan above us shone down on us, and I saw every part of her.

But I wasn't so overwhelmed that I couldn't be in the moment with her. For the first time in my life with a woman, I reveled in her, letting my eyes graze her soft stomach, her bouncing breasts and beautiful, perfectly round, darkened nipples. Her thighs tightened around my head as I ate her out and took her essence inside my body, and I relished every fucking second of her stranglehold, like *she* was the high I'd been chasing most of my life.

Loving her was like church, no church I'd ever been to, but I wanted to pray to Avery Jane Harlowe's altar for the rest of my damn life.

Her stomach tightened as she flexed her abdomen and

tried to ride my face upside down. The couch did all the work to hold her up, so I let my hand glide over her breast, and when I pinched her nipple tightly between my finger and thumb, she gasped. She suffocated me as I went to town on her clit and pumped harder, my tongue fluttering madly.

Pausing to breathe, I begged, “I need you to come, AJ. I need it more than I need breath in my lungs.”

She moaned and opened her eyes.

“I need it, I need it, I *need* it.”

She watched me lean over her, my hair falling forward and feathering her thighs, and spit on her clit. I moved the pad of my thumb over it in unhurried, smooth circles, and I slowed my fingers inside her, but pressed harder.

I’d made a sloppy, wet mess of her pussy with my mouth. The sounds and the obscene sight of my fingers slipping and gliding in and out of her forced blood to pulse through my cock again, and thank fuck, because I had plans to make messes out of her all night long.

Looking up, I begged her one more time. “I fucking need you.”

She gasped, and her hazel eyes flashed a kaleidoscope of color before I descended again, attacking her pussy one more time with my tongue. I sucked her clit so hard that it rubbed the roof of my mouth, and she dug her heels into my back when she came, whispering my name to the night.

CHAPTER THIRTY-TWO

AVERY JANE

IN MY BATHTUB under the spray of the shower, I washed Dixon, attending to the ridge and rise of every muscle with soapy hands and caressing fingers.

"Thank you," I said quietly, rubbing a bar of soap over his stomach, "for trusting me."

"I do trust you, AJ. It's me I don't trust."

"Why?"

"You have to ask?"

"Yeah, I mean, I know why you would say that, but you've been sober a long time. Don't you know yourself well enough now to trust that you won't relapse?"

"People can go years without a drink or a hit, and then somethin' shitty happens or they have a bad day, and it starts all over again. The fear will last the rest of my life. And it's not just drugs I'm afraid of. It's the anger. It's always there."

"Anger at your father?"

"Yeah. Both of 'em."

"Both?"

"Noah Lee ain't my dad. Not biologically. I think I've known it my whole life."

He'd hinted at it more than once, but this was the first he'd said it out loud. "Your mama told you this?"

"No," he said, "she's skirted it since the day I was born. I've suspected it for a long time, but when I came home a few weeks ago, that first time I saw Merv and gave her the orange flowers, it was in her eyes. It's time for me to come right out and ask her to tell me who I belong to. *Where* I belong."

I was quiet as I contemplated what he'd said, but I kept washing. His fantastical story about the magic man flitted through my mind, but finally, I turned him and rubbed the bar of soap over his back and hips. I knew he'd tell me more when he was ready.

"What are these tattoos?" I asked, chasing the dark lines inked between his shoulder blades with a fingertip. "What do they mean? When did you get them?"

He pushed into my touch as I traced the image of a broken human heart on his back, the arteries left frayed and bleeding. "The one you're touchin' is pretty self-explanatory. It's a broken heart."

"I can see that." I swatted his ass playfully. "But who's it for? Kel?"

"Naw. Don't get me wrong. I loved Kel. She gave me Stu, and she was a friend to me when no one else in the world was, but we didn't love each other. Not like that. We were just two people—two friends—caught up in somethin' they didn't know how to get out of.

"No," he said, "the heart's for Stu. After I left him with Bax, I wandered a while but eventually headed up to Alaska, and I got a job on a halibut boat. I saved most of what I made to give to Bax for Stu, but with my first paycheck, I paid for the tattoo.

"I put it on my back, 'cause at the time, I thought I could move on from the pain of leavin' Stu behind. I wanted the evidence that I loved him to be part of me forever, but I knew if I had to look at it every day, it would be a temptation. To use again or to come home when I wasn't ready. I wasn't sure which, but I knew both would hurt.

"But I was dead wrong.

"I thought about that kid every day. I went to bed every night with a sour stomach 'cause I couldn't forget him." Dixon went quiet for a minute. I couldn't even begin to imagine what he was seeing in his head, but finally, he said, "I thought about you too."

"You thought about *me*?"

"Yeah. You're gonna laugh, but I couldn't remember your name. I tried and tried, but it was like my brain wanted to protect you from me. It got so bad, the need to remember you, that I almost called my sister after years of unreturned messages. I probably should have.

"I remembered your laugh, though, and your hair. And your eyes. Your eyes have been hauntin' me for a long time."

Pressing my cheek against his back, I leaned into him. "I thought about you too. There's never really been a time when you weren't in the back of my mind. I think I've compared every guy I've ever dated to you."

"Why would you do that? There's no way I measured up."

This time, I pinched his ass, but then I couldn't resist, and I let my hand caress the taut, rounded muscle and wander down his strong thigh.

"Sorry," he said, "I'm not tryin' to talk down about myself, but I was homeless and jobless for a long time, and that's not even mentionin' the drugs."

"Yeah, but I don't measure a man's worth by his job or his house. I've looked for somethin' else from men my whole life."

"What's that?" he asked, turning to face me. He removed

my hands from his hips and placed them on his chest, and right then and there I fell in love with the feeling of my fingertips digging into his pectoral muscles and the way the hair there tickled my skin.

I peeked up at him, blinking away the spray of the shower, but he angled his body to shield me from it.

"Creativity. Imagination," I said. "I have this weird curiosity about the world, the earth, and when I'm with someone, I always wonder if they feel it too. It's not somethin' adults seem to think about, like it got lost as they grew older. My number-crunching accountant mother certainly didn't, and growin' up, its absence in my life was loud.

"Gran's flowers and your stories when we were kids filled the void. I feel it now. And I know you do too."

"Yeah, I do. I think it's 'cause of how I came up. I was always curious, and when things started to get dark in my life, the curiosity didn't go away. It changed and morphed—I sought answers to different questions—but it never left me. And now that I'm sober and learnin' how to survive life without drugs or alcohol, I lean on it. Y'know? Almost like another coping mechanism. The stories in my head get me through hard moments or sleepless nights. They help me process the world around me."

I smiled and nodded, because I knew exactly what he meant, but when he bent down, licked the water running between my breasts, and lifted me into his arms, I moaned and wrapped my thighs around his waist.

"Your voice and the sound of your laugh did that for me too," he said. "I carried it with me, and when things got bad, I'd concentrate really hard and pull up the memory. Sometimes, alone in the dark, I'd let myself feel it—that tickle in my stomach—and I'd laugh, too, like you were right there with me."

"I *was* there," I said, and I slid my arms behind his neck and pressed my lips against his. "And I dreamt about you too. I used to wake up with the sounds of us runnin' through the woods, laughin' and chasin' each other, playing at the edges of my dreams. Those were always good days."

In a rough, uncertain voice, he said, "I love you, Avery Jane. I think I always have."

I nodded, hoping the conviction of what I was about to say would give him confidence too.

"I still remember the first time I saw you, standin' in the middle of Old Fish Creek Road, drippin' lake water and wearin' nothin' but your little blue boxer shorts after you and your brothers had gone swimmin'. I was four years old. You were five, and I've loved you every day since."

"YOU'RE BEAUTIFUL," Dixon said.

Running his finger below my collarbone, he traced the thin line of my dress's black spaghetti strap. Date night had finally arrived, and I felt relaxed, ready, and proud to be on his arm.

A week had passed in a sex-fueled haze. When I imagined sex with Dixon, I really had underestimated him. The man was insatiable and *so* giving.

But we'd spent even more time reminiscing about our childhood and talking about what the future might hold for us both. He talked a lot about Stu and his hopes for their future too. Which always led back to sex because that hope was just so damn beautiful when it showed in his eyes. I couldn't help but kiss him.

Just like now. He dipped his finger below my dress's thin cotton fabric and let his skin slide over the swell of my breast slowly. My chest rose and fell rapidly as my breath sped.

Turning me a little, he checked out my ass, let out an appreciative "hmm," then ran his hand down my hip and bunched the fabric in his fist. "I can't wait to feel you pressed up against me later in this dress."

"You're not so bad yourself," I said, admiring the new navy button-down he'd bought in town and his fresh Wranglers. The way he fit into them gifted me with the most perfect view of his ass, other than when it was bare.

"You sure?" he asked, looking down at himself. "I haven't bought brand-new clothes in a while. You look elegant, and I look like any other ranch hand, dressed for supper."

"You're perfect," I replied when he lifted his eyes back to mine. "And if jeans are what you're comfortable in, then they're the sexiest pants on the planet."

"You have a happy answer for everything, don't you? You're diabolically positive."

I shrugged, grabbed my purse, then hooked my arm through his.

He chuckled. "C'mon, baby girl. Let's go get us some dinner."

"I'm not four, Dixon. You can't call me baby girl anymore."

Pressing me against the wall with one large hand, he locked my door with the other, smirked, then tucked his mouth into the crook of my neck. "Who says? I didn't mean it like I said it when we were kids."

He breathed me in and moaned, and the vibration of his voice on my skin made me wet. I rubbed my legs together while he licked me from collarbone to ear.

When he spoke again, his voice was deliciously low, rasping, and wanting. "I meant it like, 'c'mon, *baby girl*, spread those pretty thighs wide for me so I can make you come before I feed you.'"

I moaned, too, and my legs parted just like he'd said. His hand traced the curve of my hip, and he lifted my dress by its hem. Raising it above my waist, his hand disappeared beneath my lacy underwear, and he licked his lips and bit them. He rubbed rigid fingers between my pussy lips, smearing arousal over my clit and studying my face as he fingered me. Heat flushed my cheeks and I gasped.

"D-didn't you say you made a reservation at Paulo's?" I mumbled, nearly lost to the sensations his pumping hand between my legs caused.

"We can be a few minutes late," he breathed. "Isn't that what life's all about? Livin' every moment to the fullest?"

"You're makin' me insane," I panted and thrust against his hand, chasing euphoria.

"No, ma'am. It's you makin' me wild right now in this dress. Don't blame me. It's all your fault." He pumped harder, and I groaned and fumbled with his fly, trying to tug the zipper down, but an orgasm rushed out from deep inside me. My toes curled, scraping against the soles of my sandals. My hands dropped lax at my sides, and I began to slide down the wall.

Dixon seized the opportunity to kiss me, holding me up, and my dress strap slid down my arm. My breast slipped out because in my attempt to be sexy for him, I'd chosen not to wear a bra.

"Fuck. I want inside you so bad right now, but I don't have a condom. I've been too greedy for you, and we used 'em all up."

My purse had fallen to my feet sometime between when he pushed me against the wall and when he made me come, but I nodded to it. "I do. In there, but if you want to fuck me bare, you can."

He moaned again, pressing his forehead to mine.

"I take birth control because I get really bad period cramps, and the medication helps with that."

"I won't get you pregnant?"

I shook my head. "It's as effective as a condom, and I've never had unprotected sex with anyone. Do you trust me?"

"I do," he said as he lifted me, pressing my back to the wall again. "But do you trust me the same? There hasn't been anyone since Kel, and I got tested at a free clinic in Oregon before I came home. I didn't wanna bring any kind of sickness around Stu, but I wouldn't blame you if—"

"I trust you."

My legs slipped around his hips. I reached between us, unzipped his jeans, and pulled his cock free from his boxers. Hard, hot skin met wet and soft, and as he slid inside me, he cursed.

"Goddamn, AJ. It's never felt like this. Nothin's ever felt this good when I wasn't high."

"It's you and me," I whispered. "We fit together because we were meant for each other."

He didn't reply. He couldn't because he was focused on the slide of his tongue in my mouth and the glide of his cock between my legs. He fucked me like he existed for that purpose alone, snapping his hips with every slow, languid pump inside me.

I was mindless, listening to the rough sound of his breath in my ear, the quiet thud from my elbow bumping the wall, and the scuffling of clothes over skin. All of it drove us higher, until it felt like all we were was a singular pursuit of release.

My body gripped his aggressively with every grunt and

rasp of his breath, and my hands sought his bare skin wildly. I dug my fingernails into the backs of his arms below his shirt sleeves, trying desperately to pull him closer, so close he could crawl beneath my skin.

I begged him, "Come inside. Please, Dixon. Make me come."

His hands slid over my ass cheeks, and he squeezed while he took my mouth again. I bit his lip hard enough when I came to make him hiss and kiss me deeper.

"*Please*."

My last plea drew his eyes to mine, and he gazed into them and called out when he came. Mine fell shut. My body held his in safety as he released inside me.

"Damn, baby girl," he whispered, breathless. "You ain't as innocent as you make out to be."

With one eyebrow arched, I shook my head slowly.

"We better go or else my hunger for food's gonna turn into hunger for *you*, and we'll never leave this house."

"Doesn't sound like a bad thing to me."

"Maybe not, but I think your stomach begs to differ."

My stomach rumbled loudly, proving him right, and I flashed him a pouting face, but when he kissed my cheeks, I sighed and melted into him.

He had also been right when he said I was a dreamer, but he'd just made every dream I'd ever had come true because, when his lips were on me and he was inside me with nothing between us, it was like he'd never left.

Like he'd stayed right here in Wisper with me, where he'd always belonged.

CHAPTER THIRTY-THREE

DIXON

DINNER WAS A DREAM STATE.

I'd never felt so normal, like any other confident, shit-together man.

It seemed funny, but being with AJ, laughing and flirting, catching each other in long, wanting glances and tangling our feet beneath the table at the Italian restaurant on Main Street in downtown Wisper, with the whole town noticing, made me feel more like a father than I had two hours before.

AJ gave me the confidence to believe I could do it. I could be a dad. I could hold down two jobs, save some cash in a bank account, and become a somewhat upstanding citizen of the world.

I barely remembered the pasta primavera I'd eaten, and by the time we walked out of Paulo's, bellies full and minds on getting back to AJ's place, I practically skipped to my car parked out back, wondering if Stu liked Italian. He probably did. He seemed to like anything, as long as it was edible.

I texted Bax and asked if Stu was still awake. He texted back that, no, Stu had a long day at school and then Merv helped him with schoolwork, which made him cranky, so he passed out right after dinner. Bax said if I wanted to talk to him, I could call Stu on Bea's phone when I got up in the morning, so that was my plan.

Both Bax and Bea seemed open to my being in Stu's life. Bea had even brought him to the community center yesterday while I worked, and I let him beat me at air hockey. He shared my lunch with me while Bea ran an errand in town, and all the other employees fawned over him, told us how much we look alike, and then Stu and I colored with some of the day care kids.

It was perfect, like we were any other father and son.

AJ's mom had called while we ate. She left a message about AJ's website and something about an "also-bought plug-in" going haywire. I told AJ to call back while I went to start my car; I still hadn't fixed the air conditioning, so I rolled down the windows and let cooler air fill it up. The day had been sweltering, the sun shining down hard with not a cloud in sight, but night brought a light breeze and a small reprieve from summer's relentless heat.

I couldn't remember ever wishing for a season, but now I imagined the yellows and golds of the trees in fall and the silkiness of cool autumn air in the Tetons, and I looked forward to it like Christmas break from school when I was a kid. I could see it in my mind—crisp September mornings spent on Lee Lake with Stu, fishing and telling stories beneath a canopy of pines and the stiff mountain cliffs beyond holding us in their embrace.

I wondered if I'd get to go trick-or-treating with him. I'd never wanted anything more than seeing my kid dressed up as some colorful character from the stories in his head. Couldn't wait to feel the excitement rumbling around him, that jittery squall in his little heart that all kids felt before a night out on the streets of downtown, when the only acceptable outcome was a pillow case filled to the brim with free sugar.

My date, however, was a very close second in her slip of a black dress and the sandals she'd worn with it, like a goddess from Greek mythology. Those strappy leather shoes showed off her perfectly polished toes and wound up the line of her leg, the one that, no matter how hard I tried not to let it, led my eyes to her knees and then inevitably, her hips. My heart would race and my dick would harden when I imagined the warm haven between them, and then I'd forget all over again what we'd been talking about.

I couldn't remember now when I rounded the side of Paulo's and saw—

"Get your fuckin' hands off her!" I rushed to AJ, pinned up against the building by the man who I'd just seen at a courthouse in Jackson. The same guy who'd sworn to a judge he'd leave AJ alone.

My steps faltered when Cody Mahone's low man, Justin, grabbed me from behind, laughing and breathing on my neck, like some deranged marauder. I knew it was him because I could smell the stench of Camels on his breath and wafting off his shirt.

Before I could get a handful of his face and turn his jump-scare around, he pinned my arms behind my back and tripped me with a swipe of his boot in front of my feet. When he released my arms, I fell forward and my face hit gravel.

And that was when my old friend, rage, came out to dance.

Like a movie playing at half speed, I looked up to see Cody's knee between AJ's legs. He slapped her face with an open hand, and I saw red.

He'd been drinking—I recognized the posture, the way his movements stumbled and rolled—and he pointed his finger in her face, spitting crude obscenities at her. His intoxication was plain to see as he swayed a bit with each abusive move he made, but he had enough wherewithal to keep AJ right where he wanted her.

As I tried to get up, pressure on my back held me down, and I felt Justin's knees crushing my rib cage. He thought he'd gotten the drop on me, but he hadn't yet met the *real* me.

The town had come alive with talk when I walked back into it: *Dixon Lee is nothin' but trouble. He's a hooligan. A scrapper. He's been nothin' but a dark stain on this town since the day he was born.* I'd heard it all.

I tried not to let the gossip get to me, but the people of Wisper weren't wrong, and I was about to prove it to them.

Once I'd maneuvered my arms underneath my chest and pushed up, Justin lost his balance. He tumbled off me, and I sprang to my feet. Leaning over him, I laughed at the surprised look on his face. He scrambled to his feet, too, and I backed up, but I grabbed him by his T-shirt and hit him so fucking hard with my closed fist and sharp knuckles to his soft temple that he crumpled like a sack of potatoes and passed right out.

One down.

A ringing in my ears drowned out whatever Cody was spitting at AJ, like a hissing cobra, but I didn't really need to hear him to know that the way he was touching her was unwelcome and painful.

He grabbed a fistful of AJ's hair and jabbed his pointing finger into her cheek. I saw the indent it made on her skin and watched him press his mouth next to it.

AJ wouldn't look at me. She couldn't see anything because she'd lowered her eyes to the ground. She didn't want to challenge him and make things worse.

I, on the other hand, had every intention of fucking his shit up.

My ears let up for just a second, the ringing quieting and trying to subside. Maybe it was my body's way of trying to ease the anger so I'd change my course, and maybe this time I wouldn't make the stupid choice.

Unfortunately, the silence only lasted long enough for me to hear Cody's insipid voice when he said, "You stupid cunt. Fuckin' whore, embarrassin' me like that in front of my mother?"

What came next was a slur and a blur of sound and motion.

I had no clue how Cody ended up beneath me, could barely remember dragging him away from AJ by his hair, but I straddled him and pinned him with my legs, and I just kept punching.

Like the universe had given me the thing I needed to release all the bad shit I'd been feeling.

All the jealousy I felt about Bax getting to hear my son call him "Daddy" poured out of me. The anger I felt at myself, at Bax, and even Brand and Abey for simply being who they were, for being so fucking lucky they knew who their father was, even though he had been the worst father in the world.

All of it propelled me to hit this fucker harder.

Somewhere in the back of my mind, I knew I should've stopped. If my sister had to arrest me and I ended up in court, I could land in jail again. No one would be surprised. And this time, I didn't even have the excuse of being high.

I didn't deserve Stuart, but after this beating, it would be a final thing.

But this man and the way he spoke to this woman—the

beautiful, loyal, tenderhearted woman I loved down to the scars on my soul… He didn't have the fucking right.

Reason had left the building.

My weight held the asshole to the ground beneath us. He clawed at me, scratched and dug his fingers into my skin to try to stop me as my fist made contact with his nose again and again, but the rage wouldn't let me really feel the pain. I felt the bridge of his nose fracture, though, when my knuckle crunched it, but it didn't stop me.

I saw Merv's face front and center in my mind, her lies like a symphony swirling around her. The pain they caused me was the sour, out-of-tune note that ruined it all and made the music suck.

But I also saw her beautiful, shining smile I still remembered from childhood, and I watched as Noah Lee berated her and demeaned her. He flat-out fucking verbally abused her in front of her kids. And he hit her. She tried to hide it from us, but I knew. I'd always known.

This jackoff, this Cody fucking Mahone, represented the hateful man I'd grown up with. And then, in my mind's eye, he *became* the man I despised, the father I'd had to mourn when he was still alive. Cody became the wife beater, the shit-talking dick who'd hurt my mama. Who'd hurt my sister. Who'd hurt me.

If he could have, Noah would've made me cease to exist so he wouldn't have had to feel like a failure whose wife found the love and care she needed in another man.

Whoever the fuck that was.

Cody Mahone had earned the misfortune of representing the one person who it seemed still had the power to make me insane.

But deep inside, I knew Cody wasn't Noah.

Finally, the truth of that realization hit me head on, the

way Cody had tried to but hadn't quite managed, because I was bigger and angrier than his lazy ass had ever been, and I'd vowed long ago never to allow another man to beat me down.

The world around me began to pulse. Reality shimmered around the edges of my rage, and Stu's sweet voice echoed in my head:

"You're my dad, aren't you?"

"Can I call you Deedee? Yeah, D.D. for Daddy Dixon."

"I love you, and I don't care if you're my uncle or my dad."

Tears streamed down my face. I tried to tell myself it was the release of all the diseased thoughts in my head making me cry, but the truth was that it was acceptance.

I accepted that this was my life. That Noah was dead and gone and I'd never get to face him and tell him what a sorry sack of shit he was, and that he hadn't deserved my brothers and sister. He hadn't deserved our mama. And that as of this moment, he had no power over me anymore. I wasn't afraid of him.

I had to accept that I couldn't go back. I would never get the first five years of Stu's life back. And maybe I didn't deserve them in the first place. Maybe Bax was right from the start—Stu didn't belong to me. Maybe he never had. Maybe Stuart Lee was a gift to the world that I had only been authorized to bring into it, but after that, I was shit out of luck.

As I came back to myself, my arm became heavier and heavier, and my grip on Cody's shirt loosened. He begged me to stop hitting him while the small crowd that had formed around us, all the people who moments before had been peacefully enjoying their fancy pasta, began to back away from my anger, like it was a monster all its own, booming like thunder, deafening the world and justice and goodness.

The soft sound of AJ's voice cut through the anger, like a hot knife and my heart had been made of butter. I fell back on my ass in the gravel as she knelt beside me, and Cody scrambled to his feet.

"Dixon." Tentatively, AJ wiped my tears away with gentle fingers, looking in my eyes for any signs my monster would come back. But there were none. The monster had just performed his last show. All that remained where he'd lived my whole life was a tiredness I couldn't quite describe and an emptiness now ready to be filled with other things.

"It's okay now," AJ whispered, holding my face, calming me with soft caresses of her thumbs over my cheekbones.

Cody wiped at the blood flowing out of his nose with the back of his hand and aimed his vitriol at me. "I'm gonna sue you so fuckin' hard, your goddamn great grandkids will be poor. And *you*," he spat at AJ, "say goodbye to that hole in the wall you call a store. It's mine now. I'm gonna own it when this is all said and done, and then I'll turn your fucking Main Street into my personal storage garage." Embarrassed, he looked around at the wary faces in the crowd, his eyes jumping from one onlooker to the next. "You're all just a bunch of ignorant hicks!"

"Kiss my ass, Cody," AJ said. She stood, and he pointed his finger in her face again, but something told me I didn't need to worry about her being afraid of him anymore.

"You don't talk to me like that, Avery. After everything I've given you, this is how you speak to me?"

AJ laughed, reached up and wrapped her hand around his still pointing finger, and twisted it. He yelped and curved his body away from the pain. But AJ was quick. She used his momentum to spin him, and then she released his finger and pushed so hard with her dainty sandal in the middle of his back that he stumbled forward, right into my sister-in-law's waiting arms.

Dressed in her uniform with her gun slung high on her thigh, Roxi towered over him as he cowed to the pain. I hadn't noticed her before the fight, but maybe she'd been at the station down the street and heard the ruckus. She spun him, once again aiming Cody's indignant sneer at AJ, and slapped cuffs on his wrists behind his back a little harder than was probably necessary.

"You're goin' to jail, Cody," AJ shouted as she righted her pretty dress and swiped her hand over her beautiful, soft blond hair. The douchebag had messed it up, and it made me want to start up on him all over again. But AJ looked even more radiant as she stood her ground and found her fight. "Nobody believes your bluster and lies. And nobody in this town gives a shit who your mommy and daddy are."

Quietly and without lights, an ambulance pulled into the parking lot. A man and a woman climbed out and moved Justin onto a stretcher, but he came to as they tried to load him into their rig. He wiggled and argued and finally slid off the stretcher, grabbing his phone from his back pocket. He was on that thing faster than a black hare in snow, and I could just imagine who he was calling.

Cody laughed maniacally. He probably had a good inkling about who his cousin was calling too. Blood spurted from his right nostril as he focused his icy stare back on AJ. "You're gonna regret this. You mark my words, bitch."

"Honey, the day I dumped your sorry ass was the happiest of my life, and the memory of you bein' hauled off to jail will continue to bring me joy until the day I die. Now g'on. Git. Nobody wants you here."

CHAPTER THIRTY-FOUR

AVERY JANE

GRAN AND MAMA showed up at the station five minutes after Abey reluctantly led her brother into a cell in the back room. There were only two cells in there, so for a short time, until Cody's lawyers or his parents showed up, he and Dixon had to face each other. Fortunately, another deputy, Frank Sims, was back there with them to stand guard.

As far as I could tell, Dixon hadn't said a word, but Cody could be heard all the way to the street, still puffing his chest about retribution and making threats against Dixon's family.

Mama ordered me to tell her what happened, but all I could think about was Dixon.

"Is Dixon okay, Abey?" I asked while she removed her tool belt and gun and locked them in a desk drawer in the main room of the station. The receptionist, Shelley, sat behind her computer screen, clearly listening, but she pretended to type.

"Physically," Abey said, "yes. He'll be fine."

"And e-emotionally?"

She looked up at me, exhaustion playing at the edges of her eyes. "I don't know."

The weariness in her voice made me feel like screaming. This was a setback for her family. And how would Dixon handle it? Jail and possibly court?

Would this be the thing that led him back into his addiction? Would the fight with Cody derail his confidence, his happiness, his safety? Was it all my fault?

Had he just lost his chance to make things right with Stuart?

Maybe I should have left Dixon alone. I'd practically pushed him into loving me, and now, had I ruined the rest of his life?

Deputy Roxi had been trying to calm my mama down and get her to sit and at least attempt to relax, but she had probably already decided that wasn't going to fly.

"He'll be okay," Roxi said as she stood next to me and patted my shoulder softly.

"I don't know about that," Abey mumbled. "Mr. Mahone hasn't shut up about pressin' charges."

"But he attacked me! He violated the restraining order. And Justin came at Dixon from behind and surprised him. That's gotta count for somethin', right?"

"You mean the guy who was completely unconscious when Roxi showed up?" Abey challenged.

"Yeah, he's Cody's cousin."

Abey closed her eyes and shook her head. "It does count," she said. "And Cody will do some time for disobeyin' the restraining order, but that doesn't stop him or his family from pressin' civil charges against Dixon. And I'm not sure you and I are talkin' about the same fight, because the one my deputy just described to me was the definition of excessive force. Dixon could've stopped after the first punch. But he didn't, and I'm pretty sure Mr. Mahone's nose is broken, at the very least."

The sound of my voice was steady, but it came out of me wrapped in barbed wire. "He deserved worse."

"That may be," Abey said, "but it's not Dixon's job to deliver justice."

"Abey." I grabbed her arm. "Can I take him home? Please?"

She laughed mirthlessly and shook me off. "Home? Where is that? He won't *come* home. The boarding house? No offense to Mrs. Ellison, but that ain't his home. It's not anybody's besides Mrs. Ellison's."

"I meant *my* house."

"Your house isn't Dixon's home either, Avery Jane. What? Did you expect that you'd just crook your finger and everything would be alright? He's an addict. He's somebody's father. He can't play house with you just so you can relive your glory days."

The sheriff's comment was a blow. Was that what I'd been doing—playing house?

Mama jumped to my defense. "That was uncalled for, Sheriff Lee. Avery has loved that boy since the first day they met. She wants what's best for him."

Eyes firmly on mine, Abey said, "I'm sorry. It was uncalled for, but is your mama right? You want what's best for Dixon?"

I nodded. "Yes. It's all I want for him."

"Even if it means him walkin' away from you?"

ABEY FINALLY LET me back to see her brother, and when I found him locked behind bars, he wouldn't look at me. He sat bent over, with his elbows on his knees and his head hung.

His hair lay loose and tangled over broad shoulders rising and falling slowly with every breath he took.

Deputy Sims stepped back and pressed himself into the corner of the room to give me space, but the guy was huge. Besides, there was no way Dixon and I could have any privacy with Cody right there, still spouting bullshit.

But I couldn't let Cody deter me. Not anymore.

I needed to look in Dixon's eyes. I needed to see for myself that he was okay.

"Tweedledum?" I said softly, but Dixon didn't move.

Cody snorted, then caught the blood seeping from his nose with the neck of his shirt. He tried to swallow but decided instead to spit the blood in his mouth on the floor. "That's your pet name for your boyfriend? Fitting. He is dumb. It was the dumbest fuckin' thing he's ever done, comin' at me like he did. Layin' hands. I'm gonna sue him for every penny he's got."

He lifted his head toward the ceiling, trying to pinch the bridge of his nose to stem the flow, but he winced at the pain.

Finally, Dixon huffed a laugh. "Go for it, asshole. After dinner tonight and my piece-of-shit car, I've got less than two grand to my name. You've probably got more in your change jar in your bedroom at your mommy's house."

Cody's eyes narrowed. "You may be destitute, but I know who your brother is, and he's got plenty of money. I also know about Spitfire Ranch, and I'll be runnin' it by the time we're through."

Dixon didn't respond. He looked up at me through the cell door. "You okay?"

Stepping closer, I nodded and smiled pathetically. I hoped it conveyed how utterly sorry I was that I'd gotten him into this mess.

He stood and approached the door too. "Your dress," he

said, pointing to the strap that had been ripped in my struggle with Cody. Roxi had given me a safety pin to fix it so I wasn't flashing the whole town, but dirt and dust covered the material and made it look gray. "It's ruined."

"Serves you right," Cody sneered. "Only whores dress the way you did tonight."

Dixon's hands balled into fists, but Deputy Sims beat him to the punch. He yanked the Billy club out of its holster on his belt and slapped it against Cody's cell bars. The sound of wood hitting metal reverberated around the small room loud enough to make me cringe. "Sit down and shut your mouth," the deputy ordered, then stuffed a towel through the space between two bars for Cody's nose.

"I can fix it," I told Dixon, ignoring Cody completely as he all but fell onto the rickety cot in his cell. He seemed a little too scared of Deputy Sims to reach for the towel on the floor.

"Good," Dixon said. "I like that dress."

The radio on Deputy Sims's shoulder coughed with static, and then we heard Roxi telling him to bring Cody out. "His ride's here to take him to County. He'll be spendin' the night in their presidential suite after a stop at the hospital to crack that broken nose back into place."

Cody groaned, and I smiled. He deserved jail. No doubt his lawyers and his family would be working overtime to set him free, but at least for tonight, he'd have to live with what he'd done.

I kept the smile on my face while Deputy Sims opened the cell door and dragged Cody out by the neck of his shirt. "Have fun," I said unapologetically, and I winked as Frank cuffed him again.

Cody had nothing more to say to me, and as soon as they had gone, Dixon's eyes met mine through the bars.

"I'm sorry," he said.

"You have nothin' to apologize for. *I'm* sorry. Sorry I got you into this mess. Are you okay?"

"I… I'll be fine," he said, but he cast his eyes to the floor.

"Your hands." I pointed to his knuckles, bruised already and still covered in Cody's dried blood.

Dixon held them up and looked at them, but then he swiped them over his jeans, trying to brush the dark red crust off. "I dunno what this means for me. Nothin' good, that's for damn sure."

"It wasn't your fault. You didn't do anything—"

"I didn't do anything *wrong*?" he argued. "Do you live in some kinda la-la land so filled with hearts and flowers that you can't see out? I *beat* that man tonight. I could've beaten him to death."

"But you didn't."

"In the eyes of the law, I'm not sure how much that matters."

"You were protectin' me."

"God," he breathed, "did you see my sister's face? I let her down. I've let them all down. And Stu? I'll be lucky if Bax lets him so much as say my name after this."

"Don't say that. I'll explain it to Bax, to all of them. They'll understand."

"What exactly will they understand, Avery Jane? That I had a choice tonight, and once again, I chose wrong? That instead of choosin' my family—*my son*—I chose violence? I chose to let my demons out. I chose the easy way out."

"Dixon, you didn't—"

"Goddammit, Avery. Stop! You're doin' it again, and I can't stomach you tryin' to make up excuses to forgive me. I need you to go. I'm sorry, but I need to think this through, and I can't do that with you here."

An invisible wall came slamming down between us, the same one I still recognized from high school that Dixon used to wield like a shield, and it cut our connection right down the middle. “Dixon?”

“Please, AJ? Please just let me be?” His hands gripped the cell’s bars, and I slid mine over his, ignoring the dried blood and dirt.

“I’ll go,” I said, “because you asked me to, but don’t you dare think I’m givin’ up on you.”

CHAPTER THIRTY-FIVE

DIXON

HOURS PASSED. It had to be close to one in the morning, and Abey still hadn't come to talk to me.

Maybe she had nothing to say. Maybe I'd finally pushed even her away. I hadn't meant to, but I'd put my sister in the shittiest position, and now she'd be faced with having to choose her job over her family. And it would kill her.

Lying on the floor, staring at a dirty ceiling while normal people went on with their normal lives ten feet away from me was nothing new. Being close enough to see and smell the normalcy, hear the humdrum of it all, but not close enough to touch it could be maddening.

I'd had a short taste of that normalcy, and for the first time in my life, I'd loved every goddamn second.

Fuck it.

Maybe I hadn't been meant for "normal."

Maybe Merv's lies were bigger than even I could've imagined. Maybe my real father really had been a magic man, a sorcerer, or an elven prince, and with his blood running through my veins, what humans experienced as "normal" had grown into a sickness inside me.

Maybe I'd never been meant to fit in.

But daydreams and made-up bullshit didn't include Stu. How could he fit into my stories? He was real and mortal, and he needed real love and connection, not faeries and elves.

AJ too. And it hit me: She was where I had always belonged. She owned my heart; tonight had proved it, and no matter where she was, there would always be a place for me with her.

I pushed her away because of the question pounding into the back of my skull every minute of every goddamn day, the one I feared would always loom over my head:

Did I deserve it? Did I deserve either of them?

Voices in the hallway stopped my mind from running away with itself, and I sat up and braced for impact as they came closer.

When the door finally creaked open and Bax walked in, I stood, feeling more alone than I ever had in my life. My brother didn't say anything, but he watched as I hid my still-bloody hands in my pockets.

"Hey, little brother," he said, "looks like you've had an eventful night, but we came to spring you."

"We?" I asked as two men unknown to me followed after Bax, and then Brand crowded into the room behind them.

"Brand, Abey, and me," Bax said. "Merv doesn't know about this yet. I'm sure the rumor mill will clue her in by mornin', but for now you'll stay with Brand. Roxi's already made up their couch for you."

"This is Brent Harbour," Brand said, motioning to the younger of the two men, and then he nodded at the older guy. "And this is Gentry Vicks. Brent's local, from Jackson, and Gentry's a criminal attorney. I'm sorry it took so long, but they needed some time to familiarize themselves with what happened and with yours and Mahone's histories."

Stunned, I asked, "You hired lawyers for me?" Where was the judgment? Where were the "I told you so" glances between my brothers?

Where was the disappointment?

"'Course we did," Bax said, like it meant nothing. But it was everything.

"But what about… I mean, I broke the law. I-I hit that man. I'm guilty. And what about Stu?"

"What about him?" Bax said. "He's five. He doesn't need to know anything about tonight."

"But you'll still let me see him?" I didn't want to sound like I was begging, but I was and it sounded exactly like that. "You're not gonna keep me away?"

Bax stepped closer to my cage and reached his hand between the bars, like he wanted to reach out to me, but then he lowered it and let it rest on the metal. "You're his dad, ain't you?"

"Yeah, but—"

"And someday, when he's older and he asks, you can tell him that you protected a woman from her abuser. What's so bad about that?"

"The DA isn't issuing charges," Brand said. "Abey's already spoken to the judge. There's no bail to post. If anything comes of what happened tonight, it will be civil, and trust when I tell you this, brother: I have more money than Mr. Mahone could even dream of. He won't win.

"Besides," he said, clapping the younger guy on his back, "Brent here tells me that Cody Mahone has bigger fish to fry. Apparently, he got some young woman pregnant. She used to work for his mother and developed a little crush on that moron, so they'll be busy dealin' with that mess. The woman is over eighteen, but barely, and she and her parents are goin' after the Mahones in court for all kinds of things. What happened tonight will blow over, but if it doesn't, we've got you covered."

I hadn't realized I'd begun to cry, not even when I fell to the floor on my ass. It took Abey pushing past all the men standing outside my cell. She unlocked the door and crouched in front of me, the keys hooked to her belt loop tinkling like a faerie's wings. I looked up at her, and she took hold of my hands.

"I've been on the phone all night with Judge Petersen and others. I'm sorry I left you alone in here, but I've needed time to work this out ethically. But that's what we did. You're free to go.

"And look, I know Brand wants you to stay at his house, but just sayin', Devo and I have a couch too. In fact, we have a guest room, and the bed in there is like sleepin' on a cloud."

She grinned, and I threw my arms around my baby sister and held on tight.

WHEN I STEPPED outside the station, my hands still damp from scrubbing them in the restroom sink, the warm night air on my skin sent a blast of calm through me, but it was the woman standing with her back to me, holding a large, floral tote bag and texting on her phone, that eased my worried heart.

Bax, Brand, Abey, and the lawyers moved further down the sidewalk to talk and give me a minute, so I walked up behind AJ, hoping she hadn't heard my approach.

"Avery Jane Harlowe," I said sternly, "I thought you were goin' home."

She turned, but she didn't move. She looked unsure. And she had good reason.

"I'm sorry," I said. "I didn't mean to scare you tonight."

Carefully, she said, "Cody deserved every punch. What scared me was you pushin' me away."

Yeah, it scared me too.

"My only excuse is that I'm not used to relyin' on other people. For a long time, it's just been me. I thought I had to stay away from the people I love. I doubt every decision I make and every single thing I do, and I've been so worried to hurt people by my actions and decisions. I didn't wanna hurt you."

She dropped the phone and bag. Something soft but heavy inside thunked on the sidewalk, and AJ rushed to me. Her body slammed into mine, and my arms wrapped around her like they'd done it a million times.

Into my shirt, she mumbled, "I couldn't leave you in there alone."

"I'm filthy," I said, trying to put some distance between us so she wouldn't get dirty too. She'd showered and changed; the ruined dress was long gone, and in its place were jeans and a white José's Diner long-sleeved Tee. Her hair lay shiny and clean, and it flowed behind her like a waving curtain of silk.

"I don't care. Now hug me properly, and then you can change. I did go home, but it took me less than five minutes to know that *you* are my home. So instead of sittin' there and freakin' out, I hopped in the shower, washed that asshole's disgusting cooties off me, got dressed, and then banged on Mr. Henly's door until he opened up his store so I could get you some new clothes."

Pulling her close again, I rested my chin on the top of her head. I breathed in her wildflower scent and wondered if it was some kind of laundry detergent she used. But no. It was just AJ.

"You did that for me?"

"'Course I did," she said. "Did you think I'd just leave and never speak to you again? What you did tonight—Maybe you don't see it the same way, but you stood up for me. You fought for me. You could've walked away. You probably should have—you have Stuart to think about now—but you didn't."

"I could never. I love you."

Pushing up on her toes, she untangled her arms beneath mine and wrapped them around my neck, placing a sweet kiss on my lips that lingered there like magic all its own. The look in her eyes was unguarded and open, and they lit up like moonlight when she smiled.

"I know you do. I love you too, so don't you ever tell me to go away again. Wherever you are is where I wanna be, so let's get you dressed, and then your sister mentioned a big ol' bed at her house with our names written all over it."

"They don't need to do that. I can stay at my place. Cody's in jail. I'm not worried about him comin' back for us. Or I could stay with you… if you're cool with that."

"I'm very cool with that," she said, "but I think your family wants you close. They've been really worried about you. It took Deputy Sims practically puttin' Bax in a choke-hold to stop him from goin' after Cody when they were shovin' the prick in the back of none other than big, bad County Sheriff Michaels's cruiser for his personal escort to jail."

"Really?"

"Yeah, and Bax told me later that everybody knows the Mahone Ranch and that nobody likes or trusts them. If the law doesn't deal Cody some justice, you might have to worry about your brother roundin' up a bunch of cowboys and startin' a posse to go after that idiot."

I laughed. I could picture it perfectly and it filled me up with pride and hope.

"Okay," I said, pulling my fingers through soft strands of her hair, "but tomorrow, there's a pretty big conversation I need to have with my mama. Will you be there?"

"Yes, I will. Just like I want you to be there when I confront my dad. I've decided to try to find him. There's some things I need to say to him."

I kissed her and mumbled against her lips, "Look at us, doin' the healthy shit."

"For you and me," she promised, "and for Stu, I'd do anything."

OPENING my eyes the next morning, the quiet hum of my sister's air conditioner tried to lull me right back to sleep. I stretched and felt every sore muscle and my scraped-up knuckles, and the reality of last night woke my ass right up.

I sat, and the blanket warming AJ's still sleeping body pooled around my hips.

It seemed odd to me that the sun could be so bright and happy, shining in Abey's guest room window, when things last night had been so dark.

But that was life—lights and darks, and sometimes they ran together, mixing and moving within each other, creating numberless colors for us to exist in.

Waking up next to such sweet, unconditional love didn't feel wrong this time. AJ was all those colors mixed up in one flawed and dynamic woman. With her leg tangled between mine, her soft snore rumbling beneath the covers, and her hair spilled over her pillow like pale, yellow sunlight, I felt redeemed and forgiven and… *home*.

The scars she'd said she didn't care about, and the new ones probably forming on my face from last night, felt less glaring than they had yesterday.

I touched my cheek, expecting to find scabs or tears in the skin from having it shoved into gravel, but there was nothing. Just a little puffiness.

Rising from the bed carefully, I searched the room for some kind of reflective surface and found a vintage cheval mirror in the corner. That had to be Devo's style. My sister had always been a ten-dollar-Walmart-mirror kind of girl.

Stepping closer, I squinted, trying to see new imperfections, but all I could find were two thin, tiny scratches over my cheek bone. And the old scars on my face and arms seemed duller and less pronounced. Maybe AJ was right, and my scars had already started to forget me.

At first, I thought, *It has to be a trick of the light,* but as I inspected myself, my eyes following the story of addiction written in lines, mars, and marks on my skin, and the two slices from a boot knife I'd received as payment for stealing someone else's dope, I realized they'd faded over time, and they seemed to fade even more right before my eyes because I wasn't letting them lead.

The angry, sorrowful, shamed part of my life was over. I could hold my head high. I could allow myself to want good things, maybe even expect—

Abey's front door closed in the living room, and I heard Bax's voice and then Stu's.

"He awake yet?" Bax said.

"Where's Deedee?"

"They're still sleepin'," Abey whispered. "Shh. Give him a few more minutes, okay, Stu? Deedee's tired this mornin'."

"Okay," my son whispered back to his aunt, but then Devo broke the hush.

The door slammed closed this time. "Babe! Wait till you see the monster tomatoes I just harvested for breakfast. They're huge! And we've got cucumbers and green peppers. I picked spinach, too, for Roxi's frittatas. She and Brand just got here. They're outside, talkin' to Merv."

"Devo!" Abey yelled in a whisper. "Dixon and Avery Jane are still asleep. Can you talk a little louder?"

"Oh shit. Sorry."

"Aunt Devo said 'shit,'" Stu informed everyone, and then the door opened and closed again, and Athena chimed in.

"Y'all got orange juice? I need vitamin C. Shaylene says it's good for my skin."

Good things.

Yeah, maybe I could get used to them.

"In the fridge," Abey replied.

The bedcovers rustled, and then AJ's voice washed over me like a caress.

"Whatcha doin'?" she asked, and I turned to see her sleepy hazel eyes focused on me.

"Nothin'. Just wakin' up." I stepped back to the bed and slid in beside her. I pulled her close, loving how strands of her hair tickled my chest when she rested her head there.

"Sounds like your entire family's out there."

Suddenly, the low boom of Rye's voice could be heard louder than all the rest.

"I get this is a family thing," he said, "but can a cowboy snag a few pieces of that bacon before a long day?"

"You *are* family, dumbass," Bax replied, and as expected, Stu reported the curse.

"Daddy said 'ass.'"

"You up for it?" I asked AJ.

Looking up at me, love and loyalty shining in her eyes,

she vowed, "Name the place and time, Tweedledum, and I got your back."

"I think we need new nicknames."

"What? Why?"

"'Cause nobody ever told me how sexy Tweedledee could be." I leaned down, and she lifted her face to mine for a kiss. I nipped her bottom lip for good measure too. "It feels mildly inappropriate since they're cartoon characters meant for kids *and* they're brothers."

"No," she said with mock indignation. "I like our nicknames. Besides, do kids these days even know who Tweedledee and Tweedledum are?"

"You might have a point."

Reaching for my hand, she threaded her fingers between mine. "Repeat after me," she said. "'Yes, darling, you're right.' And now, memorize those four words. You're gonna need 'em."

"Yes, darlin', you're right," I said, and I stole another kiss. "Today's the day, AJ. I'm gonna sit down with Merv later. I want you there. Abey, Bax, and Brand will be there too. I'm thinkin' it's probably best if y'all wait outside so Merv doesn't feel ganged up on, but I could really use your support."

"You got it," she said, and she draped her arm over my stomach and squeezed me tight.

Kissing the crown of her head, I murmured, "Thanks."

The bedroom door creaked open an inch, and then Stu's head peeked through the gap.

"Deedee's awake!" he announced. "They're awake!" He threw open the door and bounded across the room, jumped onto the bed, and crawled over AJ and me. "Mornin' Deedee. Mornin' Avery. Aunt Abey's makin' bacon, and Aunt Roxi's gonna make somethin' called free-tah-tahs."

AJ giggled as Stu wiggled himself into the crook between us while I lifted my T-shirt from the foot of the bed and tugged it on. He slid his little hand behind my head when I relaxed back against the headboard, wrapping it around my shoulder.

"How you doin' this mornin', kid?" I asked, wanting so badly to kiss my son's cheek. I wasn't sure if that was okay, if he'd welcome that kind of thing from me, but I didn't have to worry too long about the answer to the question because he turned toward me and planted a wet peck on my cheek.

"Good," he said happily. "Hungry." He pulled his arm free and flipped around, then bounced on his knees, looking back and forth between AJ and me. "C'mon! Get up. You like bacon, right, Deedee?" He launched himself off the bed and ran for the door, but then stopped and spun back around. "Wait. Duh. Who doesn't like bacon?"

Bea's face appeared in the doorway after Stu sprinted away. "I'll just close this so y'all can have some privacy." She smiled and pulled the door shut.

AJ didn't speak, but she didn't need to say a word. The bright smile on her face spoke volumes about the good things coming right at us.

Her lips twisted into a sexy smirk. I smiled, too, feeling the weight of all those good things, but they didn't feel heavy anymore.

They felt perfect.

She moaned and licked her lips. "Yum. Bacon. My mouth's waterin' already."

CHAPTER THIRTY-SIX

DIXON

"TELL me the story about the magic man again, Mama."

High noon had descended over Lee Valley like an ominous Edgar Allen Poe reference. For once, the sun hid behind ragged clouds high in the sky, and cool mountain air had finally broken through the heat of late August. The promise of an even cooler September clung to the atmosphere surrounding my sister's house like a needy puppy, tongue wagging.

Merv's mouth opened and closed without a sound. I refused to look away, even though I could feel how uncomfortable she was now that it had finally come time for her to voice the truth. She knew AJ and my brothers and sister were on the front porch, listening, and that had to give her even more pause, but they swore they wouldn't dare interrupt.

Bea, Roxi, and Devo had taken Stu and Athena to the lake and promised not to bring the kids back until they'd received our all-clear.

"You used to tell me the story before bed," I pressed. "You remember?"

"'Course I do." Merv swallowed, and I heard the lump of

nerves go down her throat. "It wasn't make-believe. I think you already know that."

"I suspected, but I'd really like to hear it from you. The whole truth. No more magic or dragons or princesses."

"I'm sorry, son," she said. "But I wanted desperately for you to know you had been conceived out of love, not some common affair, but you were so little and couldn't understand the concerns of adults. A-and your daddy, he knew. He knew I'd been unfaithful, and he blamed you. But then Abey came along, and things got better… for a little while at least."

"Not for me."

"No, I expect you're right about that," she said. "But that's why I made up the story, so you'd feel special and know you were loved and cherished."

"I didn't feel cherished, Mama. I knew you loved me, but I have never understood why you let him treat me the way he did. You smothered me. You tried to micromanage me, but you never once stood up against Noah. You never fought for me. Why?"

"Self-preservation?" She frowned and looked down at her full coffee mug. "There was a time when your daddy and I were really happy," she said. "At least I thought we were. But back then, things were different than they are now. There were certain expectations for a man and wife. Bax and Brand came along, and life moved on. You know? But that's when I learned who I'd really married, when my husband finally understood the stress of havin' two little kids on a farm that didn't provide what a family needs.

"When that all caught up to us, your daddy became resentful."

"He *wasn't* my dad," I said. "You keep callin' him that, and it makes me wanna scream."

"Noah, Noah," she rushed to correct herself. "Noah

burned bridges with his family and friends, wouldn't let anyone in. Wouldn't let *me* in. It was him who demanded a big family. He was the one who wanted me barefoot and pregnant all the time, because that was what society expected of a farmer and his wife, but I think he also resented me for the burden he felt, for showin' him he was failin'.

"Abey and I have talked about this some, but I think that's why Noah reacted the way he did when he found out she was gay. He saw the way your brothers adored me, the way you used to, and he wanted that too. He was jealous of you and me.

"The look on his face the day your sister was born? It was like God had handed her to him personally, and for years he treated her like precious gold. So I think that's why he reacted the way he did the day he found her kissin' another girl in the barn. It made him feel out of control. In his eyes, it was another failure and the loss of somethin' he probably didn't think he could ever lose."

My mother's eyes met mine, and there was profound shame in them. "I was relieved when he died. What kind of a person am I that I was glad my husband was dead? But it was exhaustin', livin' with him, tryin' to dodge his bad moods, and he made himself a victim. A victim of life. If another farmer boasted about doin' good business, it made Noah angry.

"The whole world was out to get him. He was jealous and prideful, and he never took responsibility for his shortfalls. He wouldn't ask for help from anyone, and so he sat right here on this land and watched his dreams die, and he never once lifted a finger to stop it."

"You still haven't told me about my real father," I reminded her, "but we'll get to that. I wanna know why you stayed with him… with Noah."

It was the million-dollar question, and the one I'd wanted to ask since I was five years old.

"Leavin' wasn't an option, Dixon. My parents, our church—it just wasn't an option. Or I didn't think it was. It wasn't how I'd been raised. A wife was meant to stand by her husband no matter what. And besides, we had good times too. It wasn't all bad. Don't you remember?"

"No." I shook my head, a look of frustration surely showing on my face. "I remember hopin' he'd wake up one day and decide to love me, but every memory I have of that man is steeped in darkness and cruelty. His hatred and fists still haunt my dreams."

Her expression fell, and all that remained was hurt and regret, but the time to sugarcoat our past had come and gone.

"I remember his anger and his resentment, Mama, which leads me right back to the heart of the matter. Who is my *real* father?"

She didn't move. Didn't speak. She just looked at me, maybe seeing my birth father's face? I wasn't sure, but the unknown had begun to work its way beneath my skin. I didn't think I could take one minute more.

"I'm beggin' here, Merv. I *need* to know. I want to know where I come from."

She had to have known this was coming, and she'd had my entire life to prepare. I wasn't letting her brush my history under the rug again. Everything in our lives had been leading us to this conversation.

I deserved the truth. It had taken me a long time to believe I deserved it, but I believed it now. Stuart had helped me see it.

Merv nodded. Finally, she began to speak, and I was just as mesmerized by the cadence of her voice as I had been when I was a kid.

"You know, when I was younger," she said, "I was a looker, and your real daddy, he paid attention to me. To Bax and Brand. He made us smile, and we hadn't been doin' a lot of that back then.

"His name was William. He was a friend of Noah's from childhood. He was an up-and-comer on the rodeo circuit. Everybody called him Willy Bronc, and when that man looked at us, at me and my babies, he saw a beautiful family.

"When Noah looked at us, all he saw was an expensive burden.

"Willy had come for a month or so one summer to help with the sheep. We got along well, and we got to know each other a little, and that was when I noticed how he looked at me.

"He didn't mean anybody any harm, but the lingerin' looks became longer; I noticed it more and more, and I saw want in his eyes. But no matter how unhappy I was in my marriage, I didn't think I could ever betray my vows. I hadn't even done anything wrong at that point, but your dad—I mean Noah—he noticed the way Willy looked at me, too, and Noah became… *rageful.*

"One night, Willy found me out behind the old barn, cryin' in private so Bax and Brand wouldn't wake up and hear me.

"He fetched ice for my black eye, and he soothed my broken heart, and then he showed me what it really meant to be loved by a man. Physically and emotionally. And over the next two weeks, my life lit up like it never had before. Noah was busy with the lambs. We had parasites bad that year and we lost too many animals, and Noah became consumed with frustration and anger, so much so he didn't notice Willy and me fallin' in love right under his nose."

Merv shifted in her seat, clasping and unclasping her

hands repeatedly, clearly agitated with her own story and the blatant hypocrisy. She'd spent her life telling me that God expected honesty. The irony wasn't lost on me. Maybe she should've picked a different sin.

She went on, the shake in her voice showing me how emotional she was. "I don't think Bax or Brand remember Willy. They were still little boys, but they loved him. He treated them like the gifts from God they were, *not* like burdens. He taught them ridin' tricks and how to rope and make special knots. Then one weekend, Noah went to a Farmers of America convention over in Cheyenne, and he asked Willy to stay back and keep an eye on things. I couldn't believe my ears. I thought for sure it was a test.

"Willy convinced me it wasn't, that Noah was too proud to think that his best friend and his wife would… Anyway, Willy did exactly what Noah had asked him to: he kept his eye on *me*. He made us a picnic, and the four of us drove into the mountains so the boys could fish for trout. And for one whole day, everything felt perfect.

"But Noah came home early the next afternoon. He found us laughin' and cookin' ribs on the grill out behind the house, and he saw Willy's arm around me and his hand on my hip."

She winced as she saw the memory, and one lone tear fell from the corner of her eye.

"Noah nearly killed the only friend he had left that day. Bax might remember callin' the sheriff because he was scared by the way his daddy screamed and hit Willy. They came and took Willy away in an ambulance, Noah spent a night in jail to cool off, and it wasn't a month later when I found out I was pregnant with you."

It hit me then where all the anger I'd always felt had come from. I'd learned it. And right then and there I vowed to myself never to hit another man as long as I lived.

"Noah knew you weren't his. He could do simple math, but he would never lay a hand on a pregnant woman, thank the Lord. And when you were born, I named you after Willy's brother who died in a car accident the year before. Noah had grown up with Willie, so he had to know where the name came from, but he never said a word.

"The only thing he ever said on the matter was that if I ever told anyone, includin' you, that he would kill you. I didn't want to believe him, but somethin' told me I should."

Merv took a sip from the untouched mug on the table in front of her, and when she set it back down, the heavy ceramic clacked against the wood. Her hands shook, and a drop of dark coffee sloshed over the lip. She reached for a coaster at the end of the table and slid it underneath her mug, so the ring of liquid beneath wouldn't mar the hard walnut.

Summer whispered in through open windows and thin screens. Birds twittered and chattered as they flew above the house, cows lowed far off in the distance, and dogs barked. Inside the house, though, the silence was still and thick.

"Noah didn't have any interest in carin' for your brothers when they were babies," she said, "and he didn't bother with you at all when I brought you home, but as you grew older, when Noah looked at you, all he saw was the man who wanted to take us away, who almost *did* take us away.

"Sometimes, I still wish we'd gone with Willy, but I didn't stand up for him to Noah either. Willy and I never spoke again. I was heartbroken for years. I still am if I let myself think about it, but then I remember that if I hadn't stayed with Noah, we wouldn't have Abey."

Merv took a deep breath, and when she released it, somehow, *I* felt lighter.

"So, you see, son, Willy *was* a magic man. He made me happy when nothin' else in the world could have, and he gave me you, and from the moment you took your first breath, you were a light in my darkness because you had come from the most beautiful love."

I hadn't realized tears had begun to fall down my cheeks until Merv reached up to wipe one away. "I love you," she said. "I'm so sorry. I don't know how else to say it, but I'm sorry that I lived in a daydream. I'm sorry I didn't stop Noah from hurtin' you and makin' you feel bad about yourself, but I don't regret one moment of my life because without all that heartache and pain, I wouldn't have my children and my grandchildren, and y'all are the very best parts of me."

My mind raced. I couldn't be as angry with Merv as I wanted to be if I thought about it either, because I couldn't imagine a world without my sister, and it was dangerous for me to imagine how life might've turned out if Noah Lee had never been a part of it.

"Where is he now?" I asked. "Willy?"

"I don't know."

"You've never looked him up?"

"'Course I have," Merv said, "years ago. He never married. I hoped it was because he still loved me, but I also hoped it wasn't, because I didn't want to be the cause of more heartache for him."

"He doesn't know about me?"

"No, Dixon. He doesn't know. He became a household name in rodeo circles, but he's my age, so if he's still alive, he's retired."

"What's William's last name?"

Merv sighed and finally gave up the most important detail. "Messer. William Messer Jr. He came from a ranch near a little town in southern Wyoming called Reliance. I don't know if he went back there or if he lives somewhere else. I couldn't bring myself to look for his address because, if I knew where he lived, I was afraid I'd go to him. But just like you, I let him down, and I couldn't face that."

William Messer, Jr.

Finally, I had more than just a suspicion. All the stories in my head swirled around those fifteen common letters and then settled around my father's name like a flock of starlings.

Suddenly, the ogre of my memories began to shrink and recede in my head until he was no bigger than a figurine, and then he disappeared completely when he shrank back into the dank cave he had come from. He was still there. I couldn't erase Noah Lee completely from my memory, but maybe now his face and ugly sneer wouldn't flash through my mind ten times a day.

"Son?"

"I wanna find him. William," I said, opening my eyes after watching the human shit stain formerly known as Noah Lee walk out of my subconscious.

"Okay," Merv said uneasily. "I mean, you know he could be dead."

"I know."

"Or he could want nothin' to do with you because of me. Maybe he has a wife now or other kids."

"Yeah, Mama. I know, but it doesn't change the fact that I need to look in his eyes. Preferably without you between us."

"Oh," she muttered, nodding and staring down at the table. "I-I understand."

I finally noticed the sad, defeated set of her shoulders. Maybe I wasn't the only one holding on to old stories. Maybe she'd had a hope or two left inside her that William Messer, Jr. could fold right back into her life all these years later.

"I'm sorry," I said. "I don't mean to hurt you by sayin' this, but I need to face William alone. You left me to face Noah alone, so that's how I need to do this too."

"You're right. You should do that. I understand."

"Merv?"

She shook her head. She couldn't look at me, so I stood from my chair at Abey's dinner table and crouched in front of the woman who'd loved me so much, she loved me right into sickness. I held her hands, feeling the dryness of her skin and trying not to irritate the arthritis festering inside her joints too much. "Thank you for finally tellin' me the truth, Mama. I know it wasn't easy for you."

"I'm sorry," she whispered. "You can't know how sorry, but for the longest time, I thought I had to keep the truth from you to protect you. And I thought I was protectin' both our hearts, 'cause if you knew Willy… if he knew you, he would've loved you, but it would've taken all our safety away. I couldn't risk it.

"A-and some of it was selfish. If he knew you existed, nothin' would've stopped him from comin' for you. I would've had to watch you bein' loved by the only man I wanted to love me. But I betrayed him. He couldn't love me, and I didn't think I'd survive watchin' him love someone else. So I tried to love you enough for both of us.

"For a long time, that's what I thought I'd been doin'. When Noah died, I thought I could tell you the truth, but I never did, and it just got harder and harder. And then you left, and it was my fault, and I—

"Oh God, what have I done?" Her hands lifted and she covered her face. Sobs burst out of her chest. "The things… you've had to… t-to live through. All that pain. I'm so sorry."

"Mama, it wasn't your fault. Not completely. I made choices as an adult that shaped my life, that made me an addict. I didn't *want* to know the truth. I wanted to stay angry. It wasn't until Stu came along that I figured it out.

"That's how I knew Noah wasn't my father. I knew

because there was no world where I could ever treat Stu the way Noah treated me. I could never have treated Stu's mama the way Noah treated you."

She hugged herself, trying to quiet down the sobs, but it wasn't working, and I heard my brothers and Abey on the porch. Someone had begun to pace; I knew because like clockwork, every fifteen or twenty seconds the same floorboard creaked. My siblings could hear our mama crying, and like I wanted to, their instinct was to do or say something to make it stop, but they were also trying to respect my wishes and stay out of it.

Carefully, I hugged her. "I can't make this okay for you. You'll have to figure out how to forgive yourself, Mama, but I love you and I forgive you. I have to, 'cause if I don't find grace for what you did, the anger will come back, and I can't risk that.

"Not with Stu watchin'."

CHAPTER THIRTY-SEVEN

DIXON

AN OLD, beat-up trailer sat like some white-trash mirage in a desert, parked alone in the middle of a dirt valley in nowhere Wyoming, with only one horse catching shade in a rickety lean-to next to it.

AJ waited for me in the van. She had multiple pep talks locked and loaded. I doubted I'd need one, no matter how this conversation went, but her support was the strength in my steps as I approached my father's front door.

The magic man, who didn't look now like he had much magic left in him, opened his screen door ten seconds after I rapped my knuckles against it. He was Willy Bronc for sure. He looked like the man in all the old photos I'd found online from his rodeo days, just older, but the light in his eyes had gone.

Silence had followed him to his door. I heard no noise at all. Not his breathing. Not the wind. Not the whir of a fan or an air conditioner in this unseasonable heat and humidity. For once, I found myself wishing for some kind of sound to kick on, to distract us both from the truth and intensity of what I'd come to say.

William Messer, Jr. seemed worn out and tired, and he stood there, looking at a man unknown to him, and waited for me to speak.

"I'm sorry to bother you, sir," I said, trying to keep my voice even and true, "but are you Mr. William Messer, Jr.?"

With narrowed eyes, he answered, "I am. And you are?"

"I, I'm… Shit." *Fuck, this is harder than I thought it would be.* "I'm your—"

"Dixon," he breathed, "is that you? My eyes ain't what they used to be, and you look mighty different than you did even five years ago."

Faster than the speed of light, my heart tried to punch through my ribs. "Y-you know who I am?"

"C'mon in," he said easily, like some long-lost boy showing up on his doorstep was no big thing. "I expect you've got questions and a mountain of a story to tell me, and I'll listen."

"Yes, sir."

As I stepped over the threshold of his double-wide into the wan light of his place, the back of my neck pricked from the easing of the dry, baking noonday sun. I cast my eyes around his living quarters, realizing that was exactly what his house amounted to: living quarters. There were no warm, homely things to offer me welcome, save for—

"That's my mother," I said, pointing with a shaking hand to a piece of art on his wall, painted in the same style I'd learned about in high school, a renaissance rendering of Merv standing in a field, wearing a white summer dress, laughing with tall grass surrounding her and the sun at her back.

The painting was the only thing inside my father's house that I could seem to focus on, framed in fake gold and hanging right in front of me like some priceless Degas ballerina.

"Sure is. I painted it a while back, but it's the one that seems the realest so it's the one I like to look at every day."

"*You* painted this?"

I was no art expert, but the painting showed an innate gift and a deep understanding of shadow and color, and it was the last thing I had expected to find when I got it in my mind to track down my father.

"Sure did," he said. "Did some of you too. Look behind you."

Speechless, I turned, expecting to find a TV, but all I saw was a pile of Louis L'Amour paperbacks stacked up ten tall on a rickety end table next to a dingy, tan corduroy armchair. The ridges and edges of the fabric had long been smoothed away by the weight of William's life, but the matching chair five feet away looked like it had never been sat in.

The whole place reeked of a time long passed, when cowboys ruled this land, and ranches and rodeos were the only social media known in these parts. A man living alone didn't decorate or try to make his house feel inviting because he was never in it. He was out on the range, working cows or tending to his horse. And on the rare occasion he wasn't doing those things, he could be found at the nearest watering hole, drinking and shit-talking his hard days with his buddies.

But between two windows offering an unguarded view of the Wind River Range, another painting had been hung. Maybe three-by-two-foot, the image showed a boy with wavy brown hair and blue eyes like his mama's. He held a thick hardback book, and he looked off into a sunset, daydreaming of the characters he'd been reading about.

I knew he was daydreaming because the boy in the painting was *me*, probably thirteen years old. Still too young to ruin his life with alcohol, drugs, and lies, but not so young he hadn't thought about it yet.

Stepping closer to see it better, I said, "But you— How did you— Why did you never say anything? Why didn't you tell me who you were?"

"And here's the hard part," William said, and he walked to his chair and sat. I swore I heard his old bones creak, but then he motioned for me to take the other chair. "Take a load off. This story, like any proper one, might take a while to tell.

"Before I start, though, can I get you somethin' to drink? Ice water? It's a scorcher today."

"No, sir, I think it's best if you just start talkin'."

"Fair enough."

A deep breath whistled down his lungs when he drew it in, but then he released it and began to tell me where I came from.

"I fell in love with your mama when she wasn't mine to fall in love with. God, how I *loved* her. I'd had women. Plenty of 'em, but Mervella, she was… I'd never seen anything more beautiful in my life.

"I didn't mean to fall in love with her. Noah was my friend then, before I learned the truth about how he treated her, and I never would've chosen to hurt him, but there was never really any choice to make.

"I saw her, and I knew.

"But I'll have you know I didn't go after her. Not right away. I worked alongside Noah for weeks, helped him on the farm. And I tried not to notice Mervella every minute of every day. I really tried. But she wore me down. She was such a good mom to your brothers, firm but fun, and her laugh? First time I heard it, I knew God made it just for me. I thought to myself, I'll never forget that sound. And I never did. I can hear it still."

"If you loved her so much," I said, "if you wanted to know me, why? Why am I just meetin' you today? I don't mean to interrupt your reminiscin' and all that, but get to the shit that matters to me. You knew who I was when I knocked on your door, so I think you owe me that much."

William nodded, but a little defensiveness sounded in his voice when he answered. "My best childhood friend tried to kill me for fallin' in love with his wife." He watched my eyes when he said it. "I can see you already knew that, so maybe your mama finally told you the truth of it all. And even though Noah didn't love her, not the way she deserved to be loved, she still wasn't mine. I didn't have the right to love her.

"I did my damnedest to forget. Went back to chasin' my eight seconds. But after the rodeo and after I'd broken so many bones in my body I lost count, I struggled to know who I was and where my life was headed. My head had grown so big with small-town fame, and I had all that money, which I blew first chance I got.

"And Mervella, she was never gonna leave Noah. I knew that. And she hurt me the day the ambulance took me away. She didn't stand up to him, like I'd been dreamin' she would.

"Mind you, I knew she was scared to go against him. She was scared of a lot back then, and he abused her. That was all muddied up and messed up in her head. I knew that, but still it hurt when she didn't speak up for me and tell him she loved me.

"And she *did* love me," he said, shifting in his chair, moving from one hip to the other, "like you read about in books, with the speed of an avalanche and the strength of one too. I knew that, but after it was all said and done, I just couldn't reckon it. I couldn't let the hurt part of it go.

"And the drinkin' didn't make it any easier to forgive her. It let the hurt inside me turn into anger and betrayal, and then it became rage, and I drank more to numb it."

"You're an alcoholic," I said. It wasn't a question, and it didn't surprise me in the least.

"Yes, son, I am. Recovering, but still a drunk. Got sober for good, oh, ten years ago now."

"So then why didn't you come to find me?"

"Oh, I did. Found you alright. You were standin' not ten feet away from me in the diner in downtown Wisper. Your brother, he'd just gotten his driver's license, so he took you for a milkshake. I didn't know you were mine, but the man at the diner, he struck up a conversation with you boys, and he asked you how old you were. You said twelve. And then he got back to work behind the counter, but right before that, and I'll never forget it, he said, 'Tell your mama I said hello. How is Mervella?'

"I damn well knew that name and never met another with the same. I looked at you and your brother and counted back in my head. Math told me you were mine. And I saw the differences in your features.

"I wasn't surprised Bax didn't recognize me; he was so young when I knew him, but as soon as the man said your mama's name, the little boy I'd known him as revealed himself to me. He had Mervella's eyes, too, like you do, but the shape was different. His build was different, too, slimmer than yours, lankier, at least back then, but you were broader in the shoulders. And you've got my nose."

He touched the bridge of his nose and smiled. "Yours is a little more crooked than mine, though, but still the same if you really look. And I *wanted* it to be true. I knew the way I'd loved your mama and the way she'd loved me—I knew it had to have some great purpose."

I shook my head. Yeah, the grand love story was great and all, but he seemed to be forgetting the more important part. "My nose is crooked because Noah Lee broke it."

My father didn't have anything to say about that. He stared at me, but pain showed on his face like a dark sky before a storm.

"You knew? You knew what kind of monster that man could be?"

He cleared his throat. "I did."

"You knew you were my dad, and you knew he abused the woman you loved, but you... what? You just turned around and walked away?"

"I s'pose it seems that way to you. I tried not to. Sat out in my truck for hours, tryin' to figure what to do. You and your brother left, and I followed you to the edge of town. Y'all turned left, and I turned right. At that moment in time, I was sober, but it never lasted. And seein' you, hearin' you speak and knowin' in my gut you were mine... Well, it ended that particular bout of sobriety.

"I went home and drank until I forgot again. Forgot how much I loved your mama. Forgot how pure our love had been. And I forgot that you might need me. All I remembered was the pain."

He really was my father. We'd been built the same inside and out.

"Okay, so then when you got sober ten years ago?"

"Then *you* weren't in the best place, and then you disappeared. I tried keepin' tabs on you, but you didn't keep steady work or friends. You flitted in and out of your own life, and I lost track of you for a while."

"And you didn't think learnin' that my dad *wasn't* Noah Lee, that I didn't share DNA with that asshole, that it couldn't help me?"

William stayed quiet a moment, rubbing the palms of his hands over his thighs, the jeans below them stained dirty and worn soft.

"I came to tell you once. Caught up with you and followed you into the bar in town, the kind of place I'd vowed never to see the inside of again. I approached you at the bar, started to try to talk to you but you were so drunk, maybe high, too, and you turned, faced me, and said, 'Fuck off, old man. G'on back to the rodeo.'"

"I'm sorry for that," I said. "And you're right. If you found me at Manny's Bar, I'm sure I was wasted, but you couldn't stand up to some young punk? You couldn't tell me to shut up and sit down?"

"Would you have listened?"

That shut me up. No, I would not have listened. I would've hit him. Shit, if I'd been high enough, I might've killed him for talking to me like that.

He nodded. He knew just as well as I did that his words back then wouldn't have done any good.

"It wasn't long after," he said, "that I lost track of you. You never went back to that little apartment you used to rent over on High Street; I checked once or twice a month, if I could get a break at my job, but I never saw you again. And then the last time I was there, I saw the landlord haulin' out some old furniture and a bunch of trash, and when I asked, he said the old renter had skipped out so he was puttin' the place back on the market.

"I tried a thousand times to call your mama. It just... Well, just 'cause a man is sober, it don't mean that all the things that made him a drunk go away. I expect you already know that. So, the shame of leavin' your mama and all my misguided pride, it wouldn't let me call her. I never did. And until you showed up here today, I never saw you again."

Goddamn. Everything he said made so much fucking sense that I was struggling to stay pissed off. He was describing *me*. Misguided pride had helped me make a lot of bad decisions too.

Jabbing my thumb over my shoulder at the painting of Merv, I said, "But you loved her. There's no other art on these walls. It's painfully plain that she's the love of your life. So, if you were keepin' tabs on me, you would've heard that Noah died. Why couldn't you call her then?"

Raising his arm quickly, he swung it around his living room. "What did I have to offer her?"

But Avery Jane and Stu had taught me that all a man needs is love.

"There's a simple answer," I said, and when the words left my mouth, their weight lifted off my shoulders. "When you figure it out, maybe we'll see you. You know where we are. Oh, and by the way, you have a grandson now, if you care."

I stood. I wasn't disappointed. Maybe a little, but I'd learned a long time ago not to expect too much from fathers.

Besides, there was a beautiful woman outside, waiting in an air-conditioned flower van for me, and making her wait wasn't a habit I wanted to get into. And the little boy waiting for me two hundred miles away could ease my sorry heart with one smile. I wanted—*needed*—to get back to him.

No man would ever make me miss another moment of Stu's life for as long as I lived. I'd vowed it to myself and to Stu, and I wasn't planning to go back on my word.

William Messer, Jr. didn't say anything more as I walked out of his trailer, and the hot sun touched my skin again, but this time it kissed me and wrapped me up like a soft blanket on a long winter's night.

When I got back to AJ's van and hopped in, I took hold of her hand and squeezed.

"One father down, one to go?" she asked uneasily, worried about the outcome of my conversation with William.

"Let's go home."

"You don't want to tell me what happened?"

"I do and I will, but it doesn't matter."

Smiling at the woman I loved, I knew it was finally true. Who my father was or wasn't didn't make a bit of difference in my life. The only things that mattered to me were the people who loved me, who I loved right back, more than I ever thought I could. If I had AJ and Stu in my life, I was luckier than any prince or king.

And there was nothing, not one damn thing, in this world that could ever make me say different.

EPILOGUE

DIXON

SPRAWLED on Stu's bed at Bax's house, my legs hung over one side and Stu's dangled over the other, but we both stared up at his bedroom ceiling, trying to come up with an ending for the story he'd helped me write.

I'd been working on it for two months. The story came to me in the days and nights I spent alone in the Cascades, but in my downtime over the last couple months, I typed it out on AJ's old computer and read it to Stu before bed most nights. For a five-year-old, the kid had a lot of feedback. Although, most of it was pretty good, so I'd stay up late, rewriting and fine-tuning.

But now, the thought of turning it into an actual book that strangers might read scared the shit out of me, and the fear had given me my first attack of writer's block.

"What about if the elf prince wins a big contest," Stu suggested. "It could be a fishin' contest. He'd get a big prize, and then the maiden would kiss him. The end. Bada bing, bada boom!" He flipped onto his stomach and pushed up on his elbows. "Now can *we* go fishin'?"

I laughed, hoping that, in his eyes, things would always be so simple. "Sure, kid, but this time you're tyin' your own lure—"

The bedroom door creaked open, and my brother tossed a sketchpad at my head. "I'm comin' too," Bax said, "just as soon as you have a look through that."

"What is it?" I asked, sitting up and grabbing the pad before it fell to the floor.

Stu army-crawled and sat next to me. He flipped the notebook open to the first page, which was a drawing Bax had done of—

"What is this?" I said again, but I knew exactly what I was looking at. "This is my character. It's Jaze the Brave of Loftovel." Running a finger over my brother's drawing, the words I wanted to say got caught on awe. "Th-this is *exactly* how I picture him in my head. How did you know?"

Bax shrugged. "Y'all been in this room for the last two months, chatterin' and tellin' stories, and I heard you complainin' to Abey about needin' character art and mock-ups for the book. So, there ya go."

"Good job, Daddy," Stu said, and he hopped off the bed and skipped over to pat Bax's arm. "I'm gonna go get the worms."

Bax chuckled when Stu left the room. "Kid's got food and fishin' on the brain."

"I can't believe you did this for me," I said, still staring at the drawing, and when I flipped to the second page, the fictional town of Loftovel I'd been dreaming up for years came to life. Bax had even drawn a life-like version of the high towers and castle Stu and I had built out of Legos. "This is amazing."

"Thanks."

I stood and looked at him. "Seriously, Bax. I knew you could draw, but this is next level."

"Well, good then. Glad you like it. I didn't mean to eavesdrop, but I walked by one day when you and Stu were goin' on about the story, and I guess I kinda liked it, so I grabbed my sketchbook and sat outside the door while you talked. And then you were here all the time, and sometimes I get bored. Plus, I mean, I kinda owe you."

"You owe me? Owe me for what?"

"Y'know, for my…" He shifted on his feet and stuffed his hands in his jeans pockets. "I owe you for what my dad did. How he treated you, and I never knew how bad it got. Maybe I didn't wanna know. I just… I'm sorry."

"Thanks for sayin' that, but it wasn't your fault, Bax. You think you could've stopped him?"

"No," he said. "No, I probably couldn't have, but I'm still sorry you had to go through that alone."

"Thank you." I wrapped an arm around his shoulder, holding onto his drawings in my other hand like they were diamonds. "I don't blame you. I never have. So, let's put the subject to rest. I talk about it enough in therapy."

I'd also talked more about it with Merv. She helped me fill in some blanks in my memories, but we hadn't gone too in depth yet. I thought it might be good to do that in the therapist's office.

William had shown up. He met Stu, and he and Merv started going for walks. What they did or talked about on those walks was a mystery. She was tight-lipped about it. I thought he might be seeking a little redemption himself. Time would tell.

He and I had talked a little, but if he wanted to be my father, he had miles to go to get there. I knew what I deserved now.

"You know you're gettin' more annoyingly well-adjusted by the day?" Bax asked.

This time, I shrugged. "Don't we have some fish to catch?"

Stu popped his head in the door. "Yeah, we do, so let's go! Oh, and AJ's here, and she brought her new fishin' pole." He rolled his eyes. "It's pink."

"I don't think the fish care," Bax said.

Stu rolled his eyes again, this time more dramatically. It was his new thing. If he didn't roll his eyes six times an hour, he did it ten times the next.

"Yeah, but pink's a girl color."

"A pink pole will catch fish same as a blue or green one," I added.

"I like pink," Bax said. "You like pink, Deedee?" He elbowed me lightly in my ribs, letting me know we were good, and I smiled, 'cause even though it pinched a little, it felt right. Ribbing and jabbing each other was what brothers were supposed to do, like we used to when we were Stu's age.

"Love it," I said. "I kinda have to since it's AJ's favorite color. Everything that woman owns is pink."

"Her van's not pink," Stu said. "Her cat Fancy's not pink. Her flower shop's not pink…"

This time, I rolled my eyes. "Somebody needs to teach this kid the meaning of sarcasm and the difference between figurative and literal."

"Ooo, fancy words for a redneck," Bax joked as we descended the stairs.

Stu ran ahead to hug AJ, waiting for us in the living room, and he made sure to give her pink fishing pole the side-eye.

"Y'know," Bax drawled, "I think you should pay me for

my artwork. I'm thinkin' five million dollars when you get a big book deal."

I snorted. "Pretty sure it don't work like that."

"Well then, the least you can do is cook up all the fish I catch today for supper."

"As long as I get to eat some of it, you got yourself a deal."

"FIVE FISH!"

AJ beamed, looking down into her bucket of trout. She'd beaten me and Bax both. And poor Stu looked utterly dejected with only two fish dangling from the hook lures in his hand.

"I like my fish grilled with a dash of lemon and Lawry's salt," Bax informed me, smirking, and he reached over to ruffle Stu's hair. "Ready for football, Stu Man?"

"Yeah!" Stu handed his fish to me. "Deputy Frank says if we're late for practice, he'll arrest us." He darted ahead and tossed his pole into the bed of Bax's truck.

"I think he was kiddin'," Bax said, chuckling. "It's only Pee Wee football. Alright, see y'all around five. It's just the four of us tonight, Stu, and Rye. Athena's eatin' at Shaylene's, and Aubrey's doin' inventory at the bookshop. Merv said she's busy, so it should be a quiet, uneventful evenin'."

They buckled into the truck and took off, but as they drove away, Bax stopped and Stu yelled out his backseat window when Bax rolled it down.

"You're comin' next week, right Deedee? It's our last game!"

"Wouldn't miss it for the world, kid."

My son smiled like I'd just handed him the key to a free toy store. He threw me a thumb's up, and AJ and I waved as they disappeared around the bend.

Turning toward her, I asked, "Can I show you somethin'?"

"Sure, as long as you promise my fish will still be alive when we're done, or else I'll release them back into the lake now."

"You know we're eatin' those fish tonight, right?"

"Yes, but that doesn't mean they have to suffer before their deaths."

I didn't mention how the hook holes through their mouths probably wasn't a pleasant sensation. She refused to touch the fish, so I had to unhook all five.

"They'll be fine, baby girl. Promise."

She set her bucket on the ground in a nice little pocket of shade under a poplar tree. I unhooked Stu's catch and added them to the count, along with mine and Bax's, and we walked south around the far side of the lake and up a narrow road that had been recently carved into the earth by my brothers' tires. Rye had cleared the vegetation with his tractor, and Brand ordered gravel to be laid, but it hadn't arrived yet.

Sunshine peeked in and out of the lodgepole pines and quaking Aspens along the road, playing hide and seek with their boughs and branches. The air was crisp, and a perfect end-of-fall breeze rustled around us. AJ huddled into her hoodie, looking up at the dwindling leaves still left on a cottonwood. They shimmered in the light and covered us with a warm orange glow.

"Where we goin'?" she asked, and she studied my face as I answered.

"Somewhere special. At least, I hope it will be."

She was quiet for a minute, but then she said softly, "You're so handsome. I look at you, at the man you are now, and I feel peace."

Compliments weren't something I had quite gotten used to hearing yet. "Yeah well, you need glasses. Gran said it the other day."

"I do not. Just accept the compliment, Dixon, because it's true."

"I will," I said, standing still and pulling her close for a kiss, "because it came from you."

"Good."

"Good, now that's settled, last one there's a rotten egg!"

I took off and AJ followed me up the last rise of the hill, like we were five again, dancing and dashing in the forest. Her glittering laugh behind me filled me so full, I had to stop to catch my breath. She raced ahead of me but skidded on the soles of her tennis shoes when she saw the cabin.

"Whatcha think?" I said when I caught up.

"I don't remember this one. Is it new?"

Slinging my arm over her shoulders, I said, "Yeah. Brand and I just finished it. The credit goes to him though, because he's been workin' on it for a year when he had the time. He built it for us."

"But we weren't even together a year ago."

"It started out as a place for me in case I ever came home," I said, "but once I got here and he showed me, I knew it was meant for you too."

"You don't mean you wanna *live* here?"

"No," I said, chuckling. "It's not big enough for all your clothes. And I know you like to be near your mama and gran, but this can be a getaway for us. A place to chill and reset.

"I was thinkin' I could use it as, like, a writin' retreat or somethin'. I spent so much time alone in a cabin, and sometimes I miss the silence."

She looked at me, her hazel eyes darkening and reacting to the blue sky above and all the fall colors wrapped around us out here in the wood. A raven squawked nearby, announcing his displeasure and letting us know he didn't approve of our presence in his territory.

"You do?"

"Yeah," I said. "Sometimes."

"Well then, I love it." She stretched up on her toes to kiss my cheek. "Let's go inside."

I followed when she stepped forward. "You know what's even better than silence, though?"

"What?"

Gripping her hips, I turned her. She screeched her surprise, and it echoed between the trees as I lifted her and tossed her over my shoulder.

"That sound you just made, and all the sounds you're about to make once I get your jeans off. We don't have to be quiet out here like we do at your place."

"It's *our* place. But you're right. I'd just die if Gran knew we were havin' sex in her backyard."

"She knows I live there and that you're not a nun."

"I know but still, she's so innocent."

I snorted. "If there's one thing I know about Gran, it's that she's *never* been innocent. You should ask her about it sometime."

"Dixon! What did she tell you?" When I didn't answer and I pushed open the cabin door, she swatted my ass. "Spill, now."

"Ain't my story to tell."

I set AJ on her feet, and before she could get out another squeak of protest, I turned her and she shut right up.

"Oh my God. It's so pretty. I didn't expect pretty."

"What'd you expect?" I asked. I ran my hand up and down the knotted wood wall that had been sanded and washed with a cool birch stain before Bax, Brand, and I sealed it.

"Dark wood and masculine."

She walked to the only piece of furniture in the place, a comfy oat-colored chaise. I bought pillows to go with it in the colors of a pale sunset. I set it by a window that looked out at so many trees I couldn't count. I'd picked it out for her two weeks ago and had it delivered. It wasn't fancy or expensive, but it was comfortable. She sat and bounced once, testing the give, then leaned over the side to untie her shoes. She kicked them off, then tucked her feet beneath her butt.

"You like dark better than light," she said.

I shrugged. "I like whatever you like, 'cause if you like it, you'll spend time here, and I wanna be with you here. Brand showed me how to stain the walls light like this. We did a wash and then sanded it down, but it's just enough to make the place feel warm, y'know?"

I nodded at the door behind her. "There's a bedroom back there and a bathroom with a nice tub. We can soak our troubles away."

Reaching her arms out for me, she cocked an eyebrow. "Oh, we're not makin' it to the bedroom. C'mere." She extended her legs and spread them open, unbuttoned her jeans, and her hand disappeared beneath.

"I smell like fish."

"Don't care."

"You're trouble, baby girl." I locked the door behind us and walked to the end of the chaise, then crawled over her. "Have I told you that?"

"More than once." She pulled her hand from beneath the denim and lifted her wet fingers to my mouth.

Sucking those thin fingers, I let them glide over my tongue. My eyes rolled closed and I groaned at the sweet taste on my tongue. "Well, I'm sayin' it again."

She was trouble alright, spelled with a capital T, and her brand of trouble was the only kind I needed in my life.

And I'd spend the rest of it thanking her for it.

If you enjoyed *Scars Forget Us*, please consider leaving a review wherever you buy your books, Goodreads, or BookBub. Reviews are like gold for indie authors and help us reach more readers. I appreciate your time and effort. 🩶

Want more of Dixon and AJ? **Click here to join my newsletter** or sign up on **my website**. It's where you'll get all the good Wisper gossip. Subscribers will get the password to the VIP page, where you'll find extra "sexcapades" for my readers only!

You can find even more bonus content in the Wisper Dreams special edition paperbacks with pretty formatting, end pages, and character-specific chapter headers.

Wisper Dreams Special Editions with Bonus Content

Discover more at gretarosewest.com

EXTRA CONTENT

Join my newsletter for a FREE short story, *Wild Heart: Welcome to Wisper*. This is where you can get all the Wisper news and sexcapades—naughty little interludes for my subscribers ONLY!

Sign up on my website: gretarosewest.com/VIPS

LETS CONNECT!

You can also join me in my Facebook group, Wisperites Unite. We get up to a lot of fun there. Mostly we drool over sexy cowboys, but we do other things there too, I promise, like giveaways and fun games, and my Wisperites always get new book news first, teasers, and we chat about books. We'd love to have you!

Go to: https://www.facebook.com/groups/wisperitesunite

I would love to hear from you. Email me at greta@gretarosewest.com. I'll reply. Or find me on Facebook and Instagram.

@gretarosewest

ABOUT THE AUTHOR

Greta Rose West was a floundering artsy flake until cowboy Jack Cade showed up, knocking on the door of her brain, pounding on it, and then he just plain kicked it down. She's a boy mom to a grown freakin' man, who has recently gifted her with the title of GRANNY! She comes from the "Region" of NW Indiana, but Greta, her husband, and her two precocious kitties, Geoff Trouble and Sally Mae Midnight, now reside in the Indianapolis area. When she's not writing, she's reading and devouring music. She enjoys indie films no one else likes, and her favorite food is Aver's Veggie Revival pizza.

You can find her on Instagram @gretarosewest, in her Facebook group, Wisperites Unite, or on her website.

gretarosewest.com

- facebook.com/gretarosewest
- instagram.com/gretarosewest
- bookbub.com/authors/greta-rose-west
- goodreads.com/gretarosewest

www.ingramcontent.com/pod-product-compliance
Lightning Source LLC
Chambersburg PA
CBHW051755050726
47598CB00006B/2290

* 9 7 8 1 9 5 5 6 3 3 4 2 0 *